Praise for *Stars in an Italian Sky*

"Santopolo writes heartbreak like no other, and *Stars in an Italian Sky* is both masterful and unforgettable."

—EMILY GIFFIN, AUTHOR OF *MEANT TO BE*

"A shimmering love story for the ages . . . *Stars in an Italian Sky* is about the course of fate, the meaning of family, and the power of love. Bellissima!"

—ADRIANA TRIGIANI, AUTHOR OF *THE GOOD LEFT UNDONE*

"A poignant tale of love, loss, class, and fate, brimming with the colorful spirit of Italy and infused with the hopefulness of true love written in the stars."

—KRISTIN HARMEL, AUTHOR OF *THE BOOK OF LOST NAMES*
AND *THE WINEMAKER'S WIFE*

"Sensual, heartfelt, and incredibly moving, Santopolo's latest will bring you to tears."

—FIONA DAVIS, AUTHOR OF *THE MAGNOLIA PALACE*

"I was swept away. . . . You'll savor this story like fine wine!"

—LISA SCOTTOLINE, AUTHOR OF *LOYALTY*

"Filled with longing and romance, this book is a love letter to the human heart, and a testimony to the timelessness of true and lasting love."

—ALLISON PATAKI, AUTHOR OF *THE MAGNIFICENT LIVES OF MARJORIE POST*

"Santopolo skillfully weaves two love stories in which passionate and idealistic young couples contend with class differences, tension between their personal desires and familial obligations, and the ongoing ramifications of decisions made by earlier generations. . . . Sure to tug at readers' heartstrings."

—*PUBLISHERS WEEKLY*

"A romantic, sweeping story that's satisfying and heartbreaking at the same time."

—*Kirkus Review*

"A warm, poignant story of enduring love and loss . . . The perfect read for those who long to travel!"

—Rhys Bowen, author of *The Tuscan Child* and *The Venice Sketchbook*

"Powerful, emotional, and steeped in beauty and romance . . . Santopolo has written a sweeping story brimming with passion that will whisk you straight to an Italian vineyard."

—Ann Mah, author of *The Lost Vintage* and *Jacqueline in Paris*

"A testament to the power of art, of family, and ultimately, of love to endure across decades and continents—*Stars in an Italian Sky* is a beautifully written epic love story."

—Jillian Cantor, author of *Beautiful Little Fools* and *In Another Time*

Stars
in an
Italian
Sky

JILL SANTOPOLO

G. P. PUTNAM'S SONS
NEW YORK

PUTNAM
— EST. 1838 —

G. P. Putnam's Sons

Publishers Since 1838

An imprint of Penguin Random House LLC

penguinrandomhouse.com

The Library of Congress has catalogued the G. P. Putnam's Sons hardcover edition as follows:

Names: Santopolo, Jill, author.
Title: Stars in an Italian sky / Jill Santopolo.
Description: New York: G.P. Putnam's Sons, [2023]
Identifiers: LCCN 2022047507 (print) | LCCN 2022047508 (ebook) |
ISBN 9780593419175 (hardcover) | ISBN 9780593419182 (ebook)
Subjects: LCGFT: Novels.
Classification: LCC PS3619.A586 S73 2023 (print) |
LCC PS3619.A586 (ebook) | DDC 813/.6—dc23/eng/20221019
LC record available at https://lccn.loc.gov/2022047507
LC ebook record available at https://lccn.loc.gov/2022047508

First G. P. Putnam's Sons hardcover edition / February 2023
First G. P. Putnam's Sons international edition / February 2023
First G. P. Putnam's Sons trade paperback edition / March 2024
G. P. Putnam's Sons trade paperback edition ISBN: 9780593419199

Printed in the United States of America
2nd Printing

Book design by Lorie Pagnozzi

For my spectacular Gram,
Beverly Franklin,
with so much love

Stars
in an
Italian
Sky

Prologue

SERRALUNGA D'ALBA, ITALY

At Villa Della Rosa, autumn was fading. The beauty of the summer had given way to the fall harvest, but now the trees, the bushes, the vines—all of them were bare. Their yearly slumber had begun. Vincenzo wondered if they dreamed during those long months. Dreamed of sunshine, dreamed of color, dreamed of life.

When Vincenzo closed his eyes, he dreamed only of her.

Giovanna smiling at him.

Giovanna laughing, the sun on her face.

Giovanna angry, her cheeks flushed, her eyes burning.

Giovanna writing him a letter. A letter, now open beside him, that left him no hope.

But even with that knowledge, he preferred, still, to dream. To imagine that once again their hearts would belong to each other. That he would no longer have to paint her from memory alone.

He looked up at the stars and wished upon all of them that one day his dream would come true.

Chapter 1

GENOA, ITALY
Then

Giovanna's heart leapt every time the door to her father's tailor shop opened.

It was only six months ago that she, her father, and Faustina had returned from Saluzzo, where they'd spent most of the war. In the autumn of 1942, after a bomb blew out the windows in their shop and in their home above it, her father had boarded up the windows, taken what he could, and brought them all to the farmhouse his parents shared with his brother, Enzo, and his family in the mountain town where he was born.

When they came back to Genoa nearly three years later, they weren't sure they'd be able to open the shop again. The boards across the windows had been splintered, the floor covered in dirt and debris. Bombs had rained down on the city while they were away.

As they had stood staring at the shattered wood and chunks of glass and stone, Faustina spotted a half-destroyed piece of paper crumpled under the rubble—it looked like it had been there for years—and bent down to work it free. "A propaganda leaflet," she'd said, "from the Allied forces: *The government in Rome says: the war goes on. This is why our bombing goes on.*" Faustina shook her head. "The government in Rome cost us our shop."

"It's not so bad," Giovanna had said softly, walking over to her sister and running her fingers across the leaves carved into the counter, which was still standing at the back of the shop. Her fingertips came away covered in soot and dust.

Federico had wrapped an arm around each of his daughters. "The war is over," he'd said then, kissing first Faustina on the top of her head and then Giovanna. "We are still here."

"Are our customers?" Faustina had asked.

Federico sighed. "We'll see, won't we?"

And they *had* seen. Their customers had slowly come back, some looking to have their clothing remade to fit bodies that had become leaner during wartime, some wanting skirts tapered to look fashionable again, some carrying a coat or a dress or a sweater left behind by a loved one, asking Federico if there was anything he could do to keep their memories alive.

"I can help," Giovanna told a young mother whose husband had died only six months after their child had entered the world. She took the coat the mother brought and turned it into a stuffed rabbit for the little girl, its ears lined with scraps of satin, its face embroidered with gold thread. The whole time she was sewing, Giovanna wished she still had one of her mother's coats. It had been more than six years since her mother died; Giovanna had been fourteen then. She wished she'd been able to carry a small piece of her mother with her all these years, hold that piece in her arms, keep her close. Giovanna sewed her own longing into that bunny.

And now the woman had returned for it.

"One moment," Giovanna said to her, ducking behind the curtain into the back room of the tailor shop, where her father and her sister were working.

She picked the stuffed rabbit off the high shelf where she'd left it to keep it safe.

"That's beautiful, Giovannina," her father said, admiring the rabbit in Giovanna's hands. "Where did you find a pattern for that?"

Giovanna smiled. "I made one up," she told him.

It was something she loved to do: imagine a dress, a shirt, a jacket—or in this case a stuffed rabbit—in her mind's eye and then create it.

"I bet we could sell those," Faustina said, an A-line skirt resting on the sewing machine in front of her. "Do you want me to see if Betto can get some scraps of fabric so you can make more?"

"I can make the pattern for you, if you'd like to make them," Giovanna said as she headed back into the public part of the shop. "But I'd rather work on clothing, if that's okay." She loved how a beautifully fitting dress could give a woman confidence, how perfectly tailored pants could make a boy feel like a man. She would often watch people on the street and tailor their clothing in her mind or imagine new outfits for them entirely. Especially after the war, she wanted to give people that moment of self-assurance, of happiness. But she was glad she was able to make this toy so a little girl could have a physical reminder of her father.

"Here you go," Giovanna said, handing the stuffed rabbit to the woman.

The woman rubbed the rabbit's ears between her fingers and her eyes filled with tears. "What do I owe you?" she asked.

"Nothing," Giovanna said, her heart responding to the sorrow in the woman's eyes, recognizing her own sorrow there. "It's my gift to your daughter."

"You must take something," the woman said. "Perhaps a trade? I still have some plum jam from the summer. I can bring a jar by tomorrow."

"That sounds perfect," Giovanna said, recognizing in the woman a need for fairness. "My family and I love plum jam."

During the war they'd gotten used to trading—for work, for food, for clothing—a way to make sure everyone had what they needed.

The woman smiled when she took hold of the toy. "Angelina will love this," she said, putting the stuffed rabbit in her purse. "Thank you."

"You're welcome," Giovanna told her, noticing how loosely the woman's clothing hung on her body, wondering whether it was sorrow or scarcity that had stolen her appetite.

When Giovanna looked up, there was another customer waiting. A young man, about her age, with warm brown eyes, looking at her intently. The intensity of his gaze made her heart flutter. Giovanna's eyes locked with his, and she couldn't look away. It felt like he was looking straight through to her heart, to truly see, to understand. He cleared his throat and she remembered herself.

"Can I help you?" she asked.

"You can," he answered, and then didn't say anything more.

Giovanna laughed. She asked that question dozens of times a week, and no one had ever responded that way.

"Well, I'm glad," she said. She glanced down at his clothing, trying to figure him out. It was well made, expensive, but a little small. She could see his socks poking out between the hem of his pants and the top of his shoes. She wondered if he'd grown taller during the war, if he was still wearing pants that fit him when he was fifteen or sixteen.

There was a leather satchel slung over his shoulder and he took it off, placing it between them on the counter. "I was wondering if Signor Ferrero would be able to remake some of my brother's clothing to fit me," he said.

Giovanna took the clothing out of the bag. The fabrics were good quality, and the pants and vests inside weren't that much bigger than the man in front of her.

"I'm sure my father could do that," she said. "I'll get him so he can fit you properly."

"Your father?" he said before she could turn.

"Yes," she said. "My father is Federico Ferrero." She wondered who had sent this man to their store. Most of their customers knew her and Faustina well. "I'm Giovanna," she added.

"Hello, Giovanna." He said her name softly, and her heart fluttered again. "I'm Vincenzo, Vincenzo Della Rosa." Della Rosa. The name was familiar, but she couldn't place why.

Federico walked through the curtain.

"Hello," he said to Vincenzo. "I just heard you introduce yourself to my daughter. Can I assume that you're the conte d'Alba's second son?"

"I am," Vincenzo said.

The conte d'Alba! Giovanna remembered him, a tall man with thick brown hair the same caffè latte color as Vincenzo's. She'd met him twice, a long time ago, but he'd made an impression, since he was the only member of the nobility who frequented her father's shop.

"It's nice to meet you," Federico said. "I hope your father is well."

"He is, thank you," Vincenzo said. Then he paused for a moment. "But we lost my brother in the war."

Giovanna's heart went out to him. She could tell by the way he said it that Vincenzo was still grieving the loss, that his heart was still tender.

"I'm so sorry," Federico said. "Please send my condolences to your parents—and your sister as well."

Giovanna wished she could think of something comforting to say. Instead, she just nodded in sympathy.

Then there was a moment of silence until Federico said, "Did you say you wanted some of your brother's clothing tailored?"

Vincenzo nodded. Giovanna wondered if he was too choked up to answer out loud.

Federico picked up the satchel of clothing and brought it across the shop. "The changing area is over here," he said, pulling back a curtain that separated a small corner of the room from the rest.

Vincenzo cleared his throat. "Of course," he said, walking toward Federico. Before he stepped into the curtained-off area, he turned back to Giovanna. "It was nice to meet you."

"You too," she answered, feeling her cheeks get hot.

Giovanna ducked behind a curtain into the back of the store before he could see her blush.

"So the conte d'Alba's son is in?" Faustina asked, putting down the blouse she was working on.

Giovanna nodded. "His second son. The older brother died in the war."

Faustina shook her head. "I can't believe Papà is still going to accept their business when they supported the fascists. I told him that on principle he should refuse the business of everyone who was on the wrong side of the war."

Giovanna sighed. Her sister saw things so black and white. It was an argument Giovanna had stopped trying to have with her. There were definite wrongs and definite rights, but there were so many shades of gray in between, especially during wartime, when people were scared and sad and fighting for their lives or the lives of loved ones. You had to give everyone some grace until they showed you a reason not to, or at least that was what Giovanna thought. She had trouble putting those thoughts into words, though. Especially words her sister would listen to.

Faustina stood. "I'm taking a walk," she said. "Tell Papà I'll be home in time to make supper."

"Okay," Giovanna said, watching her sister put on her coat.

"This," Faustina said, closing the buttons, "is why I want to move to America."

Giovanna was pretty sure there were people there who needed grace, too, whose wartime stories contained shades of gray, but she kept her mouth shut. It wasn't worth arguing with Faustina. Not when they were kids, and certainly not now, when Faustina's opinions were so set, when her facility with words was so much better than Giovanna's.

As Giovanna picked up a pair of pants to hem, she wondered what Vincenzo Della Rosa's story was. And whether she'd ever find out.

"I would've found you, no matter what circles we were in," Luca said, sitting back down next to her, love apparent in his voice. "You're my Venus."

Cass smiled. She still couldn't quite believe that to him, she was Venus, the goddess of love, of beauty, of sexuality and desire. And that he was going to paint her that way soon. She couldn't wait to see how she looked through his eyes. And she appreciated that he thought social class wouldn't have made a difference in their relationship had they met back then, but she wondered if it was actually true. Even now she felt the differences in their upbringing. She wondered if in Italy after the war those differences would've been insurmountable. She was glad they didn't have to find out.

Chapter 3

GENOA, ITALY
Then

Giovanna was at the counter, hand-sewing a zipper into a skirt, when the door to the shop opened. She looked up and her heart caught in her throat. It was Vincenzo. Vincenzo Della Rosa.

"I seem to have a problem," he said as he walked in, "and I hope you might be able to help me."

His gaze was so piercing, so focused it made Giovanna feel important, like she was someone worth taking notice of. "What's the problem?" she asked.

He held out his wrist. "I have a meeting in fifteen minutes, and my button is loose."

Giovanna put her hand under his wrist to inspect the button, and somehow the room felt as if it had gotten at least three degrees warmer. She felt the heat radiating off his arm, off his whole body.

"I can fix that," she said, threading a needle with white thread to match the other buttons. It was all she could do to focus on the task, not prick him with her needle. But still she noticed that his fingers were dusted with charcoal, that he smelled like soap, that his warm breath was tickling her cheek. "There you go," she said, cutting the end of the thread with a tiny scissor.

"I can't thank you enough," he said. "It's hard to feel confident at a meeting with a wobbly button."

Giovanna smiled. "Glad I could help," she said.

He paid her four times the amount she'd charged and told her that he wanted to cover the cost of any future stuffed animals she made for customers who'd lost a parent. It made her wonder if he was thinking about his brother when he did that. They didn't know each other well, though, so she didn't ask. Instead, she thanked him, and he left and she went back to work.

When Giovanna mentioned his visit briefly to her sister, Faustina raised an eyebrow at her. "You seem like you were glad to see him," she said.

Giovanna turned to hang up a coat that had fallen onto the floor so that Faustina wouldn't see the smile on her face, because she was very glad to see him, and she could tell from that eyebrow raise that her sister did not approve.

Later, Giovanna sat next to the window in the bedroom that she and her sister shared, looking out at the street in front of their apartment, watching the people who walked by. It was nice sharing a room with just Faustina again after spending almost three years sleeping with their cousin Ilaria in the room, too. Giovanna missed being in Saluzzo sometimes—missed hearing about Ilaria's romance with their neighbor Aldo, who had come home from the Italian army in 1943 with a wounded leg and a confession of love on his lips. She missed digging up potatoes in the yard and then helping her grandmother turn them into gnocchi, missed visiting her mother's father and hearing stories about her mamma as a little girl as he whittled tiny birds from the wood she picked up as she walked to his house. The war had hit all of Italy, of course, and Saluzzo was no exception, but in the mountain town there were no rockets raining from the sky, no airplanes flying low and loud, sending everyone for shelter.

But when she was there, she'd missed Genoa, the Genoa of her childhood—the energy of the city, the people, the routines, the comfort in knowing that she was traveling the same streets she'd walked down with her mother, visiting the stores and people her mother had introduced her to. As much as she'd missed Genoa, though, Faustina had missed it even more, especially that first year.

"I want to stay," she'd told Federico, when he made the decision to go to Saluzzo. "This is my city."

"So you want to die with it?" he'd asked her, uncharacteristically harsh.

"I want to help it," Faustina had said. "I want to help Italy."

She and her fiancé, Benedetto, the son of a fabric merchant, had joined a group of young people who were helping families whose homes had been destroyed find places to stay and items they needed.

"You can help Italy by staying alive," he'd said. And that was the final word on it. But Betto had made his way to the mountains, too, and he and Faustina had eventually joined up with the partisans there. Without telling Federico, they both became *staffette*, couriers, often on bicycles, who were given various jobs, delivering everything from reports to packages of newspapers and propaganda materials, to food and medical supplies, to weapons and ammunition. Once, Betto had to travel all the way back to Genoa with a package of dynamite on his lap.

Faustina and Betto had asked Giovanna to join the partisans, too, and while she did pick mushrooms or collect hazelnuts for Faustina to bring to the group to eat, sewed blankets out of scraps, and knitted hats in the winter, mostly she listened to her father. "We are Swiss," he would whisper to her when they walked by a group of women in the Fasci Femminili, not because they were Swiss, of course, but because it was his code to remind her he wanted them to remain neutral just like Switzerland. He wanted their family to stay safe, and to him that meant not getting involved at all. She knew how scared losing her mother had made him—scared he would lose his daughters, and scared that they would lose him—and, unlike Faustina, Giovanna understood his feelings, his fear. She felt it herself.

"Similar as two drops of water," Giovanna's mother used to say when she saw Federico and Giovanna, their heads bent together working to fix a wobbly chair leg or mend a hole in a wool stocking. Federico would laugh and say the same was true of her and Faustina. Giovanna wondered what her mother would have done if she had lived through the war. Perhaps she would have joined the partisans, too.

Faustina came into their bedroom, humming a song under her breath. Giovanna immediately recognized it. "Bella Ciao," the anthem of the partisans, which Faustina hummed more often than not. Giovanna was glad she had stopped singing the words. Especially during the war, the song upset her. It was all about dying a partisan and being buried on the mountain next to a beautiful flower. The first time Giovanna heard the lyrics, she started having nightmares about her sister and Betto dying, their bodies shot through with bullets from a Mauser. Though it didn't take much to give her nightmares those days.

"Do you need any more help with your dress?" Giovanna asked her sister, both because she wanted to help her and also to get her to stop humming that song.

Faustina's face lit up. "I think it's finished," she said. She and Giovanna had been working on it most nights for months, ever since Betto and Faustina set a wedding date—and then found them the fabric they needed to sew the dress. It was done in two layers, a sleeveless layer that skimmed Faustina's slender body, and then a sheer layer on top that had fluttering sleeves to her elbows and a longer skirt that floated to her ankles. There was a drop-waisted silk sash, too. It was a dress that they never would have been able to afford if they'd tried to buy it, but that was the benefit of working in a tailor shop, of having a tailor for a father, who taught you to sew as soon as you were old enough to hold a needle and thread.

When Giovanna had shown her sister the design she'd thought of, Faustina was taken with it immediately. Faustina was a competent seamstress, but Giovanna had vision, just like their father. When she looked at a person, she knew exactly what style suited them best, and then she had the patience to create it, no matter how difficult the design or how much small detail work there was.

For the past few weeks, Giovanna had been working on Faustina's veil, edging it with lace and embroidery, work that Faustina didn't have the patience for.

"Can I see the dress on you?" Giovanna asked.

Faustina was only too happy to oblige. She took off the clothes she'd been wearing for the day and went to the sewing dummy that had taken up residence in their room. She slipped the gown over her head and turned her back to her sister so Giovanna could do up the tiny buttons running down the back.

When she was done, Faustina turned to face her. "So?" she asked. "Did we miss anything?"

Giovanna looked at her sister critically and then it truly hit her. Her sister was getting married, was leaving their home. She remembered their childhood games, dressing up in their mamma's clothing, playing an intricate game of make-believe where they would trade off who got to be the good witch and who got to be the evil witch. She remembered growing older, when Faustina would so, so patiently try to help her learn to read, and then would finish reading the books out loud when Giovanna got frustrated. And she remembered their fights during the war, when Giovanna was terrified of her sister risking her life with the partisans, and how tightly she hugged her when she returned.

Giovanna realized that so much of how she saw herself was in comparison to Faustina. Faustina was smart, bold, opinionated. Giovanna was quiet, easygoing, emotional. They each grew in the spaces they'd carved. And now Faustina was carving a new space—a married space, where she would grow differently, grow separately, with Betto.

"Your dress looks perfect," Giovanna said, tears threatening to overflow her eyes. The dress *was* perfect. There was no extra fabric, no pulls across her hips or her chest. Nothing left to fix.

Faustina smiled. She had been doing it more and more, since the war ended, since the partisans won, since she and Betto chose a wedding date.

Giovanna lifted the veil off her bed and placed it on her sister's head. "There," she said, wiping her eyes. "Now you're ready."

Everyone always commented on Giovanna's looks—her spiraling curls, her hazel eyes, her dimples. They said she looked like a cherub, like she belonged on the ceiling of the Sistine Chapel. But Faustina was beautiful in a different way. Her dark brown hair was thick and wavy, and her eyes a pale blue that her father said must have come from a Sicilian ancestor. The juxtaposition of her hair and eyes was striking. Somehow the wedding dress made them more so.

"Betto's cousin Roberto is coming to the wedding," Faustina said, raising her eyebrows. "He's just your age. Maybe the two of you—"

Giovanna smiled. "You want to marry me off so soon?"

"I just don't want you to be lonely," Faustina said. "I worry about you."

Giovanna gave her sister a hug. "I know," she said. "I worry about you, too. But I won't be lonely, I have Papà to keep me company."

Faustina took off the veil. "You know what I mean."

Giovanna did know what Faustina meant. She'd love nothing more than to find the man she was going to marry. But the only man who'd caught her eye recently was Vincenzo Della Rosa.

"I'll make sure I say hello to Roberto," Giovanna said, placing her sister's veil on top of the dressmaker's dummy.

Faustina smiled. "Good," she said. "I want you to be happy. I want you to find someone you love, like I love Betto."

"I want that too," Giovanna said.

She wondered if Betto made Faustina feel . . . seen. Because that was how Vincenzo made Giovanna feel, and it was one of the best feelings she'd had in a long time.

Chapter 4

NEW YORK CITY, USA
Now

"Here you go," Luca said, handing Cass a tight red gown with a slit to her thigh. She shrugged off her blazer and turned around so he could unzip the structured, navy dress she had worn to work—one of her favorites from Daisy Lane's fall collection. The rasp of the dried paint on the tips of his fingers as he touched the skin of her back made her shiver.

"You cold?" he asked.

Cass shook her head. "I'll be fine once I put this dress on." She slid the jersey fabric over her head, then walked to the perfectly made bed he'd set up in a corner of the room, the heady scent of his studio, of linseed oil and turpentine, coffee and wood, filling her lungs. In one hand, she picked up a glass of wine that was waiting for her. Her phone was in the other. A pair of leopard-print high heels were already placed next to the bed.

"There she is," Luca said. "My Venus of the twenty-first century."

Cass smiled. If she were to choose for herself, she would have gone with Minerva, the goddess of strategy, of commerce. She relied on her brain to get things done, not her body. She'd worked hard to get to her current job. And she hoped that it was that hard work and nothing more that got her there, not anyone's assessment of her face or her hair or her figure. But she loved being Luca's Venus. She loved how he saw her.

The concept for this painting was that Cass, as Venus, was swiping through Tinder while getting ready for a night on the town.

"So," Luca said as he stood behind his canvas. Then he paused. "Wait, can you pull your hair forward a little more? Over your left shoulder." Cass complied. "Are you going to see your brothers tomorrow?" he asked, focusing on the canvas in front of him.

Cass stopped herself from shaking her head and instead answered without moving her body much at all. "Probably not," she said. "Christopher and Jenna are taking Milo to go pumpkin picking farther out on Long Island. Dominick had said he would try to stop by, but he just texted that a family called him because they had an electrical fire in their wall, and he wanted to try to fix it for them tomorrow, so they won't have to spend the whole weekend in the dark."

"I'm sure they appreciate that," Luca said. "Nick's a good guy."

"He is," Cass said, smiling. Of her two brothers, Dominick was the one she was closest to. Neither of her brothers seemed to understand why she wanted to do things most people in her family didn't— go away to college, study abroad, live in Manhattan. But the difference was that even if Nick didn't get why she wanted what she did, he always defended her to everyone else, always helped her out. "That reminds me," she said. "Are you up for a trip to Island Park for the Feast of San Gennaro? Nick's worked so hard on planning it for his church. I told him we'd try to come."

Luca laughed, his eyes on his canvas while he answered. "That was one of the biggest surprises when we moved here."

"What was?" Cass asked. She was looking down at her phone, the way she was supposed to for the painting, but watching the number on her email icon increase was distracting. She locked the home screen and instead looked at a photo of her and Luca taken at the top of the Empire State Building. Luca couldn't believe that Cass had lived in New York her whole life and never gone, so he took her there for her birthday last May. The wind had blown her hair around in the photograph. She loved the look on both of their faces: their eyes had found each other, and they were laughing at how windy it was. It was the moment she knew she'd love him forever.

"That Italian Americans are obsessed with San Gennaro. In Italy, he's only celebrated in Naples. But here's it's like he's the patron saint of all Italian immigrants."

"I think he kind of is," Cass said. "Or at least he is in the New York area. We should go to the festival in Little Italy, too. That's the main one."

Luca groaned. "Again? You sweet-talked me into going last year, but now I know better. It's so . . ."

"Wonderful?" Cass finished for him.

"It's crowded and loud and they sell subpar wine and ridiculous shirts," he told her.

"It's alive and invigorating and who cares about the wine and shirts when you can eat cannoli and ride a rinky-dink Ferris wheel," she answered.

He laughed. "I can't believe I'm going to marry a woman who loves rinky-dink Ferris wheels."

Cass looked up, not sure if she'd heard right. "What?" she asked.

His eyes still focused on his painting, he repeated, "I can't believe I'm going to marry . . ." and then his voice trailed off.

"Marry . . . ?" Cass echoed.

Luca had stopped painting, his eyes wide. "Madonna! Pretend you didn't hear that."

"Luca?"

"I just blew it." He closed his eyes and raked his hand through his hair. "I had it all planned. For tomorrow evening. When you got back from your parents' place. I was going to ask you to marry me tomorrow, Cassandra. And I just messed it all up." He shook his head. "I'm so sorry. I'm such an idiot."

But a smile was already on her face. Her heart was beating double-time. This was a surprise, but the most delicious kind. The kind she'd secretly dreamed might happen but hadn't given voice to quite yet. She thought about marrying Luca all the time—how his art would mature and her career would thrive while they fed each other creatively, how they'd have little artistic children who'd want to paint on the walls and she would be the kind of mom who let them, how they'd move down the block from a playground, raise their kids to be bilingual, travel with them to Italy on school vacations to visit his family. "You are not an idiot," she said. "You're my favorite human being on the planet. And you have nothing to be sorry about. Can I say yes now?"

Luca smiled, though she could tell he was still upset with himself. He often had a vision of how he wanted something to go, and if things went sideways, it was hard for him to get himself back on track. "If I were you, I'd wait to see what I have in store for tomorrow."

Flouting his rule about a model breaking pose before the artist told her to, Cass got up and threw her arms around him.

"Tomorrow," he whispered into her hair, "we'll celebrate like this tomorrow."

"Tonight, too," she whispered back, then turned to kiss him.

She knew no matter what he had planned, she'd say yes again. And again and again and again, as many times as he wanted her to, until they were bound to each other forever.

Chapter 5

GENOA, ITALY
Then

Giovanna was sitting at the counter, sketching out a pattern for a jacket she had seen a woman wearing on the street that morning—it had a peplum at the bottom that hit her in just the right spot—when the door to the shop opened. She looked up, and Vincenzo Della Rosa was standing there.

"Hi," she said with a smile. "Did another button come loose?"

She thought she could detect a slight pink hue to his cheeks when she said that.

"I could pretend," he told her. "But . . . I was in the neighborhood and it's such a beautiful day . . . and . . . I wanted to see if you might want to accompany me to a bench on the piazza over there." He pointed out the window and down the street. "I . . . I know you probably have to work, but I thought maybe since it's your father's shop you might . . . um . . ."

Giovanna smiled again. "I'd love to," she said. She poked her head into the back room where her father was working and told him she was going to take a quick walk to mail a letter to Ilaria and would be right back.

He nodded—he was basting a dress and had pins in his mouth—and she popped her head into the main part of the shop.

"Let's go," she said, grabbing the letter she'd written to Ilaria the night before so what she'd told her father wouldn't be a lie. It was March, but the day was unseasonably warm.

"It feels like the first true day of spring," Vincenzo said as they walked outside. He put his elbow out, and Giovanna rested her hand on it. The warmth of his body against her fingertips made her stomach flip.

"It does," she said. "I'm looking forward to seeing bright spring colors again. Everyone always looks so drab in winter."

Vincenzo looked at her. "Is that why you're wearing bright red?"

Giovanna smiled. Faustina always said she wore "look at me" clothing, in bright colors and bold patterns. And maybe she did, but she also remembered the way her mother smiled when she sewed bright dresses for her as a child. "I won't ever lose you!" she'd say. And Giovanna sometimes wondered whether, if her mother truly could look down on her from heaven, bright clothing still helped her find her daughter.

"My mother liked red," Giovanna told Vincenzo.

He nodded and then softly said, "She's gone?"

"When I was fourteen," Giovanna told him. "Pneumonia."

"My brother, Leonardo, died when he was fighting in North Africa," Vincenzo said. "He was supposed to be the next conte, but now . . . it's me."

Giovanna didn't know what to say to that other than "I'm so sorry."

They'd reached the bench, and Vincenzo sat down. Giovanna sat next to him, leaving a hand's width of space between them.

"I've been trying to draw him," he said, pulling out a sketchbook from his satchel. "But I can't seem to get his face right."

Giovanna looked at pages of versions of the same face, with slight differences. Eyes a little bigger, a little smaller. Chins pointier or rounder. Cheekbones more pronounced and less.

"He looks like you," Giovanna said, reaching her fingers out to touch one of the faces. "In this one."

Vincenzo looked at it more closely. "Maybe I did get his face right, then. But . . . it was me who looked like him."

The bell from the Cattedrale di San Lorenzo rang out, marking midday. She remembered when bells had been confiscated at the beginning of the war. Mussolini had made an agreement with the Vatican that half of the church bells in Italy would be taken for war industries, but at least one bell would remain in each tower. When she heard that one bell ring for the first time on its own, she found herself surprisingly emotional. One bell, ringing on while its partner was at war, its world changing irreparably.

"You miss him?" Giovanna asked.

"Every day," Vincenzo answered. "I feel like I should be used to it now, used to the hole he left in my family, used to looking at a new future, one that should have been his but now is mine, used to knowing I can't go to him for help or advice." He sighed. "I'm not used to it. I don't know if I ever will be."

In Giovanna's family they tried to bury what was painful, but Vincenzo seemed comfortable talking about it. His honesty was freeing and loosened her heart.

"I thought it would go away, too," Giovanna told him. "The missing. But really it's just changed. Memories that used to feel painful are a little sweeter now, a little less bitter. But I do still miss my mother. All the time."

"I think we will both be changed forever by our losses," he told her, his finger tracing the shape of something over and over on the flannel of his pants. Giovanna tried to follow his finger with her eye. It looked like he was drawing a tree.

"We'll grow differently now," she said, the image of his tree in her mind.

"Yes," Vincenzo said, reaching his hand out. Giovanna reached back, their fingers touching, connecting, and then weaving together. "You understand," he said.

And in that moment she felt like he might be able to sew up the rip that had been growing in her soul. Like she could share secrets with him, and he would keep them safe. Keep her safe. And she would do the same for him.

Chapter 6

LONG ISLAND, USA
Now

The next morning, Cass sat on the train to Island Park dreaming about a future wedding. She wondered what Luca had in mind, if he had anything in mind at all. Something big and fancy in New York City? A weekend-long celebration somewhere on Long Island? Family and a few close friends at his grandfather's vineyard in Italy? She could imagine all of those, and she wasn't sure which one was right for them. She was looking forward to talking to him about it, figuring out how best to represent their love to their family and friends—what would really encapsulate them as a couple—and then going to cake tastings and florist appointments and listening to bands online.

No matter what, she knew she wanted to wear a re-creation of her gram's wedding dress—tea length with a deep V-neck and three-quarter sleeves. Gram and her sister, Cass's great-aunt Faustina, had sewn it and trimmed the bottom with lace. When Cass was little, she would run her fingers over the photograph, which had been black and white, but someone had tinted the flowers yellow and rouged her grandmother's cheeks and lips with pink. Cass had always thought her

grandmother looked like a movie star in that photograph, her eyelashes long and dark and her curly hair twisted up with a thick fringe
of bangs across her forehead. Cass wouldn't go that far. She'd wear
her dark hair loose and wavy, the way she liked it best. The way Luca
did, too.

Maybe their wedding could be in the summer. It would be less
than a year from now, but the flowers were always so beautiful in the
summer.

Cass wondered how Luca would propose. Would it be dinner out?
Or in? Was he going to get down on one knee? Or hide a ring in a
puff pastry for dessert? Maybe in a piece of tiramisu, which he knew
was her favorite?

After his slip of the tongue yesterday, he'd gone quiet, painted her
until the light faded completely from the windows.

"You hungry?" he'd finally asked her, clearly still annoyed at himself, but less so than before.

"I could eat," she'd answered, but she wasn't very hungry. All she
could think about was him, them, their future. She wondered if his
grandfather was coming with one of their family's heirloom rings. Or
whether Luca had designed her ring himself.

It was still all she could think about as she walked from the train station to her parents' house in Island Park. Years ago, they'd converted
the space above the attached garage into an apartment for her brother
Dominick, when he got in to the Long Island Electrical Apprentice-
ship program to become an electrician. The entrance was through the
main house, but Nick had appreciated having his own kitchen, his
own bathroom, an area where he could close the door and be alone.

And now it was where Gram was living. She had her own home, but Cass's parents were there if she needed anything.

As Cass got closer, she could see curtains in the windows that she recognized from her grandmother's house on the Gulf Coast of Florida. The braided-rope pattern transported her back to her childhood trips there, eating lunch under an umbrella on the beach and dinner on the back patio. Building sandcastles with her big brothers and watching her grandmother in her sewing room, adjusting Cass's too-short clothes so they'd fit again—letting down hems, adding ruffles to skirts, sometimes even making dresses from scratch.

She was the reason Cass had wanted to work in the fashion industry. Her grandmother always made her feel beautiful. When Cass had told Gram that years before, her grandmother said it was something she'd always believed—that the right outfit could make a difference in someone's life. In their confidence, their achievements. It was why Cass loved the Daisy Lane line. The clothing was classically stylish and really well made. It was the kind of clothing that could be transformational. In fact, when she'd started working there, she sent Gram a few of their pieces, and Gram had agreed. She and Gram had often mailed things back and forth and talked on the phone, but having her close by would be even better.

Cass jumped up the front steps to her parents' house, the way she used to when she was a kid—two legs, then one, then two again, like she was playing hopscotch. Before Cass could ring the doorbell, it opened and she was wrapped in her grandmother's arms.

"It's been too long, Cassandra," Gram said.

"Way too long," Cass agreed, her voice muffled by the hug.

"Let me see you." Gram released her from the hug but held on to her hands.

Cass stood still while her grandmother looked at her, and she looked back. It had been six months since Cass had visited Fort Myers for a quick weekend hello, and Gram hadn't changed a bit. Her hair was pure white, just as it had been ever since Cass had known her, and instead of cutting it short, like many grandmothers, Gram left it chin-length and curly. Her eyes were a sparkling hazel, and her skin, soft and wrinkled, was the same light olive tone as Cass's own. She'd make a great Juno.

"You look happy," Gram told Cass.

Cass smiled. "I guess I am," she said, thinking about Luca, about her job, about their lives together.

"Your parents worry about you," Gram said.

Cass nodded. "I know. They've always worried about me." She remembered when she told them she wanted to go to college in Boston, to explore a new city, meet new people. *What about Hofstra University?* they'd asked. *You could live at home.* But that was the whole point. She didn't want to live at home. She wanted something new. She wanted to find out what else there was to see, to know about, to experience. Maybe it was because she read more than her brothers and was fascinated by worlds not her own—she began reading travel guides as if they were bedtime stories, travel memoirs as if they were her own personal bibles. Nick joked that Cass was just born curious, and maybe it was true. But she'd had the same conversation over and over again with her parents for most of her life. When she wanted to live in Manhattan, her parents said: *You could commute, stay with us, save money.* But she insisted on renting her own tiny studio, experiencing the city firsthand.

Gram squeezed Cassandra's hand. "You remind me a lot of my sister," she said. "Always reaching for more, always climbing higher."

"She was a high school principal, wasn't she?" Cass's great-aunt had died when Cass was in elementary school, and she didn't have many memories of her.

"That's right," Gram said. "The minute we got to New York she started studying to become a teacher. And got a second university degree while she was working, so she could run the school one day. She was smart and she was a hard worker, just like you—always ready for the next challenge."

Cass couldn't tell if her grandmother thought this was a good thing or a bad thing. "Are you happy I'm like her?" she asked.

Gram patted her hand. "I'm happy you are who you are, Cassandra. But I know it's caused some friction between you and your parents. It caused some between me and your aunt as well. I worried about her the way your parents worry about you. I know it means a lot to them when you visit."

Cass smiled. "Well, now I have a reason to come home to see them even more. I'm so glad you're only a train ride away."

"Me too," Gram said. "Dominick and Dina and their two visited yesterday. And Christopher is coming tomorrow with Milo while Jenna's at work at the salon. And you today . . ."

"I'm sorry Luca couldn't come, too," Cass said. "I really want you to meet him." She thought about telling her grandmother about the impending engagement but decided to wait. And she'd wait to ask her about the modeling, too. Maybe over lunch.

"It'll happen soon enough," Gram said. "Now, let's get out of the entryway and into the apartment. I've been waiting for you to help me hang some pictures."

"You got it," Cass said, following her grandmother slowly down the hallway that led from the entry hall to the garage. It was hung with school photos, and Cass smiled at Nick's fourth-grade "serious guy" pose as she walked by. In it, she could see hints of how his face looked when he was fixing a faulty circuit breaker at her last apartment. "Where are Mom and Dad?"

"Grocery shopping," Gram said. "They've got something big planned for lunch." Knowing her parents, Cass guessed it was going to be an array of sandwich meats and condiments, with hero rolls and side salads and who knew what else. They always did it up when any of their kids came home for a visit, even Nick, who lived less than fifteen minutes away.

Cass stopped at the staircase to the apartment and turned to see if Gram needed any help, but she was already sitting down in a chair attached to the wall. She buckled herself in and then pressed a button. Cass walked slowly next to Gram as she traveled the length of the staircase and unbuckled on the other end. Cass's father had told her he'd installed this chair with Nick and Chris, but Cass hadn't seen it yet. And it tugged at her heart.

"Better safe than sorry," Gram said as she stood again, steadying herself against the wall.

Gram had always been like that, acknowledging her own limitations and working around them. But this one made Cass sad. Not being able to walk up and down stairs seemed like a first step to something. Something Cass didn't want to think about.

She looked into the apartment and saw her grandmother's familiar couch, her area rug, the funny wooden sculpture of a banana that Pop had bought at a flea market sitting on the bookshelf. It all seemed the same, but different, just like her grandmother. Then her eyes rested on a stack of framed paintings on the coffee table. The one on top wasn't one Cass recognized.

"Is that the art you were talking about?" she asked.

Cass walked over and lifted the first frame. Inside was a painting of a woman in a gown looking out a window at a city on fire. She had one glove pulled up and the other down around her wrist. There was a ring over the glove, a cluster of bright gemstones shimmering in the sunlight. There were spiderwebs in the corner of the painting, but the woman's surroundings were opulent.

"It is," Gram answered, walking slowly toward the couch.

Cass squinted at the signature on the bottom but couldn't read it.

"Where's this from?" she asked, lifting it up.

"It was a gift," Gram said. "From a long time ago. I found it in a box when I was cleaning out the house and framed it."

"The light is beautiful," Cass said. "Look how it plays off her hair."

Gram walked over to Cass and stood next to her, gazing at the painting.

"It was a different time," Gram said.

"Was it a gift from Pop?" Cass asked.

Gram shook her head. Her eyes looked far away, like she was remembering who it was from and how she got it. Cass waited for her grandmother to speak, to tell a story, but when she opened her mouth, all she said was, "How do you think it would look over the desk?"

Cass turned to her left, checking out the width of the wall. "I think it would fit well," she answered, wondering who gave her grandmother that painting, why she was being so secretive about it. Why she had not seen it before. Whether there was a way to coax her into telling the story.

Cass picked up a picture hook from the box on the table and the hammer and tape measure next to it. As she walked back to the wall, she saw her grandmother looking more closely at the painting, her hand touching her hair.

Something about that gesture made Cass wonder if Gram saw herself in that woman.

Chapter 7

GENOA, ITALY
Then

Giovanna was adding the cost of hemming Signora Rossi's new dress to the older woman's account when Vincenzo walked into the tailor shop again. He looked at Giovanna and tilted his head, and she couldn't stop the smile from spreading across her face. Seeing him in the shop made her heart beat faster. She'd never felt this kind of connection to someone before. It was like she was magnetically drawn toward him, body and spirit. She glanced down to make sure she'd written the cost correctly. She had a habit of accidentally transposing numbers, so she always double-checked what she wrote against the price list Faustina had written out and left next to the register.

"Thank your father for me," Signora Rossi said. "The hem looks perfect."

"I will," Giovanna answered, knowing that her sister had actually sewn that hem but keeping quiet. The customers liked to think Federico had done all the work himself.

She watched as Vincenzo held the door open for Signora Rossi and then smiled at Giovanna, a secret smile. She couldn't help admiring how he was dressed—and how his body looked in those clothes. His gray vest fit so perfectly, Giovanna could see the contours of his torso, the muscles beneath his shirt.

Vincenzo checked the time on his gold pocket watch. His hair fell forward toward his eyes. "Forty seconds until you close for lunch," he said with a grin. "Would you like some company? And perhaps something to eat?"

"To eat?" she echoed.

"Well, we both do have to eat," he said with a shrug that seemed nonchalant, but she had a feeling it was a practiced gesture, a way to play down an emotion he didn't want to share.

"Not another button?" she asked, welcoming the thought of putting her hand on his arm, bending her head so close to his.

Vincenzo laughed, but then his face turned serious. "I . . . I couldn't stop thinking about you, so I took a chance. If you're not free, I can . . ."

Giovanna stopped him. "Let me just grab my cardigan," she told him as she disappeared behind the curtain. "Papà! Faustina!" Giovanna called to the back room. "I'm taking a walk. Don't wait for me for lunch."

She knew that their lunch routine would be the same if she was there or if she wasn't—they would go upstairs to their apartment and eat quietly while Federico looked at the styles in the most recent issue of *Grazia*, making notes about hem lengths and silhouettes and any other tricks he could use to make his customers' old clothing look brand new again. And Faustina would read that day's edition of *Avanti*, the socialist newspaper. When Giovanna joined them, she and her father shared the magazine, Giovanna folding down the corners on the dresses she wanted to try to copy.

"I'm ready," Giovanna said, walking over to Vincenzo. She noticed the sketchbook under his arm.

"What are you working on today?" she asked as they walked out the door, Giovanna turning the sign from *aperto* to *chiuso*.

"I'm trying to get my father's face right," he said, flipping the sketchbook open and showing her a page with three different versions of the same man looking out at her. He had big dark eyes, sharp cheekbones, and a narrow nose, like Vincenzo. But he also had a manicured mustache and a grim expression. "He looks . . . too . . . sad," Vincenzo added.

"Don't we all?" Giovanna said, thinking about all the sorrow she saw hiding behind people's smiles, behind Vincenzo's in particular. She wondered how long it would take for the war to be far enough in the past that it didn't cast a shadow on the present. Or was its shadow so long that the lives of those who'd lived through it would always be shrouded in semidarkness?

Vincenzo stopped walking and tipped her chin up toward him. He looked at her carefully, as if assessing the level of sorrow in her soul. "Some more than others," he answered. And then he offered her his elbow.

Giovanna took it, shivering slightly as their bodies touched. She wondered how much sorrow he saw inside her. She wondered how much more was hidden inside him. They walked down the darker narrow path of Salita di San Matteo toward the open sunshine of Piazza De Ferrari. This area had been hit hard by bombs—the cobblestones broken and cracked, the old stone buildings crumbling—but just like the Ferreros, people were starting to rebuild. There were men still clearing rubble from the buildings that had been completely destroyed, others replacing windows in the buildings that hadn't sustained quite as much damage, and still others who were ready to reopen their shops, bread and pastries visible in their windows. This rebirth of the city felt like the start of spring, too, in the way that certain flowers in the parks were just green shoots growing from the ground, others with buds, and yet others with blooms ready to be enjoyed. Giovanna and her family were lucky that the damage their properties sustained was minimal in comparison. Other people would be rebuilding for years—or perhaps would decide not to at all.

"Where are we going?" she asked. They walked by a trattoria and then turned right when they hit the piazza.

"A quiet place where, if we're willing to pay, we can drink real coffee," he said, steering her down toward Piazza Giacomo Matteotti.

"Real coffee?" Giovanna echoed. There hadn't been real coffee available since the war started. Instead, they'd been drinking caffè d'orzo, coffee made of barley instead of coffee beans, which Giovanna couldn't stand, even when her father called it caffè d'oro—coffee of gold—to make it sound more appealing. "*Real* coffee is the caffè d'oro," she'd told him, even though before the war she'd mostly had it the way a child would, with lots of milk. Her father had laughed, though. "That's true," he said. "You need to have gold to buy it." And now Vincenzo was offering it to her.

"Imported from Ethiopia," he answered.

They reached their destination, a small trattoria with tables on the sidewalk.

"Signore!" A man walked out of the café to greet Vincenzo. "Is the conte here with you?"

Vincenzo shook his head. "My father's in Alba."

"Has he sent you for more coffee? I can secure at least another kilo for you by next week."

Giovanna watched the exchange in fascination. An entire kilo of real coffee? How was this possible, when her family hadn't had a cup in nearly three years? How much would that cost?

"Oh no, no, he won't need more for at least another two weeks," Vincenzo said. "But Giovanna and I would love a coffee each."

The man turned and seemed to notice Giovanna for the first time and nodded at her. "Of course," he said.

"Giovanna," Vincenzo added, "this is Mattia, the best barista in Genoa. And his wife, Beatrice, is the best cook."

Mattia smiled. "I'll let her know you said so. Is there anything else I can get you?"

Giovanna looked down at a menu that had been left on the table. It was the dessert menu—ruette, buccellato, pandolce. There had been a sugar shortage, too. She hadn't had pandolce since she was fifteen.

Vincenzo's eyes were on her. "Would you like gnocchi al pesto to start?" he asked. "It's one of Beatrice's specialties. So is the beef brasato."

"That sounds good," Giovanna said, her mind still on the pastries, the way they made her mouth taste sweet even when the last bit was gone, the memory of it staying on her tongue for hours.

"You're thinking about something else," Vincenzo said, swiping his hair out of his eye.

She smiled at him, embarrassed to admit that she was focused only on sweets, like a child. "I was thinking about dessert," she said. "I haven't had pandolce since the war began, and it's my favorite."

He smiled back at her in a way that seemed both tender and indulgent. He turned to the man. "Forget the gnocchi. We'd like to start with one pandolce and one buccellato," he said. "Actually, no. We'd like two of every dessert on the menu."

Giovanna felt her eyes widen. "Two of every dessert?" she asked.

"There's no law that says you have to eat pasta or fish or meat for lunch," he said. "And if you like sweets, you should try every one of them."

Is this what it's like to be the son of a conte? she thought. *Or is this just what it's like to be Vincenzo?* "What if we don't finish it all?" she said out loud.

"Then we'll wrap it up in napkins and take it home," he said. "Share some with your sister." He put his feet up on the chair next to him, and Giovanna heard something crinkle.

Vincenzo bent over and came back up with a newspaper in his hands. It was a copy of *Avanti*, the one Faustina was probably reading at that very moment. *Italians are indifferent to the pulverized monarchy!* it said on the front page. The monarchy—and whether it should be abolished—was what everyone was talking about these days, especially Faustina and Betto.

The institutional referendum, the one where Italians would choose between keeping the monarchy and creating a republic, was going to be on June 2, and Faustina and Betto were already trying to figure out how to make sure their friends voted—and voted for a republic. It would be the first time women would have a say in a national election, something Faustina was very excited about—and that Betto thought might change the outcome.

Last night, Faustina had convinced Giovanna to listen to a radio news program about the history of the Italian monarchy. Afterward, Betto had talked about the idea of King Vittorio Emanuele III abdicating. Giovanna hadn't paid much attention to the king before now. She knew that Vittorio Emanuele's son, Umberto, had been in charge of things for a while as the lieutenant general, even though

Vittorio Emanuele had kept his title. But to be honest, it really didn't matter much to her who was king—she still got up, worked at the shop, went to sleep, all the same. But she knew it mattered to a lot of people.

"Do you think it would be good if Vittorio Emanuele abdicated?" Giovanna asked Vincenzo, thinking about what Betto had said.

"I think most people would say so," Vincenzo answered. "The socialists and republicans want him out because they want all monarchs out, and the monarchists want him out because they think his son makes a more appealing king."

Giovanna liked how Vincenzo explained things, simply, calmly. So calmly, in fact, that she wasn't sure what his opinion was. Maybe he was like her and didn't pay that much attention to what was happening in areas he couldn't control.

"Which one are you?" she asked, as Mattia came back and placed two coffees and a tray of pastries on their table. They looked so delicious that it was all Giovanna could do not to grab one right away.

Vincenzo ran his fingers through his hair. "My father is a monarchist," he said. "Because the monarchy gave birth to the nobility. And if the monarchy were voted down in the referendum this summer, he'd lose his role in our local government. He'd lose his power. And he'd lose the money to keep up our house and our land—and most importantly to him, our vineyards."

Giovanna placed a piece of pandolce on her plate, thinking about the kilo of coffee, the cup on the table in front of her. "That means you'd lose all of that, too."

Vincenzo took a sip of his espresso and closed his eyes, as if the flavor of the coffee made it impossible for him to focus on anything else. All this talk of the king and coffee brought to mind a song Giovanna had heard people sing to criticize Vittorio Emanuele III:

> *Quando Vittorio era soltanto re*
> *Si bevea del buon caffè.*
> *Poi divenne Imperatore,*
> *Se ne sentì solo l'odore.*
> *Oggi che è anche Re d'Albania,*
> *Anche l'odore l'han portato via.*
> *E se avremo un'altra vittoria,*
> *Ci mancherà anche la cicoria.*

> *When Vittorio was only king*
> *Good coffee was a common thing.*
> *When an Emperor he was made,*
> *Coffee to a smell did fade.*
> *Since he took Albania's throne,*
> *Coffee's very smell has flown.*
> *And if we win another victory,*
> *We will also lose the chicory.*

When Vincenzo's eyes opened again he said, "In a way, yes. I'd lose the life I now expect to lead."

His eyes had a faraway look to them, and Giovanna wondered if he was thinking about his brother, Leonardo, who should have had the life Vincenzo was talking about. She also noticed he said *expect*, not *expected*. Which meant he thought the monarchists would win. Faustina thought they wouldn't. Giovanna didn't know what to think.

She realized, though, that she and Vincenzo were from very different worlds with very different concerns, and she wasn't sure how to respond to this one. Instead, she put a forkful of cake in her mouth, and now it was her turn to close her eyes.

"Delicious?" Vincenzo asked.

She swallowed, reveling in the sweetness on her tongue. "The best thing I've eaten in years," she answered honestly.

"I'm so glad," he said. And he did seem glad, like making her happy made him happy.

The air between them was still for a moment, while they both took a bite of the food on their plates. Vincenzo swallowed first.

"Would it be okay if I asked you a question?" he said.

"Of course," Giovanna answered, wondering what sort of question needed to be prefaced with a statement like that.

"Ever since I first saw you in your father's shop," he said, "when you tried to give that stuffed rabbit to the woman for free . . . the way the light hit you . . . you just, you glowed, from the inside out. And it made me want to paint you. Would you . . . would you let me paint you?"

Giovanna swallowed. "Paint me?" she echoed. She immediately thought of his sketches, the care with which he made them, the tenderness with which he drew his father and his brother. She couldn't believe he wanted to draw her as well.

"I'm sorry," Vincenzo said immediately. "Forget I said it. I know it's a strange thing—"

"No!" Giovanna said, feeling his embarrassment. "It's not strange. It was just a surprise. And an honor. It would be an honor to be painted."

"Truly?" he asked, his calm, his happiness returning.

"Truly," she told him, and smiled.

The glow on his face made Giovanna sure she'd made the right choice, even though her sister wouldn't approve—of her being painted or of her spending even more time with the son of the conte d'Alba, a man who was the definition of a monarchist. But there was something about Vincenzo, something that fascinated her—the mix of vulnerability and bravado, of being seemingly carefree, but clearly caring so much, of being so different from her but also somehow the same. He was a series of opposites, of contrasts. And she wanted to figure out why.

Chapter 8

GENOA, ITALY
Then

Giovanna told her sister she was going to visit a friend, which wasn't entirely a lie. Even so, she still had trouble telling Faustina anything but the truth. The two of them had always been close, and had gotten even closer after their mother died, working to figure out things she hadn't yet taught them, whispering about their changing bodies, about how to navigate friendships and hardships, a two-girl team, stronger together than they were apart. Faustina was the leader, and Giovanna needed her—for advice, for help, for confidence. Wherever Faustina went, Giovanna wanted to go, too, so much so that their father started jokingly calling her "me too."

Things changed during the war—and even before that, when Betto became a serious part of Faustina's life—but Faustina was still Giovanna's center, her anchor, her home. And Giovanna knew that if Faustina made her promise not to see Vincenzo again, she'd have a hard time going against her sister. So she hadn't been saying much. And Faustina hadn't been asking much, though she raised her eyebrows at Giovanna any time she saw Vincenzo in the shop. Faustina was focused on the referendum, and on her wedding, now less than two months away. There was family coming down from Saluzzo, and a dinner to plan for the night before, plus the luncheon afterward.

Giovanna was excited about the wedding, too, but her mind kept circling back to Vincenzo.

When they'd parted after lunch, Vincenzo had written a time and an address in the margin of the copy of *Avanti* and then handed it to her. "Come here on Saturday for our first session," he said. "It's my family's apartment. I'll set everything up there." Giovanna had nodded.

On Saturday the shop was closed, and Federico went to visit his wife's grave. It was something he did every Saturday since she died on New Year's Day in 1940—except for the three years they'd spent in Saluzzo during the war. Federico had made his daughters come with him to the cemetery at first, but as they got older, they both stopped visiting. "I feel Mamma everywhere," Giovanna told her father. "I don't need to go to her grave to think about her." Faustina never said why she stopped going; she just started disappearing on Saturday afternoons, confessing to her sister in whispers that it was when she went to spend time with Betto.

Giovanna decided to take a long, winding walk to get to Vincenzo's family's apartment. It was rare that she went on a walk like this alone, up and down the hills of her city. She passed by Christopher Columbus's house and wondered, not for the first time, what it was like for him to set sail into a world he knew nothing about. School friends of hers had done that recently, set sail for the United States, for

Argentina. When her friend Teresa left with her new husband, there had been a party, and one of the boys kept referring to their ship as the *Santa María*, even though it was actually called the *Saturnia*.

Giovanna took the stairs up and paused for a moment to look at the view of the harbor. From here she could see the sun sparkling off the water. One of the things she loved about Genoa was the different levels of the city, how you could walk up a set of stairs and your whole perspective changed. And here, the city changed, too. Federico's shop was in the historic area of the city, where the buildings dated back centuries, and where a lot of the bombing had been focused. Here, the buildings were newer, built in the last hundred years with more space to breathe, more space to let the light in. And the bombing wasn't as concentrated in this area, farther from the port, so there wasn't quite as much to rebuild. It felt like her city, but not. Like the difference between velvet and velveteen.

It somehow made sense that Vincenzo would live here, in this neighborhood that felt so different from hers. She knew there were other members of the nobility who had flats in this area. Other contes and marcheses and their families. Other people whose lives Giovanna couldn't even imagine living.

There was a piece of her that wondered if Faustina was right about Vincenzo's family and if Giovanna should put an end to this and stop spending time with him. What really was the point? Initially, Giovanna had thought he had just been looking for someone to talk to, someone with whom he could be honest precisely because she was so removed from his everyday life. But the more he'd come to the shop to see her, the more they'd talked, the more she wasn't quite sure what he wanted from her—and the more she felt that frisson between then, that spark of something that was not just friendship. She was intrigued enough to find out.

Giovanna had daydreamed once or twice about a school friend's older brother, and there was Iacopo, one of the boys Ilaria knew, who had kissed Giovanna the night before she left Saluzzo to return to Genoa. Giovanna hadn't liked him all that much, but enough that she let him kiss her. She was curious and he was kind—and it was nice. But the idea of kissing Vincenzo felt entirely different.

When she got to the large stone building with balconies overlooking the street, she pressed the button with his family's apartment number next to it, and soon Vincenzo was in the lobby, letting her in the door. He was wearing a pair of tan pants that were splattered with paint and what looked like a white undershirt. She couldn't help noticing the dark hair on his forearms, the outline of his muscles under his shirt. His smooth skin, a shade darker than hers. He looked like a man, and she still felt like a girl, as if even though she had just turned twenty-one, she hadn't quite finished growing up yet.

"I've set up my canvas to capture the light from the windows," he told her. "I want to draw you in my parents' parlor, looking out at the city."

Giovanna nodded. She glanced down at her outfit: a dress she'd made herself out of a cream-colored fabric with tiny yellow and orange flowers on it. The top had a collar and buttons, and the skirt was full and came down to the middle of her calf. She wasn't sure what someone was supposed to wear to have herself painted, but this was the most fashionable dress in her closet.

"I have a few dresses for you upstairs," he said. "They're my mother's. I think she's about your height, though a bit bigger otherwise."

His mother's clothing? Giovanna hadn't expected that. "Are you sure your mother won't mind?"

Vincenzo shook his head. "She hasn't worn any of this in years. She hasn't been to Genoa since before the war. She may not even know what's in these closets anymore. And styles are different now anyway."

When he opened the door to the apartment, Giovanna couldn't believe the opulence. There were crystal vases, art in gilded frames, and the most elegant furniture she had ever seen.

"This place is . . . beautiful," she said, searching for a better word but not finding one.

"Beautiful, yes," Vincenzo said, "but also dusty." He ran his finger across the top of a wooden side table and left a mark in the dust. "Every time I come here, I feel like I'm trying to rewind a clock, but time doesn't move backward."

"One of the women who came into our shop last week, Signora Grieco, she called the years of the war 'the lost years,' as if they didn't exist. But that's not true," Giovanna said as she admired the beautiful tapestry curtains that framed the windows.

"No," Vincenzo said. "I know many people who wish they were the lost years, who would give anything not to remember what they lived through."

"Like the Italians who are Jewish," Giovanna said, feeling ashamed. She knew about the Italian Racial Laws passed in 1938 that said what Jewish Italians could and couldn't do. Mussolini had made those laws and the king didn't fight him. Her friend Sarina had had to leave school. Sarina's father had lost his job at the newspaper where he'd been a typesetter for years. Giovanna hadn't thought it was fair, but she had been twelve and hadn't entirely understood what was happening or why. Her mother had brought some clothing and a basket of food to Sarina's family and found out that they were planning to go north, over the Alps and into Switzerland. Giovanna and her family had prayed at church that weekend for their safety.

Later, after Giovanna and her family had left Genoa for Saluzzo, Jewish Italians were taken away. There was a community of about sixty Jewish people in Saluzzo, most of whom were taken by the Nazis in 1943. Faustina and Betto worked with the partisans to try to save the families they could—particularly those with young children. But in her last letter, Ilaria said that half of the community had been killed during the war, and many more hadn't returned. That was the same with the Jewish families Giovanna had known in Genoa. Most hadn't returned, and those who had, came with stories of living in internment camps in Borgo San Dalmazzo and Fossoli. They were the lucky ones. Giovanna had seen horrifying photos of the liberation of the German death camps—mountains of skeletal bodies and starving children with sunken eyes whose faces she saw in her nightmares. Now that the war was all over, now that she saw what had truly been happening, there was a knot in her heart for all she didn't do. For all she didn't question, even when she was twelve.

She didn't like to think about it, but she had to. There were so many feelings to untangle: the deep guilt that she didn't do more with Faustina and the partisans, the shame that her fear—and her father's fear—had stopped her.

She thought back to what Faustina had said when Vincenzo first walked into the shop—that his family had supported the fascists—and wondered if they would have made different choices in retrospect, too. Given another chance, she hoped she would have been more like Faustina. It was why she felt like she couldn't judge others. She was already so busy judging herself.

Vincenzo was quiet for a moment, too. "Part of why I've been back in Genoa so often is because my father wants to export the wine from our vineyards. He wants to sell it in America. Just before the war started, he'd begun conversations with Signor Menasci—he used to live in this building on the floor below us. But he was Jewish and left with his family as soon as the Italian Racial Laws were enacted. My father got a letter from him recently. He and his family are living in New York now. He asked us to see if we could locate some family members for him, some cousins he hasn't heard from since before the war. My father is going to see what he can do."

Giovanna shook her head. She thought about those pictures again. About the missing cousins, about Sarina and her family, and tears came to her eyes. "We will carry this with us for always."

Vincenzo used his finger to trace a Star of David in the dust on the table behind the sofa in the living room. "We will carry the sorrow and the guilt forever. It will always be there. But I hope we don't let it take over everything." He blew on the dust, blurring the image he'd traced.

"You hope that happiness can coexist with sorrow?" Giovanna asked.

"Yes," Vincenzo answered, looking at her as if he was grateful she understood what he meant, and as if she brought him some of that happiness. "That's why I want to paint you, here. I want to pair the opulence, the elegance, the splendor, and grandeur of this apartment with the spiderwebs and the dust and a city burning outside the window. I want to show you in a gown, watching it. Witnessing, seeing, but staying safe."

"You are painting our guilt," Giovanna said.

"I am painting my sorrow," Vincenzo answered.

Giovanna nodded. She knew that there were people who could speak about their feelings and others who could not, others who needed art or music, dance or story to show their emotions. Ilaria was like that. She was a beautiful musician, a violinist, and Giovanna could only truly tell how Ilaria was feeling when she heard her play. Her choice of music, the movement of her body, it was a window into her heart—a deeper window than her words. Vincenzo, Giovanna realized, was like that, too, only he needed to paint his heart. She was glad she'd said she would model for him. "What do you want me to do?" she asked.

He took her hand, his skin soft and warm, and led her into the parlor, where he'd set up his canvas. There were three gorgeous dresses lying on the couch.

She looked up at him. "Can I . . . touch them?" she asked. One was silk, one velvet, and the other layers of delicate organza, so thin it must have been sewn by hand.

He laughed. "Of course," he said. "You're going to wear them. Or, at least, one of them. Let me see the colors against your skin and hair."

Giovanna lifted up the dark blue velvet dress, the sumptuous fabric warm in her hands.

Vincenzo shook his head. "Not that one."

She picked up the pale pink silk.

He shook his head again.

She ran her hand along the ruffles of the organza dress, light blue with a wide white satin sash. She held the fabric up against her cheek.

"Yes," Vincenzo said, "That one. My sister's room is the second door on the left, down that hallway. Do you want to try it on in there?"

Giovanna nodded and walked down the hallway, looking at the framed paintings. She stopped at one that looked a little like Vincenzo, but older.

"That's my grandfather," Vincenzo said, noticing her standing there. "The last conte before my dad. This had been his apartment, too. I think he was about thirty in that painting."

"You have the same chin," Giovanna said, her eyes going from the art to the man standing in front of her.

Vincenzo smiled and touched his chin.

"Did you know your grandfather?" she asked him, thinking about her own grandparents, her mother's mother, who was gone before she could remember her.

"Only when I was very small," he said. "He was the one who started taking our vineyards more seriously, selling the wine locally instead of just keeping it in our wine cellar and giving it to friends, planting more vines. I remember picking grapes with him during the harvest—he used to put me up on his shoulders."

Giovanna watched Vincenzo's eyes as he talked about his grandfather and smiled. She could tell he loved his grandfather. She wondered what his eyes did when he talked about her. But then she shook the idea out of her head. They'd only known each other for a few weeks. Still, she couldn't deny how being with him made her feel, how he had claimed space in her thoughts. "Will you run the vineyards one day, like him?"

Vincenzo nodded and then squared his shoulders. "I will. I'll run the vineyards, I'll live in this apartment, I'll inherit everything my father has, which belonged to my grandfather before him and his father before that."

"Is that what you want?" Giovanna asked him, curious.

Vincenzo shrugged. "It's not a matter of wanting or not wanting. It just is," he said. "A tree doesn't choose to grow olives, it just does. I'm the same way. I'm an olive tree. Or, I guess, the backup olive tree, always in my brother's shadow until now."

Giovanna thought about that, about what it might feel like to be the "just in case," and then to become the heir. And to know what your life would entail—and what it wouldn't. In some sense, there was probably a feeling of stability about it. Relief, knowing that there weren't many choices to make. But in another sense, she could see how it could feel stifling, especially if he'd had other dreams that would now be cut short. The thing with olive trees is that they didn't know any different. They didn't see a plum tree and wish their own fruit were sweeter. People did. They had their own hopes and desires.

"What about your art?" Giovanna asked him.

"I like to paint," he said. "And I'd hoped . . ." He shook his head. "My family needs me now, and I'll do whatever has to be done."

"I'm sorry," she said. "That your choices were taken away." She looked back up at Vincenzo's grandfather and wondered what dreams he'd had that weren't realized. She felt Vincenzo's eyes on her, and when she turned to him, she saw that they shone with unshed tears. He blinked them away.

"No one has ever acknowledged that before," he said. "That I lost more than just my brother in the war."

Giovanna wanted to comfort him, give him the space to mourn the losses that he felt so acutely. "You lost a lot," she said quietly. "You talked the other day about the life you expect to lead, but really you expected a different future entirely."

"I did," he said and looked up at her, his eyelashes wet.

"And it hurts to lose it," she said.

"It does." Vincenzo cleared his throat. "I'm sorry for getting so emotional."

Giovanna smiled softly at him. "You never have to apologize for that to me. There's a lot we don't talk about in my family, too. When I was in Saluzzo, during the war, I used to walk to the cemetery and sit against my grandmother's grave and tell her and my mother all the things I was afraid of. Just saying it out loud always helped. I bet it would've helped even more if there had been someone alive I could tell."

"You can tell me," Vincenzo said. "I'll listen."

Giovanna looked at him and their eyes locked. In that breath, it seemed like their souls had touched. "Me too," she said, and then she turned into his sister's bedroom to try on his mother's gown. What was the difference, really, between someone who was noble and someone who wasn't? History? Money? Power? Expectations? They were the same at their core. They both needed someone to talk to, someone who would listen and hear more than was said.

As Giovanna slipped into the organza gown, looking at the tiny horse figurines that lined the shelves, she wondered whether a friendship between her and Vincenzo was possible. She reached behind her back to tie the sash and thought of the heat of his arm beneath her fingers when she'd sewed his loose button. What would his parents think of their son spending time with the daughter of a tailor?

Chapter 9

Cass returned to Manhattan weighed down with leftovers from lunch. Her parents had given her containers of macaroni salad, cheese, fruit, and rainbow cookies from her favorite bakery, Agrigento. There was even a Tupperware container filled with leftover drumsticks from their dinner the night before. "We want to know you're eating well," her dad had said as he'd packed up the tote bag, slipping in some of the rosemary, basil, and mint he grew in the backyard.

When she went away to college, he'd had boxes of Omaha Steaks shipped to her apartment when she started living off campus. And perhaps at her father's urging—or perhaps of her own volition—her grandmother had sent her homemade pesto, with typewritten instructions on top of each Tupperware container explaining how to heat up the frozen basil, pinoli nut, garlic, and parmesan mixture and add the proper amount of olive oil to give it the right consistency and flavor. Next time she visited, Cass decided, she'd ask her grandmother to make pesto with her, just so she'd always have the recipe—and the memory—to savor.

Cass shook her head as if to clear out the sorrow that had been creeping into her thoughts since she saw her grandmother. The realization that life was finite. That there would be a time when she would exist in this world without Gram. Pop had passed away when Cass was twelve, but somehow the fact that Gram would one day be gone, too, had never really registered until now. It was an idea she hated.

As Cass got off the train in Penn Station, her phone chimed. She looked down and saw a text from Luca.

Almost home?

Yes, she responded. At Penn.

Her stomach flipped with anticipation. The impending marriage proposal had been pushed to the back of her mind briefly while she was on Long Island. But now it was giving her butterflies.

Would you mind picking up some olive oil on the way?

She smiled. They went through olive oil the way some people went through milk. But she knew for a fact they had more than enough in the kitchen cabinet. He was stalling for time.

Sure, she wrote back.

She got off the subway and went to the local convenience store where they stocked the extra virgin olive oil she and Luca liked best. Then she walked down Houston Street to their loft, taking in the basketball game on the court next to the playground, the yellow cabs pulling over to the curb to let people out, the shops and restaurants, the Freedom Tower standing tall in the distance.

She had dreamed this life when she was a bridge-and-tunnel kid, coming into Manhattan from the Long Island suburbs. Taking a quick detour, she passed Lafayette, turned right on Mott Street, and walked up the steps to St. Patrick's Old Cathedral. The church was just as grand as the ones she'd visited in Europe.

Throughout her whole life, Cassandra's mother impressed on all three of her children that you shouldn't just ask for things in prayer—you should be thankful when your prayers were answered. Her favorite psalm for saying thank you was the *Benedic anima mea*. First on her mother's urging, and then by her own choice, Cass followed her mother's advice. Whenever she was particularly grateful—in school, in work, in love—she walked into the closest Catholic church and said thank you.

Cass entered the cathedral, genuflected, crossed herself, and sat down in a pew. She let the calm and the beauty of the holy space wash over her. "Benedic, anima mea, Domino," she murmured. The ancient language on her tongue always made her feel an even deeper connection to God. "Et omnia quæ intra me sunt nomini sancto ejus. Benedic, anima mea, Domino, et noli oblivisci omnes retributiones ejus." *Bless the Lord, my soul, and all that is within me, bless his holy name. Bless the Lord, my soul, and never forget all he has done for you.*

Cass stood and walked back out onto the street, feeling the way she always did after leaving church, after praying—as if the chaos of the world, of her life, had melted away and she was emerging a more centered, grounded version of herself.

Cass traveled the rest of the way home feeling that calmness in her soul. She took the elevator to their loft and had just put her key in the lock when the door swung open. Luca was dressed in a gray suit and pale yellow button-down, the collar open in a way that made him look fancy and casual at the same time. There was music playing, something classical Cass didn't recognize, and then she stepped into the living room and gasped. Luca had turned their entire living room into a Rothko-inspired Luca Bartolomei painting. Huge sheets of canvas had been sewn together and painted, and then hung from the ceilings, hiding the walls and the furniture.

"I wanted to create something for you," he said. "Just for you. Not for the galleries, not for the collectors. And when I started painting, it just kept getting bigger and bigger. Like my love for you. It's too much to contain on one canvas. It fills my whole self, my whole life. And this is the only way I know to show that to you."

Of all of the ways that Cass thought Luca might propose, she had never thought of this. She spun in slow circles, taking it in. The stripes of color, while like Rothko in form, were the ones that Luca used most in his art. Deep reds, royal blues, brilliant teals. His color palette always seemed to hold the boldest version of every color. And now here she was, inside a painting. Inside a painting he created for her. To show her the magnitude of his love.

Cass stopped her slow turn when she was facing him again. "This is incredible," she said. "You are incredible."

He took a ring out of his pocket and held it toward her. "Will you . . ." he started, then paused, as if looking for the exact right words.

"Marry you?" she finished, wondering if he was so nervous that the words of both languages flew out of his mind.

He laughed. "Yes. Simplest is best sometimes. Will you marry me?"

She felt tears well in her eyes. "Of course," she said.

He took her hand and slipped a ring on her finger. She looked down at it. There was a diamond in the center of a cluster of gems—ruby, sapphire, emerald, topaz. It fit perfectly.

"This is gorgeous," she said. She thought she'd seen something like it recently, but she couldn't quite place where.

"My nonno brought it with him today," he said. "He had it sized for me. It was his mother's, and his grandmother's before that. My grandmother used to wear it when I was younger, and I always loved it. She promised me I could have it one day to give to my wife. Even though she's gone, Nonno remembered her promise. And I loved the idea that this piece of jewelry would welcome you into our family. A bit of our history that's now part of yours."

Cass admired her hand with the ring on it. Her finger felt different, a little heavier, but she liked it. She liked having that reminder of Luca on her hand. The reminder that he was her family now, officially. They were united.

"I love that," she said and kissed him. "Thank you to the jewelry for the warm welcome."

She looked down again and watched the stones catch the light with the slightest movement of her finger.

"Speaking of welcoming into families," he said, "there's just enough time for you to change before we're going to meet our families at Osteria Morini."

"My family, too?" she said, surprised.

"Well, our parents and grandparents," he said.

Cass couldn't believe she'd spent the whole afternoon with her family, and neither her parents nor her grandmother had let it slip that they'd be coming to dinner that night, that they knew what Luca was about to do. They probably had wanted to preserve the surprise, but she was shocked none of them had said something accidentally.

"What about our siblings?"

Cass's brothers and Luca's sister hadn't met yet, and Cass wondered what Nick and Chris would think of Alessandra. They couldn't be any more different.

"We'll save siblings for a real engagement party," Luca answered with a smile.

"Good plan," Cass answered. Then she sighed. "I love Osteria Morini."

Luca laughed. "Why do you think I picked it?"

"You were pretty sure I would say yes, huh?" Cass said, kissing him again.

"Let's just say I had a preview last night. I was hopeful the response would be the same."

Cass laughed. "Your hope was not unfounded," she said.

That was how Luca made Cass feel. Hopeful. Hopeful there was a place where she could fit, a family they could build, someone who would love her because of the choices she made and the dreams she had. With Luca, the future she dreamed about seemed possible.

Chapter 10

GENOA, ITALY
Then

Vincenzo was supposed to meet his friend Bruno for a drink at a new jazz club that had opened up not far from the port. Bruno was late, as usual, so Vincenzo waited with a glass of wine at a table for two. He thought about Giovanna and wished she were there, sitting across from him.

She'd come by again today, her second week modeling for him. And when she walked out of his sister's room his breath caught. There was such beauty in the soft way she entered a space. Neither one of them had said anything as she walked toward him and then stopped at the window, where he was waiting.

"What are you looking at?" he'd asked her.

"The destruction of La Superba," Giovanna had answered, her eyes still facing the window.

Vincenzo loved that name for Genoa and loved that Giovanna had used it. "We'll rebuild the city," he had said. "We'll rebuild all of Italy."

And he knew they would rebuild—his father's vineyards, their export business, the damaged churches and destroyed streets.

Giovanna had turned to him, so beautiful in his mother's pale blue gown. "I wonder how it will change," she said.

He did, too. He wondered if it could mean his parents might approve of him being with Giovanna, instead of Isabella, the perfectly sweet daughter of his father's friend—a marchese who owned the Fratelli Lorenzi automobile company—whom his family wanted him to marry. He hoped so. He hoped that after the referendum his family would not need to be so protective of their status, would feel secure enough to give them—him—more freedom. If the monarchy was abolished, he really had no idea what to expect.

"We'll see, won't we?" he'd finally replied, and then walked to his canvas on the other side of the parlor.

Giovanna walked toward him, the gown tied tightly at her waist with a white satin sash, one pristine white glove ending at her elbow. She looked the part. She looked like she could walk into any social gathering on his arm and fit right in.

"I know we haven't yet begun, but perhaps it's already time for a break?" he'd said, reaching his hand out to caress her cheek. He hadn't intended to, but he felt drawn to her.

"You tell me, Mister Artist," she'd answered, intertwining her gloved fingers with his other hand.

"Definitely time," he'd murmured. With every fiber of his being, Vincenzo wanted to kiss her. He imagined their heads tipping toward each other slowly, as the space between each second got longer, and then his lips meeting hers, warm and soft.

But he was afraid. Afraid to start something he couldn't finish. Afraid it would ruin this beautiful thing they'd created. Sitting in the club, Vincenzo took out his sketchbook and started drawing Giovanna's head on his chest, his lips in her hair.

"Sorry I'm late," Bruno said, dropping into the seat across from Vincenzo.

Vincenzo quickly slipped his sketchbook back in his jacket pocket.

Chapter 11

Cass was getting dressed for dinner but kept getting distracted by the ring on her finger. The bathroom light made it cast rainbows on the marble counter.

Whenever she went out with Luca's family, she felt like she had to be particularly well dressed. His mother, Marina, always looked like she'd stepped out of the pages of *Vogue Italia*. Her pants were perfectly tailored, her tops were made of silk and cashmere, and her accessories were coordinated in a way that made it look like she wasn't trying, though Cass had a feeling a lot of time went into planning those outfits. Marina, along with Luca's father, Pietro, worked in Nonno's wine export business. They managed the North American distribution, with Marina as her father's deputy, in charge of sales, and Pietro running operations. Marina was a trained sommelier, too, and with her mix of style, intelligence, and confidence, Cass understood how the brand had grown sixfold under her watch.

Cass put on a garnet-colored knit dress from Kate Spade, the first designer she had ever worked for in an internship during college.

Then she clasped a gold necklace, the Immaculate Heart of Mary that her parents had given her for her first Holy Communion, around her neck and whispered an extra thank you. "Holy Mary, mother of God, thank you for all the blessings I've been given. Especially Luca." She went to reach for a pair of heels in her closet—but then Luca came up behind her, swept her hair to the side, and kissed her neck.

"What shoes do you think?" she asked, leaning back against him, feeling his warmth envelop her. Her fiancé. He was her fiancé. And soon he would be her husband.

"Those brown boots," he said, pointing. "The ones you got when we were in Firenze. My mother will love them."

She leaned out of his embrace to pull the boots from the closet. They had a stiletto heel, and the leather was patterned with tiny leaves and flowers. She sat on the bed to zip them up, and then she stood and looked in the mirror. It was an edgier pairing than she usually chose, but it looked good. And it was always nice that Luca thought Marina would like her outfit. She could never quite get a handle on how Luca's mother felt about her—and she knew it meant a lot to Luca that his family like her.

"I'm your canvas tonight," Cass told her fiancé. "What else?"

He looked at her and smiled, then pulled a braided belt out of her closet that was made of brown, orange, and gold-dyed leather, and took a pair of gold earrings from her jewelry box that brought to mind filigreed leaves. After that, he went to another drawer and took out three bangle bracelets, one in orange and two in gold.

"There," he said. "You look like autumn. Even your golden eyes are on theme."

Cass laughed and batted her eyelashes at him. Their styles were different. Cass usually chose just one statement piece, the rest of her clothing simple and classic. Luca liked things a little louder, a little more creative, putting belts and shoes and bracelets together in a way that made them seem like they were meant to be worn that way.

Cass quickly did her makeup and applied a red-orange lipstick that completed the look.

"Sei bellissima, stellina," he said as she walked out of the bathroom and back into their bedroom.

"Does everyone know why we're having dinner?" she asked.

Luca smiled. "I think they've guessed," he said. "I did ask your father for permission to marry you, and my grandfather brought the ring with him from Italy, plus you sent everyone that photograph of your hand before, so . . ."

Cass laughed. "Right. I did." Her brain was so overcome by joy it wasn't quite working properly. "Oh," she said, just remembering. "My grandmother said she'd think about posing for your painting. She was funny about it. Said no one had asked her that in a long time, but then she wouldn't say anything more when I wanted to know what she meant by that. So maybe when you meet her tonight, you can give her some more details—or *get* some more details."

When they got to the restaurant, Cass saw her parents and grand-mother sitting with the Bartolomeis. Marina, wearing a silk blouse in a pattern reminiscent of a mosaic, was talking, gesticulating.

Cass's parents were nodding. Her mom looked nice in a dark green sweater and black pants, with a long necklace that had little gems dangling off a gold bar, one for each of her children and grand-children, and her dad was wearing a navy sport jacket with a blue checked shirt and khakis. They looked like what they were: good, solid, bighearted people. But the contrast between her parents and the Bartolomeis was clear.

Marina stopped talking, and then everyone at the table turned to look at Gram. She was wearing a cobalt blue dress that Cass knew she had sewn herself some years before, which is why it fit her so well. Even at ninety-two, Gram could turn heads.

Whatever she had said was funny, and the group laughed.

"Where's Nonno?" Cass asked.

"Probably jet-lagged." Luca shrugged. "We'll see him tomorrow."

"It's the couple of the hour!" Cass's dad exclaimed, standing up as she and Luca walked over.

Everyone else at the table stood, too, except for Gram, and hugs (for her parents) and double kisses (for his) were exchanged. Luca bent down to say hello to Gram, and she held his hands tightly. "You're as handsome as Cassandra says," she told him, and everyone laughed. She patted the seat next to her, and Luca sat in it, Cass next to him with Marina on her other side. "So tell me about this painting you want me to be part of," Gram said.

And Luca explained the image, the idea behind the whole group of paintings, and that his grandfather would be part of it, too, while the rest of the table listened.

"That sounds lovely," Cass's mom said, then turned to the Bartolomeis. "You must be so proud."

Marina nodded. "We're glad he finally seems to be able to make a living at it. I'd been hoping he'd want to join us in the wine business, but my father insisted that we let him follow this path."

Cass could feel Luca shrinking next to her. "Nonno's a smart man," she said as she grabbed Luca's hand and squeezed it. "He must have an eye for talent."

Luca squeezed back.

"I'm sorry he couldn't make it tonight," Cass's dad said from across the table. "We're looking forward to meeting him."

"Transatlantic travel takes a lot more out of him than it used to," Marina said. Then she turned to Gram. "I think you two will get along. Cass says you grew up in Genova?"

Gram nodded.

"My family has had a flat there for generations. You may have gone to some of the same cafés."

"Perhaps," Gram said. "I'll have to see if I can remember the names of any of those cafés. It's been a long time."

"Cassandra!" her mother said, nearly jumping from her seat. "Your ring! I just realized I still haven't seen it in person!" The photograph of her finger Cass had sent earlier hadn't done the ring justice.

Cass lifted her left hand above the table, toward her mother.

"It's been in my family for at least a hundred years," Marina offered.

"It's beautiful," Cass's mother said. "So unique."

Gram reached out to hold Cass's hand in hers. "It must've been a popular style for a while," she said. "I knew someone in Italy who wore something very similar. I may not remember cafés, but I remember jewelry."

The waiter came by. "I heard we're celebrating tonight," he said, bringing a bottle of champagne with him.

"Champagne?" Pietro asked. "We didn't order this."

"I ordered it before we sat down," Cass's father said.

"May I see?" Marina asked. The waiter obliged. She looked at the label and then at Cass's father. "You wouldn't mind if we drank something Italian, would you?" She turned to the waiter. "May I see your wine list?"

"My mom's very picky with her wines," Luca said with an apologetic smile. Cass could tell he was uncomfortable. Cass looked around the table. Her parents seemed confused. Her grandmother looked annoyed.

Marina scanned the list. "This one instead," she said, her finger stopping on a riserva brut Ca' del Bosco. "A sparkling wine from Franciacorta."

A good choice, of course. Cass wouldn't expect anything less from Marina. But she nudged Luca when she saw the price. He knew what she was trying to tell him, and he immediately said, "Since I invited everyone out tonight, I just want to make it clear that I'm the host, and I'm paying."

"Oh no," Cass's dad said. "We can't let you do that."

"Don't be silly," Marina added.

"Nope," Luca said. "On me. Has to be, or we're leaving. Right, Cass?"

"Right," Cass said, smiling at him. She pressed her leg against his under the table. Usually it didn't make much of a difference how much money Luca's family had compared to hers, but once in a while something like this came up. She'd have to talk to Luca about their wedding, make sure that he was thinking what she was thinking: the two of them would pay.

"In that case"—Cass's mom turned to her father—"we should let him pay. We can't very well celebrate their engagement if they leave."

Cass's dad smiled. "Of course," he said.

Marina shrugged, a delicate rise and fall of her shoulders. "Come volete," she told her son.

Cass knew what that meant. *Do what you want.*

"Grazie, Mamma," Luca said.

Cass would give him a big kiss for that later. Her parents did just fine—they had enough money to own a house, put food on the table, help their kids out when they needed it, go on a vacation every summer, buy Christmas gifts. But she knew that paying more than two hundred dollars for a bottle of wine was something they would balk at and then talk about for years. The champagne her father had ordered was seventy-five dollars, and she knew that was a splurge for him.

The rest of the dinner went on without much incident. They finished with tiramisu, which Cass found out was also Pietro's favorite dessert, and then Cass's dad went to get his car, so Gram wouldn't have to walk too far. "Would you like a ride home?" Cass's mom asked. "We can drop you off before we head back."

"That's okay, Mom," Cass said. "You have a long drive ahead of you, and it's late."

"We'll take them," Pietro said. "We have a car coming in a moment."

Cass somehow felt caught, like taking Pietro's ride would be choosing Luca's family over her own. She knew it was silly, but she was relieved, nonetheless, when Luca said that he had something else planned for the two of them, and his parents should go.

Cass's dad pulled up with the car, and Luca helped Gram out to the street.

"When do you want me at your studio?" she asked him.

"You'll do it?" he said.

"I'll do it," she affirmed.

"My grandfather is coming Monday morning, around ten. Could you do that?"

She nodded. "I'll ask Cass's father to drive me. Now that he's retired, it'll give him something to do."

Cass stood next to Luca, watching their families get into their cars, and let out a deep breath. She loved her family, and she liked Luca's, too, but having them together stressed her out. They were so different, and it highlighted the differences between her and Luca in a way that she didn't like.

She turned to him. "I love you," she said.

He smiled. "I love you, too. Now, are you ready for the last surprise of the evening?"

She took his hand. "Lead the way," she said.

Chapter 12

GENOA, ITALY
Then

It was getting harder and harder for Giovanna not to tell Faustina about Vincenzo. He was a permanent fixture in her life now, in her mind. Whenever anything happened, no matter what it was, she thought, *I have to tell Vincenzo.* Two birds chasing each other outside the shop's window, Ilaria's news that she and Aldo were going to have a baby in the summer, the beautiful emerald fabric Betto found her to make a new dress for herself. No matter how big or how small, she wanted to tell him everything, wanted to see him smile at her excitement. Her joy brought him joy, and that brought her joy. It was a continuous circle of happiness, and she found herself waiting for the moments when he would come by the store with a loose button or box of pastries he thought she and her family might enjoy.

For the third Saturday in a row, Giovanna went to Vincenzo's family apartment to be his model. Their days together consisted of painting, of long walks through streets and gardens and near the water, long talks, delicious food and wine, getting to know each other's hearts, each other's souls.

When the day's painting began, Giovanna was wearing the blue organza dress, one satin glove pulled up to her elbow, the other crumpled down by her wrist. Vincenzo was in his paint-splattered tan pants and an undershirt.

"Something's missing," he said, looking at her critically.

"Shoes?" she asked. She wasn't wearing any. It turned out she was slightly taller than Vincenzo's mother, and the gown didn't hit the floor properly when she wasn't barefoot.

Vincenzo smiled. "Not shoes . . ." He looked at her some more. "Jewelry! Come with me."

Giovanna picked up the skirt in her hands so she wouldn't trip on it or accidentally step on it and tear the delicate fabric. She followed Vincenzo down the hallway into the apartment's main bedroom, which she hadn't been inside before. It felt strange to be in a room with him that had a bed in it. Even stranger that it belonged to his parents. She felt like she was trespassing and stood near the doorway, not wanting to go too far in.

She watched as Vincenzo took a painting off a wall and then twirled the combination on a safe.

"My mother split her jewelry between here and Alba before the war, so if one place was hit with bombs or raided, she wouldn't lose everything," he said as he took a box out of the safe. "I asked her if she wanted me to bring it back now that the war's ended, but she said there was no reason to. That eventually she'd be back here in Genoa and would need it. But in the meantime . . ."

Vincenzo took a pair of sapphire earrings out of the box and looked up at Giovanna. "Your ears aren't pierced," he said. She shook her head. He put them back in the box.

"Here," he said. "This is perfect." He was holding a ring. It had a delicate gold band and a cluster of colored gems with a diamond in the center.

Giovanna couldn't imagine how much that ring cost.

She held her hand out for it, but he flipped her palm over and slid it on her ring finger. With the glove on, it fit almost perfectly.

Giovanna looked up and saw Vincenzo's eyes on her. He hadn't let go of her hand. She could feel the satin of the glove catching on the dried paint stains on his fingers.

"Giovanna." He whispered her name as if it were sacred, holy.

"Vincenzo," she whispered back. Her heart was fluttering, and she could feel the tremor in her stomach, her hands, her throat. The walks, the buttons, the lunch, the coffee, the pastries, the painting, the dancing—it felt like it was leading to this moment, his face centimeters from hers, his lips even closer.

"May I . . . may I kiss you?" His voice was soft, more air than sound. She could feel his breath on her skin.

"Yes," she said to him.

He leaned in, and she realized, in his hesitation, that this wasn't something he did often. That thought calmed her fluttering heart, allowed her to lean forward, to press her lips against his. The kiss was warm and soft, and so were his arms, wrapped around her. She hadn't known how a kiss could make her feel—as if the world started and ended right there, in that room, in the space between his breath and hers.

The kiss transitioned to an embrace, and she laid her head on his shoulder, feeling his arms tighten around her back.

"That was . . . the most beautiful thing I've ever experienced," he said.

She reached up to rest her satin hand on his cheek, their eyes fixed on each other's. "Me too," she whispered.

Chapter 13

NEW YORK CITY, USA
Now

"So what's this big surprise?" Cass asked as Luca took her hand and walked with her down Lafayette Street.

"It's a family tradition, actually. An old one." Luca smiled down at her, and she imagined generations of his family, tall and regal, smiling down at women across centuries.

"How old a tradition?" she asked.

"Old," he answered. "Going back to my sixth great-grandfather."

"The first conte?"

Luca nodded.

It amazed Cass how Luca could trace his family back so easily. Find them in history books, their names engraved in the walls of churches, their likenesses chiseled into marble and preserved on canvas. Her family, meanwhile, came from a long line of untraceable tailors and stonemasons, or at least that was what she'd been told. They could've been farmers or chambermaids for all she really knew.

"Hmm," Cass said, thinking about the generations of women before her who had participated in this tradition—Luca's aunt, his mother, his grandmother. She couldn't imagine what it could be, but she liked the idea that it would tie her to them, to Luca's whole family. "Will you tell me more?"

Luca shook his head. "I said it was a surprise. It wouldn't be a surprise if I told you, now would it?" The streetlights were on, taxicabs were zooming past them, and music spilled out from a bar on their right.

Cass looked over at Luca, and he smiled. The streetlight glowed behind him, making it look like he had a halo, like in Renaissance paintings of saints. *I could build a campaign around this*, she thought. It was a thought she had a lot, the kind she would tuck away in her mind until she needed it at the office. And then it would inspire people to dream about being the best versions of themselves, the person they wanted to be. When Cass was younger, her grandmother used to tell her that the way she dressed was her calling card to the world. And she could use it to telegraph whatever information she wanted to share. Did she want to look mature? Carefree? Serious? Flirty? Like she was trying to impress someone? Or like she wasn't? You can play psychological games with what you wear, giving people a particular impression before you even open your mouth.

The light behind Luca shifted and sparkled against a puddle of water in the street. *Do the clothes make the man?* she imagined a voice-over saying. *Or does the man make the clothes?* Cass knew that being your best self came from the inside, of course, but when you felt good on the outside, it had the potential to change you on the inside, to raise your confidence so that you carried yourself better, owned any room you walked into. It was something Cass felt acutely during her junior year abroad in Italy, when she got a job working in a boutique in Florence, on Via Della Spada, and used her employee discount to buy a handful of classic pieces—a black wiggle dress, a fitted charcoal blazer, a tan pencil skirt, a white silk blouse; when she wore them, she felt like she could do anything. When she was deciding how she wanted to spend the rest of her life, those outfits, that feeling, influenced her choice to go into fashion. She knew the power of clothing and wanted to share it with everyone.

"How about twenty questions?" she asked him. "To see if I can guess the surprise." The two of them played this game often. *Twenty questions on who called me today. Twenty questions on where Alessandra and her family are going on vacation. Twenty questions on the gift my mother just sent me in the mail.* They'd played it on their first date. "Twenty questions," Luca had said, "on what compelled me to find out who you were." The answer was the confidence with which she walked through the room. "There is nothing I find sexier," he told her, "than a woman who knows who she is."

Cass told him she wasn't sure that she did know who she was. But he shook his head. "I can tell by the way you move," he'd said.

And the more Cass thought about it, the more she realized he might be right. Once she came home from her junior year abroad, she told her parents she was moving to Manhattan, that she wouldn't be the bookkeeper for her dad's and brothers' contracting company, and that she had gotten a marketing job in fashion. In that way, she and Luca were very similar—both pursuing their own dreams, not conforming to what their parents wanted them to be.

Luca's grin grew, and he paused in his walk down the street to give Cass a kiss on the cheek. "Okay, twenty questions. Go."

"Is the surprise an object?" she started, as they walked past a pizza joint.

Luca shook his head. "Not really."

"Not really or not at all?" she asked. The answers were supposed to be yes or no, but sometimes they had to equivocate, which was allowed but made the game harder.

He thought for a moment. "Not really," he said again.

Hmm. Cass wasn't sure where that left her. "Is the surprise an experience?" she asked.

"Yes, mostly," Luca answered, squeezing her hand.

"Mostly!"

He laughed at her indignation. "I know, I'm not making it easy, but just trying to be honest."

Another yellow cab raced by, and Luca tried to hail it, but it kept going.

"Are we staying in New York City?" She was trying to narrow down the options, all the while thinking about what kinds of things could be a tradition in his family. A late-night Italian cooking class so she could learn to make a family recipe? A dance lesson for a specific dance at their wedding? A drive to the mountains to spend the night under the stars?

"Yes," Luca said.

That narrowed things down a little, but not much. She didn't really think they were traveling far anyway, with his grandfather in town. "In Manhattan?" Cass asked.

"No," Luca answered.

"Brooklyn?" she asked.

"Yes," Luca said. "That was five."

He managed to hail a cab and held the door open for Cass, then slid inside after her.

"Are we making something?" she asked as she fastened her seatbelt. *Pasta*, she thought, *chocolate . . . wine!*

"Yes," Luca said. "I bet you can guess it now."

"Are we going to Red, White, and Rosé?"

"Yes!" Luca said triumphantly. "Stefano is opening the wine press for us. We're going to make some wine. My parents, my grandparents, my great-grandparents—and on and on—all crushed grapes together when they got engaged and made their own special vintage of wine, one they never sold and never shared."

That was fascinating. Special wine. Secret wine. That no one would taste but them. Cass wondered what Marina and Pietro's wine tasted like. "Shouldn't we fly to Italy for this? Make this in your grandfather's vineyard?"

"Stefano has imported my grandfather's grapes for us, so it's the next best thing. And, quite frankly, it's a lot easier to get the grapes to us than to get us to the grapes. It's perfect timing, too, because they just started harvesting them."

Cass smiled and wondered if getting engaged during the grape harvest was a family tradition, too. "So, how does this all work?"

"Well, it's up to us," he said. "That's the fun of it. We're making this for ourselves, and there won't be any other wine like it in the world."

Something she'd realized while dating Luca was that his family loved bespoke gifts like that. Things that were one of a kind, created just for them, or an experience they alone could have. She figured that when you had enough money to buy pretty much anything you wanted, the uniqueness of a gift was what made it special; the thought that went into it was what set it apart.

That realization was what led Cass to ask for her grandmother's help last year to make Luca a birthday present. She had gotten all of his paintings screened onto fabric, and then had them sewn together into a quilt the week he'd gone to Italy for a bachelor party for his cousin Serena's fiancé. When Luca opened it and realized what it was,

Cass saw tears in his eyes. "No one has ever created art with my art before," he said, before taking Cass into his arms and holding her there. He'd told her later that it was the moment he knew he was going to marry her.

"Is Stefano going to be there?" Cass asked as they rode across the Brooklyn Bridge. Stefano and Luca had grown up together before the Bartolomei family moved to the United States, and then Stefano studied under Luca's uncle before coming to the United States himself and working at the vineyards on Long Island's East End, a couple of hours' drive from where Cass grew up. After that, he decided he wanted to start his own winery in Brooklyn. He bought grapes from all over the world to make his wines, including some from the Della Rosa vineyards. He had a tasting room, live music—and a great write-up in the *New York Times* that had put his business in the black within a year.

"Nah, he's closed early tonight for us, which means he and Dorian are out enjoying themselves somewhere else this evening. He gave me the key." Luca held up a keychain with a bulldog on it. Stefano's first love was winemaking. His second love was Dorian, and his third was his bulldog, Fabio.

The cab stopped in Red Hook in front of a metal gate. Cass got out of the car and was amazed, as she always was when they visited Stefano's winery, at how different Red Hook looked from their neighborhood in Manhattan. There were no skyscrapers, just small streets of residential buildings near more commercial strips of shops and bars and restaurants. And then here, in this area, a few blocks from the water, there were warehouses that had been taken over as restaurants and a high-end wedding venue—one that served Della Rosa wine, actually.

Luca unlocked the gate and set off a motion sensor light, illuminating the big wooden front door of the brick winery that had a sign taped to the door saying *Closed for a private event.* Then he unlocked that door, too, and inside the winery, it was filled with flowers: fresh red, white, and pink roses. Dried rose petals were strewn across the floor.

"This isn't part of the tradition," Luca said with a smile. "This is just Stefano having fun."

Cass laughed.

The two of them walked through the outer part of the winery, where the tastings happened, and into the back room where the wines were made. On a stainless-steel table in the middle of the room was a bottle of moscato d'Asti and a note from Stefano.

> **Congratulazioni!**
> **You make the must, I'll do the rest.**
> **Un bacione,**
> **Stefano**

So they were going to make must, and Stefano would age it for them and turn it into wine. Cass was into this, even though she wasn't sure how the must process worked—or how to work any of the presses or machines.

"The family tradition," Luca said.

"Yes?" Cass answered, looking around the room, wondering what they would do first.

"You remember when we went to Italy last fall during the grape harvest?" Luca was leaning against the stainless-steel table.

Cass nodded. Tons of people had been picking grapes in the vineyard, and then large machines mashed them into must. All except for two barrels that they used for Il Calpestamento, The Stomp, where the two people who picked the most grapes during the harvest competed against two members of Luca's family to see who could produce the most juice. One person was in the barrel with no shoes on, and the other person caught the wine that came out through the spigot with a bucket. For a long time, Luca's nonno did the stomping with his wife doing the catching, but once she died, Luca's uncle, Giorgio, and his wife, Vanessa, took over. They didn't make any wine from those two barrels, but apparently, they used to.

"So the tradition is that we do a calpestamento. Just us—and we get in the barrel together. Stefano set it up for us, see?"

Cass turned, and there she saw a barrel taller than she was, with a spigot attached to a hose. "This looks a little more high tech than the one in Italy that your uncle stomped in."

Luca looked at her like he wasn't sure what she meant.

"The hose," she said. "The one there, the juice just came out of the spigot for your zia Vanessa to catch."

"Oh, yes, the hose." Luca nodded. "Family traditions can get upgrades." He uncorked the moscato and poured it into two glasses that Stefano had left them. "My mother and father made their wine in Italy, with the whole family watching. But I liked the idea of doing this alone. Because I have some other upgrades to the tradition I'd like to make."

"Oh really?" she said as he handed her a glass.

"Salute," he said, clinking his glass to hers and taking a sip. "So I was thinking, what if we crushed the grapes naked?"

Cass coughed, almost choking on the moscato she'd just swallowed.

"Are you okay?" Luca asked.

She nodded, taking another sip of wine. "Sorry, just not expecting that," she said when she'd caught her breath. Luca bent to kiss her, and she put her glass on the table. Then she started slowly unbuttoning his shirt. "But things that are unexpected are often the most fun."

The two of them undressed each other, replacing clothing with wine-flavored kisses. Cass couldn't believe that this was actually her life, that Luca was actually going to be her husband. She had dated other men who were handsome, other men who were talented, who were smart, who were kind and caring, but none of them made her feel like Luca did. When her friend Kiley met him, she said, "Oh, I get it. You two are from the same collection." And Cass had laughed, but she thought about that often. It seemed true, somehow; no matter how different their upbringing, they were from the same collection.

Cass felt cool air blow across her body, and her nipples hardened. Luca took one in his mouth.

"Are we making love or making wine?" she said softly, her head falling back in pleasure.

"Both," Luca whispered, as he kissed his way down her stomach. She ran her fingers through his hair until his tongue reached the most sensitive part of her, and she had to grab onto his shoulders to stay upright.

"Sit down," she whispered, "please."

Luca did as she asked, sliding to the floor, and she sat on his lap facing him. He rocked into her, and the pleasure took her breath away.

"I love you," he said softly into her ear.

"I love you more than anything," she answered. "More than anyone."

They both came soon after, their bodies momentarily still. And then Cass collapsed against Luca, her head on his shoulder.

He held her tight, kissing her hair. "Now," he said, "are you ready to make wine?"

After one last kiss, she stood and helped him up from the floor. The two of them climbed the metal ladder and lowered themselves into the barrel that was about a quarter full of grapes. Cass had never felt a sensation quite like it: the squishy firmness of the grapes giving way under her toes, the juice flowing toward the bottom of the barrel.

Luca climbed down next to her.

"Should we stomp?" she asked.

"Let's dance," he said.

He started humming softly, a song they'd discovered that both his mother used to sing to him and her grandmother used to sing to her: "Stella, stellina, la notte s'avvicina." *Star, little star, the night is coming...* And then he put his arms around her, skin against skin. She laid her head on his bare shoulder—she was wearing nothing but the engagement ring he'd given her that night—and the two of them slow danced, their feet moving together to a song that connected them both, their past to their present, creating their own vintage of wine.

Chapter 14

GENOA, ITALY
Then

Vincenzo and Giovanna spent the next three Saturdays together. "Meet me tomorrow at the Spianata dell'Acquasola," he'd said the first week, when he brought by a sketch of the shop he'd made from memory the night before, a gift that told Giovanna that he'd been thinking about her while they were apart.

"Meet me at the port," he said the next week.

"Meet me at Salita di Santa Brigida."

Each time, he packed them a picnic lunch of bread and cured meat and olives and cheese and wine, and they would find somewhere to sit and talk and he would draw and she would watch the people going by.

"Did you know that Santa Brigida was originally built for both nuns and monks? They lived in separate cloisters, but right next to each other." Vincenzo said as he sat on a bench that had been placed on the cobblestone street. He was drawing the stone building and the wrought-iron railing in front of him. The street was small and close, the stones graded like low, wide steps, leading up to a proper staircase at the far end. Sitting here, Giovanna could imagine herself as one of those nuns, living there so long ago.

She nodded. "And then the pope sent the monks away," she said. "Too much temptation."

"My grandfather told me that story," he said. "I always wondered where they went."

Giovanna laughed. "I asked my mother the same thing when she told it to me. She said she imagined they found a beautiful new monastery to live in, right on the sea, with birds waking them up each morning, just as the sun peeked into their windows."

"She was a good storyteller," Vincenzo said.

"She was," Giovanna answered. This street felt hidden away, like they were in a moment outside of time. "I think back, now, on the details she included in her stories, and it makes me wish I'd asked her how she came up with them, whether they were things she'd read somewhere, or if she invented them in her mind."

"There are so many questions I wish I'd asked my brother." Vincenzo took a small box of biscotti out of his larger satchel. "Would you like one?" he asked. "I bought the last two that were dipped in chocolate."

Giovanna took one. "How did you know I like them better that way?"

Vincenzo smiled. "Just a suspicion," he said as she took a bite. "Did you know that it's been a month since the first time we kissed?"

Giovanna nodded while she swallowed her bite of biscotti. It seemed incredible that it had only been a month. She felt different now. Bolder, braver. She felt like maybe she could make choices herself, without asking Faustina's advice. "Nearly two months since we met," she answered.

Time was flying. It was only two weeks now until her sister's wedding.

"I'm going to have to go up to Alba next week," Vincenzo said. "So I won't be around on Saturday. I'm going to miss you."

"The weekend after that my sister's getting married," Giovanna said, "so I think that will be two weekends of missing each other."

Giovanna was already preparing herself for the ache that being without him would cause.

"I wish I could be there with you," Vincenzo said.

Giovanna looked at him. She could see the desire in his eyes. But, of course, he wasn't family, and he wasn't her fiancé, so he had no place at her sister's wedding. It would be nice, though, to have him by her side.

"I wish that too," she said.

She looked at him, wondering what he was really saying. Only family—and close family friends—were invited to weddings. The only way he'd be able to come was if they were engaged. Was that what he was hinting at? Did he want to tell his family about her? Did he want her to tell her family about him?

Vincenzo used his forearm to push his hair out of his face and didn't say anything for a while.

Giovanna thought maybe he was going to change the subject, even though he was the one who started the conversation, but then he said, "Do you and your father want to come to my family's vineyard the weekend after your sister's wedding?"

Giovanna was quiet for a brief moment and imagined it, the brilliant greens of the trees and grass and grapevines, the cool air of the country. His parents smiling, welcoming her and her father to their home three weeks from now. Or would they?

"If I come," Giovanna asked, her heart hammering, "will it be because you told them about us?"

Vincenzo paused, dusting the crumbs from the biscotti off his pants. "I think this time, no," he said. "My parents . . . they have someone else in mind for me, and I have to navigate that."

Giovanna nodded, though her heart squeezed with jealousy as she wondered who this other woman was, who his parents wanted him to marry. Was her father a count, too? Was she beautiful and elegant in the way people seemed to be when they were born wealthy?

But Vincenzo had chosen to spend his time with Giovanna, not this other woman. So really, it didn't matter what his parents wanted. It mattered what *he* wanted. "Okay, so let's say my father and I come as your new friends from Genoa. What did you have in mind?"

Vincenzo put the box back in his satchel. "We're having a bit of a party. Not a *party* party, more like a gathering to help bottle the 1944 vintage. It was a good year for the grapes, so it'll be a delicious wine.

"Anyway, a lot of local people will come, my father will put out some food, and everyone gets a job—wine in the bottles, corks on the top, wax on the corks, and then labels on the front. My father asked me to design the labels."

Giovanna could see his pride in that request. "What did you design?" she asked, her mind off the party for the moment.

"I drew a rose framed by the sunrise," he said. "Della Rosa d'Alba. Our name and our title. I used the imagery of both words and added our family crest at the bottom."

"That sounds beautiful," Giovanna said.

"I'm happy with how it came out," he said. "I can't wait for you to see it. And to taste this wine. Everyone who comes will get a taste." He rested his hand on hers. "So, do you want to come? If you don't want to bring your father, perhaps your sister and her husband would like to come instead."

Giovanna looked at him, the chiseled bones of his cheeks and chin, the thick hair parted to the right, the intensity of his artist's eyes. She marveled at the fact that she was here with him, that he wanted her here with him.

"It's a lovely invitation," she said. "I bet my father would be happy to come." She knew Faustina and Betto would not.

Chapter 15

GENOA, ITALY
Then

The following week, three days after Vincenzo left for Alba, a letter came in the mail for Giovanna. When she opened it, she found a drawing inside of Vincenzo sitting on a bench in a garden with a blackened-in silhouette of a taller man next to him. The only words were the title of the drawing: *Only Me.* She stared at it for a long while, until she realized what he was telling her: how hard it was to be at home without his brother, Leonardo. How he felt his absence while he was at his family's villa.

A few days later another drawing came: Vincenzo asleep in bed, and above his head, Giovanna laughing in a ray of sunlight. The title was *Joy Comes in the Night.* He had dreamed about her. She made him happy.

The drawings kept coming every few days. Each a new message, a new piece of Vincenzo that he was sharing with Giovanna. She kept them under her mattress so no one else would find them, taking them out only when she was alone in the apartment. Vincenzo was sharing his heart with her, his mind, his whole self.

Giovanna wanted to do the same. She couldn't draw, and she was terrible at writing letters. Her talent was with needle and thread. So she took extra fabric from a dress she had made for herself and sewed him a stuffed rabbit. The day he came home, she wore the dress that matched the bunny, and when he came by the shop, when he took her out for lunch, she gave it to him. "So you'll always have someone to talk to," she said, "even when I'm not around."

Vincenzo smiled at Giovanna, but his eyes shone with tears. "This is the most thoughtful gift anyone has ever given me," he said.

And he ate lunch that day with the rabbit on his lap. "I don't want to let it go," he said.

Giovanna wondered if he was talking about her, too.

Chapter 16

NEW YORK CITY, USA

Now

Cassandra took Monday off. Her grandmother was coming to their apartment to be painted, and she wanted to be there.

She was in the kitchen making herself a cup of espresso, what Luca referred to as "un caffè" in a way that always made Cass think of the barista at the coffee shop down the street from where she had lived in Florence.

"One for you, too?" she asked.

He nodded, sitting at the table and running his fingers through his slept-on hair. When Cass awoke in the morning, she was up—eyes open, brain racing, ready to start the day. Luca took his time waking up, all soft edges and yawns until at least an hour later.

"Do you think we should have some breakfast for everyone?" Cass asked, sitting down next to Luca, handing him a coffee cup and resting hers on the table between them, her fingers wrapped around the warm ceramic. She tried not to unleash the full force of her energy on him in the mornings, and she knew he tried to get himself moving a little more quickly for her.

"Maybe some pastries?" Luca suggested, taking a sip. "That and coffee should be fine. I want to spend as much time as I can painting, so they don't have to come back too often."

"Sounds good," Cass said. "I'll stay out of the way."

Luca patted her hand. "You're never in the way."

She smiled and drank the last of her espresso. "About a dozen pastries?" she said, standing up. "I can go now."

"Sounds good," Luca said. "I'll get dressed when I'm done with this."

She leaned over and kissed him, tasting coffee. "Sorry I'll miss the show," she said.

He smiled. "I'll save you a seat for the nighttime performance."

She thought for probably the millionth time how lucky she was to have found Luca—someone who loved her, respected her, supported her, understood her—and who made her laugh, too. "Can't wait," she told him.

When Cass got back, Luca's grandfather was there, sitting in the kitchen, drinking espresso with his grandson. The two men didn't really look alike, but when they were next to each other, you could see a similarity in the shapes of their eyes and the line of their jaws. She paused in the doorframe of the kitchen, box of pastries in hand, listening to them speak Italian, catching most of their words, if not every detail—Nonno was asking after Stefano, whether the winery was doing well, and how the calpestamento went. Cass's cheeks warmed at the memory.

"Cassandra!" Nonno had looked up and noticed her in the doorway. He stood to greet her, leaning on a carved wooden cane for support. When she walked closer, he took her hand in his and kissed both her cheeks.

"Did you come alone?" Cass asked. She'd switched into Italian for him, and felt self-conscious—she knew her accent and her sentence structure were off. She translated from English to Italian in her head. The only time she had really felt comfortable in the language was at the very end of her year abroad, when she was able to think in Italian, dream in Italian. But once she came back to America, everything in her head was English again.

"Marina called me a black car," he answered. "It was door-to-door service. So"—he turned to include Luca—"do I look like a modern-day Roman god?"

Cass gave him a once-over. He was wearing a three-piece gray suit with a light blue shirt and a blue-and-yellow-patterned tie. Maybe this was where Marina got her sense of style. If there were a fashion magazine for men in their nineties, Nonno could've been a model for it, especially with his mane of thick white hair.

"I'd been thinking a little more of a casual god," Luca said, "but I like it. We'll have to see what Cass's grandmother is wearing. We may need to do a little shopping for her in Cassandra's closet. And some adjustments to the sketch to make the three-piece suit work."

Cass moved over to the counter and put the pastries onto a plate, arranging them in a small pyramid. "This is from our favorite bakery," she said. "Mille-Feuille. Their croissants are delicious."

Nonno picked one up. "Did Luca ever tell you I had an aunt who moved to France? She's been gone forty years now, but I loved to visit her in Paris, especially when I was a child. There was a little bakery down the street from her apartment building where we would get fresh croissants every morning when I traveled there."

"That sounds like such a wonderful memory," Cass said, thinking of her last trip with Luca to Paris, when he was meeting with a gallery owner and they saw one of his cousins for dinner. His name was Henri, and after they'd split two bottles of wine among the three of them, he told Cass that his great-great-grandfather had come up with the idea for the French Revolutionary calendar. "Each week was ten days long," he told them. "And each month had three weeks."

Cass had woken up the next morning thinking about that. "Was that real?" she'd asked Luca over coffee.

"Weirdly," he had told her, "yes. And everyone who ever meets Henri usually gets more of an earful about it than you did."

If the aunt Nonno was talking about was Henri's great-grandmother, the calendar inventor would've been on the other side, the French side, of his family.

"It is a wonderful memory," Nonno said. "So much of my life is memories now. But I try to keep making new ones. That's why I'm here."

With that, the doorbell rang. Cass wiped her hands and went to answer it, finding her grandmother and her father on the other side.

"Since I'm the chauffeur, I hoped I might be able to stay for the day," her dad said. "I brought a book, so I won't get in anyone's way." He held up a copy of *Never Never*. He was a serious James Patterson fan and read everything he wrote.

"You're welcome to watch," Luca said. "Would you like a coffee?"

"He means espresso, Dad," Cass clarified.

"I'd love one," Dom said, walking over to the table where Nonno was standing, one hand on his cane, the other on the back of one of the chairs.

Cass walked over to Gram and gave her a hug. She was wearing a beautiful dress that looked almost like it belonged in the 1940s. It was calf-length with three-quarter sleeves and buttons down the front. The fabric was a deep wine color with tiny cream-colored polka dots. Cass was almost certain this was another one Gram had made herself, years before. Nonno was looking at Gram from his place in the kitchen. Cass wondered what he was thinking about her, what his first impression was.

"Come," Cass said to her grandmother. "Let me introduce you to your Jupiter."

The two women walked into the room. "Gram," Cass said, switching back to Italian, "this is Luca's grandfather, Vincenzo. Nonno, this is my grandmother, Joanna."

"A pleasure to meet you," he said, taking her hand in his and kissing it.

Gram was staring intently at his face. "Vincenzo Bartolomei?" she asked him.

Nonno shook his head. "I'm Luca's mother's father. Vincenzo Della Rosa d'Alba."

Gram grabbed onto Cass's arm so tightly she had to bite her tongue to stop from crying out. "Oh," she heard her grandmother whisper.

"What's wrong?" Cass asked, switching back to English.

"Will you walk with me to the living room?" her grandmother said quietly. Her face was white, and Cass wondered if she was feeling ill.

"We'll be right back," Cass said to the rest of the room, and then she walked down the hallway with her grandmother.

"I've seen a ghost," Gram said. She was shaking.

"What do you mean? Gram, what's wrong? You're scaring me."

Gram took a deep breath. "I need to sit down," she said.

Cass steered them both into the small room that she and Luca called the office; it was filled with bookcases and file cabinets, a desk and a love seat. She helped Gram down onto the love seat and then sat next to her.

"What's going on?" she said.

"I know that man," she said to Cassandra. "I knew him. Vincenzo. Della Rosa. In Genoa, just after the war."

"And?" Cass asked, no idea what her grandmother would say, but horrible thoughts were forming in her mind. She'd never seen her grandmother this shaken.

"He broke my heart when I was twenty-one." Gram took a shaky breath. "He said some of the most hurtful things anyone has ever said to me. His family was awful, too. I thought his face looked familiar, but I wasn't sure. When he said his name, all those feelings from seventy years ago . . . they just hit me again. I felt like I was twenty-one and my world was falling down around my ears."

Gram was breathing heavily. Cass's mind was whirling. How was it even possible that her grandmother had dated Luca's grandfather? That made no sense. And she made it sound like they were seriously together or something.

"You . . . dated him?" Cass said.

"I did," Gram answered, "so to speak."

"How did you even meet?" He was a count, or at least the son of a count. How would that have happened?

"He came to get his clothing tailored in my father's shop," she said slowly. "And we . . . we liked each other. First he came to see me while I was working behind the counter, then we took walks around Genoa, then we went out to eat, and then . . . then he started painting me."

Cass's thoughts were spinning. She didn't even know Nonno

painted. Did Luca? Did Marina? Her brain spiraled and spiraled and then landed back on the painting in Gram's apartment. The one she wanted to hang, the one she'd looked at while touching her own hair.

"The painting we hung last week—"

Gram nodded. "That was the first one he painted of me. The only one I kept. I'd finally decided I could try to enjoy it, after all these years. I was finally able to detach the feelings from the art. But maybe I was tempting the fates. I should've kept it wrapped in paper under my bed, where it's been for more than half a century."

Cass took a deep breath. She wasn't sure what to say. What to do.

"What was wrong with his family?" she asked, wondering now if there was a dark secret she should know about before marrying Luca.

Gram sighed. She was breathing normally now. Her panic seemed to have subsided slightly. "Nothing, really. They were snobs, is all. They didn't think I was good enough for him."

"He probably wasn't good enough for you," Cass said, putting her arm around her grandmother's shoulders.

Gram shook her head. "He was the son of a count. I was the daughter of a tailor. In those times, I wasn't on his level. I'd hoped things would change—that after the war people would see things differently. And for a while I thought they might. I thought he was different. But it wasn't true."

Cass thought about what Luca had said—how he would find her no matter what circles they traveled in. She wondered again if that would have been true.

"Do you think he knows who you are?" Cass asked her grandmother, not sure what to do now, how to save today and talk to Luca and make her grandmother more comfortable.

She shook her head. "He doesn't know me as Joanna," she said. "To him I'd be Giovanna. And the last name I had then was Ferrero, not Fanelli, so hearing your last name wouldn't have meant anything to him either. I'm sure I look different enough, now that seventy years have gone by, that without my name as a hint, he wouldn't even think it was me. I wouldn't have recognized him if you hadn't introduced him as Vincenzo."

"So," Cass said, looking her grandmother in the eye, trying to read her face. "Do you want to pretend you're someone else?"

Gram thought about it. "I won't say that I recognized him," she said. "Unless he recognizes me."

There was a knock on the door, and then Luca poked his head in. "Is everything okay in here?" he asked.

Cass nodded. "Gram was having cold feet," she said. "But she's ready to model now."

"Yes," Gram said, "that's right. You know, I once modeled for a painter years ago. In Genoa."

Luca reached down to help her up. "Well, maybe you could tell us about it while I paint."

Gram was standing now, her hand on Luca's arm. Cass wondered if he reminded her of Vincenzo when he was younger. Or if she was replaying the dinner at Osteria Morini in her mind and seeing it all through another lens.

"I love the dress you chose," Luca said, oblivious to what might or might not be going on in Gram's head. "Did you make that one?"

"I did," Gram said, and Cass could detect a hint of pride in her response.

"Well, I think it's perfect for the painting; it goes nicely with my grandfather's suit. And the colors complement each other beautifully. Would you mind wearing some of Cassandra's jewelry as well?"

"Not at all," Gram said, walking toward the studio with Luca, "as long as it's okay with her."

"Of course it is," Cass said, smiling at her grandmother. "You're welcome to anything of mine you'd like."

"Thank you, Cassandra," Gram said, walking out of the room with Luca. "You know," she told him, "the first time I was painted I wore family jewelry, too. The artist's family's, though, not mine."

Cass stayed in the office for a moment, wondering how this was going to play out. How Gram was able to play it so cool after the revelation she'd had. And what was going to happen when Nonno figured out who Gram was. She spun her engagement ring on her finger. And then it hit her where she had seen something like it before: the ring in the painting at Gram's house. Her engagement ring was the same ring her grandmother had worn then, the same family jewelry Nonno had lent to her so many years before.

Chapter 17

SERRALUNGA D'ALBA, ITALY
Then

Giovanna and her father traveled by train from Genoa to Asti, both of them lost in thought most of the way. The trains weren't running to Alba, but Vincenzo had said he was happy to pick them up and drive them the rest of the way—and had a cousin who would drive them back to Genoa that night. It was a lot of travel—and would be a very long day—but it was worth it, at least to Giovanna.

"This was such a nice invitation," her father said partway through the train trip, when the buildings were getting farther and farther apart. "Though I must say, it was a surprise."

"Vincenzo said that he was grateful you made him look so good again after the war," Giovanna told him, again. "And thankful that we've all been so helpful when he's needed a tailor in Genoa. It's too bad Faustina and Betto are in Varazze, but I don't think they would have wanted to come anyway." When she initially brought up the bottling party, she hadn't completely explained why they'd been invited, but her father had seemed up for it anyway. Clearly he was curious but wasn't entirely sure how to ask what he wanted to know.

Giovanna wondered if she'd have been more comfortable telling her mother. Or if her mother would have been like Faustina, still too angry to see shades of gray.

"He has come to the shop often," Federico said, "for lost buttons."

"He has," Giovanna agreed. She'd teased Vincenzo about how many buttons fell off his shirt the other day and he'd blushed, which confirmed her suspicion that he pulled them off to have an excuse to visit her at the shop, when they couldn't get together otherwise. "We've become friendly because of it."

"It's always nice to have new friends," her father replied.

"It is," Giovanna answered. It was nice to have friends who painted you, who sent you artwork, who dreamed about you, who made you feel like the most beautiful person in the world. Just thinking about Vincenzo made her feel warm inside, the way being with her sister or her father did, but more so. If their love was a candle, his burned as bright as a star.

"The conte hasn't been to the shop since the war," Federico said. "It'll be nice to see him again. And the contessa."

Giovanna wondered what it felt like to be called *contessa* not just as a term of endearment but as a title.

"Vincenzo said that his father hasn't been to Genoa yet," she told her father. "He's been managing the vineyards, while Vincenzo has been rekindling their connections at the port to start exporting."

The conductor came through the train announcing that Asti was the next stop.

"His father must think a lot of him to trust him with those relationships," Federico said.

"He must," Giovanna agreed, feeling a sense of pride.

* * *

The train pulled into the Asti station, and Federico and Giovanna exited with a handful of other travelers. They followed the group down the stairs, and then Giovanna spotted Vincenzo, waving at them from a red Alfa Romeo.

"Look over there," Giovanna said, waving back.

They walked closer, and Vincenzo got out of the car to open the door for both Giovanna and her father. "So glad you could make it," he said.

Giovanna slid into the back seat.

"It was so nice of you to invite us," Federico answered, settling into the passenger seat. "And I'm glad it was the weekend after Faustina's wedding. It's wonderful to be part of real celebrations again."

Vincenzo closed the door behind him. "I agree, sir," Vincenzo said, walking back around to the driver's side of the car. "And congratulations to you and Faustina. You must be so happy."

"I am," Federico said. "My wife used to say she was as happy as our least happy child. Once she was gone, I fear I took on that role. And both my daughters seem quite happy now. I'm a lucky father."

Giovanna wondered if he was trying to give Vincenzo a subtle message, telegraph his tacit approval, in the event it was needed.

"How far to your father's vineyard?" Federico asked.

"About half an hour," Vincenzo answered. And then he smiled at Giovanna in the rearview mirror. "I won't go too fast—I know I'm transporting some precious cargo."

Federico laughed.

As Vincenzo drove, the three of them talked about the weather, about Faustina's wedding, about a restaurant that was reopening down the street from Federico's shop.

They drove up a winding road, and when it crested, Giovanna was able to see a valley of vineyards. "Papà!" she said. "Look!"

"Isn't the view wonderful?" Vincenzo said. "Every time I come home from Genoa and see that view, my heart lifts. That will always be my definition of home."

Giovanna thought about what her definition of home was. It wasn't a place. It was her father and her sister. Wherever they were felt like home.

"Are we nearly there?" Giovanna asked.

"It's just over that hill," Vincenzo said. She could hear the smile in his voice, a note of pride.

When the Alfa Romeo was at the top of the hill, Vincenzo pointed straight ahead. "That's our vineyard," he said. "And that's our villa, up there."

Giovanna looked up to the ridge of the next hill and her breath caught. The villa looked more like a castle than a house. It was made of pink-tinted stone and seemed to have two wings in addition to the center of the house. There was a separate chapel, too, she could see as they drove closer, with stained glass in the windows, in the middle of an orchard and a lush garden.

"Has it been in your family long?" Giovanna's father asked.

Vincenzo nodded. "The land was given to the first conte in the fourteenth century. It's been inherited by the oldest son ever since then. Or, I guess, the oldest living son."

Giovanna wanted to reach out and put her hand on Vincenzo's arm.

"I can't believe it's been more than three years without Leonardo," he added.

"Time is funny, isn't it?" Federico answered. "Sometimes it feels like I saw Giovanna's mother just yesterday, and other times it feels like she's been gone for decades."

"It feels sometimes," Vincenzo said, "like I'm living his life now. Like when he died, I gave up my own life to live his."

Giovanna thought about the clothing she and Faustina and her father had tailored to fit Vincenzo. Not only was he living his brother's life, but he was wearing his brother's clothes. She decided she would make him a pair of pants and a vest, something of his own.

"My father has been preparing me, now," he said, "to take over his title, his role in the government, the vineyard—the way he had been preparing Leonardo. It's . . . different. I'd thought, before the war, that I might go to art school. But I don't think that's in the stars for me anymore."

Federico and Giovanna were quiet.

"Anyway," Vincenzo said, stopping the car, not at the villa but at a building in the vineyard. "Here we are. I didn't mean to get so melancholy."

"Please don't apologize," Federico replied. "The war has taken a lot from us."

Vincenzo turned off the car.

"Life has taken a lot from us," Giovanna added, thinking about her mother, too.

"That it has," Vincenzo said, and then turned to look at her. "But it's also given us a lot."

His smile was soft.

She lifted her pointer fingertip to her lips and, while her father was getting out of the car, blew a kiss off her finger to Vincenzo.

There were about twenty people there, and it had the festive air of a celebration. Giovanna could feel the joyous energy of people gathering together, the way she'd felt it at Faustina's wedding.

A man that Giovanna recognized as Vincenzo's father was wearing gray flannel pants and a pale lavender button-down shirt, chatting with a couple who looked about his age and a young woman who looked about Vincenzo and Giovanna's age.

The young woman was pretty, with chestnut-colored hair tied back with a light blue ribbon that matched the cardigan sweater she wore open over a navy blue shirtwaist dress. The clothing fit her well, and she carried herself with a confidence that made the look feel effortless; it might have been the pushed-up sleeves or the fact that her ribbon hadn't been tied in a bow. Her tan leather ballet flats finished the look, along with nylon stockings.

Giovanna was jealous. During the war, there were no nylon stockings to be found anywhere, and now the demand was so high, Giovanna wouldn't have paid the price the stores were charging, even if she did have the money to spend.

She couldn't help comparing herself to that young woman and finding herself lacking.

Before Giovanna stepped away from the car, she checked over her outfit. It was similar in feeling to that of the girl with the blue ribbon, but she was wearing a deep-orange shirtwaist dress made of a fabric patterned with tiny yellow flowers, and she had on a red cardigan and red flats. Her mamma wouldn't lose her, even here in the mountains.

Vincenzo came up beside her and whispered, "You look beautiful." His words gave her the confidence she needed to follow him over to his father, who was already talking to Federico. The girl with the blue ribbon and her parents had gone.

"It's lovely to see you," the conte was saying to Federico. "It's been so long. I was glad to hear your shop was still in business after the war."

"Thank you, signor conte," Federico said. "And thank you for including us today. It's been so nice to see Vincenzo in the store so often."

"I'm the best-dressed man in Alba now," Vincenzo said with a smile. "Other than my father."

All four of them laughed, though Giovanna wondered if, in another time, Vincenzo would've said, *Other than my father and brother.*

"And you, Giovanna, must be the best-dressed young woman in Genoa," the conte said. "Look how you've grown."

"Thank you, signor conte," Giovanna said, blushing. "The vineyard is beautiful."

"It's my favorite place to be," the conte answered. He looked around, his eyes sweeping across the vines and the people and the large expanse of sky.

"I understand why," Federico said.

All four of them were silent for a moment, appreciating the view.

"I'll show our guests around and then perhaps we'll find Mamma and Chiara," Vincenzo said. "After that, of course, I'll set the Ferreros up with a station."

"Very good," the conte replied. "Bernardo can tell you which area of the process needs more people."

Giovanna followed Vincenzo, a few steps behind him. Here in Alba, there was a bounce in his step, a buoyancy to him that made her smile. As if he could feel it, he turned around and winked at her.

"I'm so glad you're here," he said to Giovanna and her father.

"Me too," she said softly.

She wished she could reach out and grab his hand.

Maybe next time. Maybe then, they'd no longer be a secret.

Chapter 18

Even though Cass had taken the day off and had planned to use it to start going through the wedding magazines her friend Kiley had dropped off, she couldn't concentrate. Instead, she kept checking her email on her phone to see if there was anything she needed to take care of at work that would take her mind off what she'd just learned about Gram. She kept waiting for Nonno to figure out that he knew her grandmother. But so far, it hadn't happened. Luca had been painting them for the last hour. Her father had been reading his book in the living room. Cass couldn't take staring at her phone, waiting for something to happen, a minute longer.

"Hey, Dad," Cass said, sitting down next to him. "How's the book?"

Her dad put the front flap of the book on the page he was reading and then closed it. "It's good," he said. "James Patterson always writes a good story. And this one has a part that takes place in the Australian Outback, so I feel like I'm learning some things."

Her father was an avid reader—there was an entire shelf in their living room on Long Island filled with James Patterson, John

Grisham, Tom Clancy, Attica Locke, John le Carré, and Sue Grafton. If the book was fast-paced with a central mystery, he was all over it.

"Are you working on your construction heist novel?" Cass asked. When her father retired last year, he said that he wanted to write a mystery set in his world. He'd started but hadn't gotten very far.

"I think I might be a reader, not a writer," he said.

Cass opened her mouth to protest, but he held up his hand.

"I'm okay with that," he added.

She nodded. "The same way I'm an appreciator, not an artist," she said. "I get it. The world needs all of us."

He nodded. "You're a good kid," he said, seemingly a non sequitur, but kind of not.

Cass laughed. She loved that she'd always be a kid to her dad. "How's Gram settling in?" she asked him.

"It's only been a week, but I think she's doing well," he said. "We have a few doctors' appointments set up for her—we want to check on her blood pressure, her hips, her joints. Getting old's no picnic."

Cass was immediately alarmed. "Nothing serious, though, right?"

He shook his head. "I don't think so."

Cass let out a soft breath. "Good," she said. "Good."

Her father cleared his throat. "Cassandra," he said, looking at his hands, "I've been meaning to talk to you and Luca about this, but maybe it's better it's just us and I can talk to you first. Your mom and I have been saving up some money for your wedding since you were born. You're our only girl, and we wanted to be able to throw you a really special party when you decided to get married."

Cass felt her eyes get wet. She hadn't known her parents had been saving money for her wedding since she was an infant.

"I know that Luca's family has a lot more than we do, and I know you and Luca are both doing well for yourselves, but . . . we'd still love to throw you a party. If you get married out by us, it'll probably go a long way. But I don't know if you want that, or if you were thinking about a party in New York City. I don't think we could afford New York City, with what we've saved."

Dom looked up at his daughter, and Cass felt her eyes start to overflow. She wiped her tears away quickly. Her dad's face was so earnest, so apologetic that he couldn't give her enough for a wedding anywhere she wanted it.

Cass threw her arms around him. "Thank you," she said into his neck. "Thank you so much." She pulled away. "I'm not sure what kind of wedding we want," she said. "Luca and I haven't discussed it. But your offer means so much to me. Thank you, Dad."

She knew that she and her parents had their differences, but there was never any question that they loved her and that she felt the same about them. There was so much of them in her—their beliefs, their values, their perspectives. And she was grateful that they were the parents she had; they were the ones who'd raised her, no matter their differences. She hugged her father even tighter.

"Oh," her dad said, "and your mom asked me to give you this." He unfolded a piece of paper from his pocket. "She said she started a list. These are friends whose children's weddings she's gone to over the years who she wants to invite to yours. The back is a list of cousins she didn't want you to forget."

Cass took the list and looked it over. There were twelve couples on one side, and about thirty names on the other. "Thanks for being the messenger," she said. "I'll call Mom later so we can chat." She hadn't started a wedding list yet and was wondering how big it would get, if this list from her mom was any indicator. And if she—and Luca— had a choice in the matter . . .

Her father nodded. "Thanks. Your mom has been waiting for this wedding for—"

"My whole life?" Cass finished.

He laughed. "Pretty much."

Cass wondered how much he and her mom had saved, and what Luca would think about this. It seemed silly to take what her parents were offering, when the money would mean more to them than it would to Luca, than—quite frankly—it would to her. But she didn't want to offend them either, especially if they'd been saving since the moment she was born, socking away a little at a time to throw her a party so many years later.

She hadn't thought about that, what her and Luca's marriage would mean to their families. What would her mom say if she knew about Nonno and Gram? Why was everything so complicated all the time?

Cass looked at her watch. It was nearly twelve thirty.

"Hey," she said to her dad, refolding the list and slipping it in the back pocket of her jeans. "I was going to pull something together for everyone for lunch. Want to give me a hand?"

"Of course," he said, standing up, leaving his book on the coffee table. "Just like I tell your mom: put me to work."

Cass saw her dad's hand swinging by his side and had the urge to grab it, to hold on, to feel, once more, like a little girl whose world revolved around her strong, smart, wonderful dad. Instead, she put her arm around his back.

"I'm glad you're here," she told him.

"Me too," he said, smiling down at her. "Me too."

And together they walked into the kitchen, still father and daughter, but somehow also equals.

Chapter 19

NEW YORK CITY, USA
Now

Cass and her dad made a salad and a frittata, and sliced some bread, and then Cass went to see how things were going in Luca's studio.

The door was half open, and she paused for a moment outside. She heard Italian music playing, a song that sounded like it must've been from the 1930s or '40s, the quality a little scratchy, like someone on YouTube had recorded an old record or something. Maybe it was from a radio show.

She looked inside and saw Luca's setup—he'd brought a love seat and a coffee table into the spot where the bed had been for Cass's painting. There was a bookcase right behind the love seat, filled with empty picture frames, all pushed together. The coffee table was covered with photo albums. Nonno was holding an iPad in front of him, and he and Gram were smiling down at it. Cass noticed that the two of them were sitting close to each other, about a finger's width apart, but not touching. She wondered whether Luca had placed them that way, or if that was how they sat naturally.

What had Gram been thinking for the two and a half hours they'd sat like that? What had it been like for her to be next to him? Someone who, Cass imagined, she used to touch with abandon, who had seen her in ways few others did.

Cass moved to open the door farther, but before her hand was even on the knob, Gram looked up. The smile on her face went from practiced to real.

"Cassandra!" she said.

Cass walked into the room. "I didn't mean to disturb you, but it's one o'clock, and I was wondering if anyone was hungry."

Nonno smiled. "I could wait to eat, but wouldn't mind a break. I'm not used to being a model," he said.

"Of course," Luca said. "Let me just mark where they were sitting."

He grabbed some painter's tape and offered Gram his hand. When she stood, he put a marker down on the indent in the couch where she had been. Then he did the same for Nonno, handing him his cane, which Cass saw had been tucked under the love seat. Then all four of them walked to the kitchen.

"Well," Nonno said, "now that I've sat for a painting, I have a deeper appreciation for models. That's a lot of sitting still."

"And you love to be on the go," Luca said with a smile.

"Who wouldn't?" Nonno said. "If it weren't for my arthritis, I'd still be out picking grapes come harvest season. I try to walk through the vineyards every evening before dinner. I don't get quite as far as I used to, but I worry that if I slow down, I'll never be able to get moving again."

Luca smiled again, but this time Cass could see some pain behind it.

"Is that why you decided to hop on a plane when Luca called?" Cass asked.

"Partially, yes, but how could I miss a chance to celebrate? To make more memories? Will you let me throw you an engagement party while I'm here? Don't worry, I'll ask Alessandra to help me plan it. That way you know it'll be beautiful."

Cass looked at Luca and raised her eyebrow, asking if he was okay with it. He nodded, and then raised an eyebrow back at her. She nodded, too. If Nonno had flown all the way from Italy to celebrate with them, they should celebrate. And he was right, Alessandra would throw a lovely party. Cass always marveled at how she intuitively seemed to know things, like what to serve when and to whom, which outfits to wear to which events, when to shake hands and when to go in for the double-cheek kiss.

Alessandra worked for the family's business in what Marina called "new endeavors"; she was tasked with looking at the traditional in a new way and had the incredible ability to take what was classic and shift it ever so slightly to make it seem new without making it feel different. A huge part of the increase in profits for the past three years had been thanks to Alessandra.

"That sounds fun," Luca answered, as they all sat down at the kitchen table. "We'd love that."

"Oh, fantastic," Nonno said. "We'll invite our family and yours, Cassandra. We'll all get to know one another."

"Thank you," Cass said. "That's so generous of you."

Dom came over to the table with the frittata he and Cass had made, still warm.

"I'd be happy to help with the party," he said.

Nonno shook his head. "It's my treat, please. One of the pleasures of my old age is getting to spoil my grandchildren—and great-granddaughter."

Dom nodded. "We should all be so lucky."

Then he sat down, too.

Cass noticed that Gram hadn't said anything during this whole exchange. What was she thinking? Clearly Nonno hadn't yet figured out who she was. Cass wondered if Gram was going to keep quiet or say something. If it were her, Cass would've had trouble not bursting out with the information.

She looked at Gram and saw her reaching toward the plate of frittata. There was a tremor in her hand that Cass didn't remember. Cass picked up the cake slicer she'd laid out to cut the frittata and said, "Who would like a piece?" She didn't want to see Gram's hands tremble, a piece of frittata fall. Especially not for Gram's sake, if Nonno truly was a man who broke her heart more than seventy years before.

"This is delicious, Cassandra," Gram said after she took a bite.

"Dad helped," Cass said.

Gram smiled at that. "You, too, Dom."

Cassandra's dad looked proud. "I started cooking after I retired," he told Luca and Nonno. "Never made so much as a meatball while I was working, but now, I help Christine make dinner most nights, and I cook for us on Tuesdays and Thursdays. I'm not bad, right, Mom?"

Gram laughed. "Not bad at all. Your father would be proud."

"How come?" Nonno asked.

"My husband owned a restaurant for a while," she said, "with his brothers. But ended up going into construction."

"Restaurants are a hard business," Nonno said. Then he turned to Dom. "What work did you retire from?"

"I was a contractor," Dom answered, passing the plate of bread around. "I built houses, remodeled kitchens and bathrooms, put on extensions, that kind of thing. My son Dominick, he's an electrician, and my son Christopher is a plumber, so we all worked together for a while. We thought Cassandra might join us and do the books, but she had different plans. My boys are doing great on their own now, though. Everyone always needs an electrician and a plumber."

"Totally," Luca said. "We needed one to rescue us when the dishwasher exploded last month."

Cass smiled at him, grateful that he changed the subject from her not being a bookkeeper for her dad and brothers. "It didn't explode. The drain got clogged and it overflowed."

"It *looked* like it exploded," Luca said. "The suds were everywhere."

Gram chuckled. "That happened to me once, too. What a mess."

"Anyway, Chris always has more than enough to do." Dom took a bite of his frittata.

"And what about you, Joanna, did you work?" Nonno asked.

"I worked at a tailor shop once," she said. "And then I made wedding gowns in the garment district for a few years, before I had children."

Nonno cocked his head. "I used to know someone who worked in a tailor shop. It was a long time ago."

Cass held her breath. Was Gram going to say anything?

"I used to know someone whose family owned a vineyard," she said.

She looked at him, her eyes steady.

He looked back, his expression shifting, like he was starting to put a puzzle together, but he didn't quite have all the pieces yet.

"Have you been there?" he asked.

She nodded. "Once, many many years ago."

Luca looked at Cass.

Dom looked at Luca.

Clearly something was going on here.

Both men put their forks down.

"Where was the vineyard?" Nonno asked, his eyes on hers.

"Serralunga d'Alba," she answered. "It was during the late spring. I helped bottle the 1944 vintage—just after the war."

Cass could see a small smile on her grandmother's lips. She was enjoying this.

"Serralunga d'Alba," he echoed. He studied her face, as if he were trying to lift away the years. "Bottling the '44 vintage."

Gram picked up her water and took a sip. "Yes," she said.

"Your name," he replied slowly. "It wasn't always Joanna."

He said it like it was a fact. Like he was sure of the statement.

"No," she said. "It wasn't." Cass couldn't quite place the emotion on her grandmother's face when she said that. It was a mixture of pain and hope and love and anticipation all at once.

"Giovanna Ferrero," he said.

And then he started to cry.

Chapter 20

SERRALUNGA D'ALBA, ITALY
Then

Vincenzo brought Giovanna and Federico over to Bernardo, who managed the day-to-day operations of the vineyard. He was keeping track of who was where to make sure that all the tasks that needed doing had the right number of people doing them.

"Hi, Bernardo," Vincenzo said, "this is my friend Giovanna and her father, Federico Ferrero. I was hoping I could work with them— perhaps on the wax dipping?"

Bernardo looked over at a list in front of him. "The wax dipping could use another two," he said. "And, right next to them, the men corking the wine bottles could use some help."

Vincenzo nodded. "Thanks," he said, leading them into the building everyone had been standing around and then down a set of stone steps into the wine cellar. Giovanna couldn't believe how huge it was down there. An enormous set of stone hallways led to even bigger stone rooms. She wondered if the underground tunnels connected all the way to the villa. She bet they did.

"This is where the barrels mature," Vincenzo said, pointing into a room on his right, where a handful of people had already gathered. "The people in there are going to bottle the wine from the barrels."

Giovanna looked into the room, and she saw that her father did, too.

"That's a lot of wine to bottle," Federico said.

"It's not as much as we harvested this past autumn," Vincenzo answered, "but more than we did the few years before that, during the war."

Giovanna wondered if people would always measure time that way—before, during, and after the war. So far, it seemed her life had four categories: before her mother died, after her mother died but before the war, during the war, and after the war. She wondered if in the future she'd look back on the moment she met Vincenzo, and that would be another marker of her life, another moment things changed. She wondered how Vincenzo measured his life. How her father did. Or Faustina. She'd never asked any of them.

"So these men will bring the wine bottles to us for corking and waxing," Vincenzo was explaining to Federico. "My father loves the look of the wax on top of the cork, plus it solves for a situation in which the cork isn't quite the right fit. With wax on top, no air can get into the wine for certain."

Giovanna turned to Vincenzo. "Do you have a finished bottle we can see?" she asked.

He smiled at her. "As a matter of fact, we do, except there's no wine inside. I put together a sample for my father yesterday so he could see how the wax looked with the new label. It's in with my mother and her friends, who'll be pasting on the labels. Let's go look."

"Papà," Giovanna said as they walked down the stone hallway, their footsteps echoing. "Did I tell you that Vincenzo designed the new label for the victory vintage?"

"You didn't," Federico said, "but I'm sure he did a wonderful job, if it's anything like the sketch he made of our shop." Federico turned to Vincenzo. "Thank you for that, for capturing this moment in time for us."

"My pleasure," Vincenzo said. Giovanna thought she might have seen him stand a bit straighter when Giovanna's father complimented his art, and it made her heart swell with love for both men.

"Hello, Mamma," Vincenzo said when he walked into the large room. There was a wooden table in the center with chairs around it. A few women were sitting, chatting with the contessa, whom Giovanna knew instantly. She was beautifully dressed and had the exact same thick wavy hair as Vincenzo, but hers was pulled back into victory rolls. Giovanna patted her own hair and wondered if she could tame it into that style.

"Hello, little mouse," his mother answered, looking up from the conversation. "Is there something you need?"

"No, Mamma," he said, his cheeks coloring slightly at the childish nickname. "Just wanted to show the sample bottle to everyone working on the wax dipping."

"Wonderful," she said. Then she seemed to notice Giovanna and Federico and stood. "Signor Ferrero," she said, "it's so lovely to see you. And Giovanna! You've grown so. I wouldn't have recognized you without your father standing there."

Giovanna smiled.

"Isn't she beautiful?" the contessa said, and the women around her nodded and murmured their agreement.

"Thank you so much, signora contessa," Giovanna answered.

"It's lovely to see you, too," Federico added.

Vincenzo picked up the sample bottle and ushered them both

back out the door. Giovanna wondered if Vincenzo's mother knew something was going on between the two of them, or at least suspected. Could she have been setting up her friends to accept Giovanna as her son's partner? Sending a message to Vincenzo that she was on the couple's side? It was so hard to know, when things were secret, who knew what, who was saying what.

"So who else is here?" she asked Vincenzo. "Those seemed to be your mother's friends. Did you all invite people?"

"This year, yes," Vincenzo said as they walked down another stone hallway. "In the early days of the war, it was hard to get the labor we needed to keep the vineyard going. Not that we were selling wine—it was mostly confiscated by the Italian army and then the Germans—but we still made it. Well, my parents invited some of their close friends to help. They got it done, and the next year, they came back to help again. In the years we had bigger harvests, they needed to invite more people to help—some people from town, Chiara's friends, my friends. And this year, with such a great crop of grapes, we had to expand the guest list even more. My mother's only request was that she and her friends get to keep the job they've been doing—pasting the labels on the bottles. They've grown quite fond of it, and to be honest, it's not that easy getting the labels on straight."

"I would've thought your father would hire workers to do this," Giovanna said.

"At some point he will, maybe as soon as next year—and we'll probably get some machines to make it more efficient—but for now, it's working for us. And our friends have a fun day of socializing and working together."

Giovanna nodded. "Well," she said, "my father and I are happy to be part of this. Right, Papà?"

"Of course," Federico said.

"I'm glad," Vincenzo said, smiling at Giovanna.

He led the two of them into another big stone room. There was a group of men who had funny-looking machines and a pile of corks in front of them. And there were five pots of melted wax on electric burners.

"So," Vincenzo said, "my sister and her friends will bring the full bottles of wine here on a cart. That group over there will cork them, and then this group over here will dip the bottles in that bright red wax, spin it until the wax stops dripping, and then place the finished bottles back on the cart to get sent over for labeling. Chiara and her friends will transport them when the cart is filled."

Giovanna looked to see if Chiara was around. She didn't know much about her, other than that she was eighteen, three years younger than Giovanna, and that she loved horses. Vincenzo told Giovanna that near the end of the war a German soldier had confiscated Chiara's horse, a chestnut Calabrese named Aurelia that their parents had given Chiara for her eighth birthday. He said Chiara cried for months after that, though she had been talking recently about training the new foal that had been born a month ago. *Before and after.*

"So what's our job?" Giovanna asked.

"Bernardo said two of us can dip the bottles in wax, and one of us can cork," Vincenzo answered.

Federico looked at the corking machine and then over at Giovanna and Vincenzo. "I've never corked wine bottles before," he said. "I'd love to try, if someone will show me how."

Giovanna saw Vincenzo's smile. He brought Federico over to one of the men already gathered by the corking machines. Then he came back to Giovanna and showed her how to dip a bottle in the wax and then swirl it to stop the drips from forming.

"So are any of your friends here?" she asked him, as they sat down next to each other, a little apart from a couple a bit older than they were, to wait for the first cart of bottles. Giovanna thrilled at being so close to him, though she wanted so badly to touch him, to lean her head on his shoulder. Something about her skin touching his made her feel calmer, breathe easier. She wondered if touching her did the same for him.

"My two closest friends left the region," he said. "Daniele is at university in Torino studying architecture, and Alfredo and his family moved to Argentina to start a new vineyard there. There are some old school friends I hang out with in Genoa but"—he shrugged—"I'd rather spend time with you."

Giovanna rested her hand on his for a brief second—his brother, his friends, all gone. Her heart ached for the loneliness he must feel. "My sister wants to move to America," she told him. "I can't imagine life here without her."

A group of three girls came into the room with a cart of wine bottles.

"You wouldn't want to go with her?" Vincenzo asked.

Giovanna shook her head. "Why would I go there when you're here?"

Vincenzo smiled back at her and gently squeezed her knee under the table. It made her whole body flutter. She quickly looked at the other couple to see if they noticed Vincenzo touching her.

A shadow appeared over Giovanna's shoulder, and both she and Vincenzo looked up. It was the girl with the blue ribbon and another girl, dressed in a similar style, but wearing a bright yellow sweater.

"Isabella didn't want to bother you," the girl in yellow said, "but I told her that you never found her a bother, right?" She smiled, and in her grin, Giovanna saw the resemblance to Vincenzo.

"You must be Chiara," Giovanna said.

Chiara looked at her. "And you are?" she asked, coolly.

"This is Giovanna," Vincenzo said, smiling at her. "Her father is the one who tailored Leonardo's clothing so it would fit me. And she's modeling for a painting I'm working on in Genoa."

Giovanna nodded. "It's lovely to meet you," she said.

"Yes," Chiara answered, and then turned back to her brother. "Well, I imagine you'll want to paint Isabella soon. Wouldn't you like that?"

Giovanna could see Vincenzo looking uncomfortable. She expected him to say no, but instead he swallowed and said, "Of course."

The girl with the blue ribbon, Isabella, blushed. "I'd love that," she said.

Giovanna looked from Vincenzo to Chiara to Isabella and realized that this must be the family friend that Vincenzo's parents wanted him to marry, part of his expected future. She wondered how she could compete with someone so effortlessly elegant, someone from his world. But then she felt the pressure of Vincenzo's knee against hers. She knew he was trying to tell her not to worry. But she did. She looked at Isabella, and she did worry.

Chapter 21

NEW YORK CITY, USA
Now

"What's going on?" Luca asked. "Dom?"

Dom shrugged, bewildered. "Mom," he said. "Are you okay?"

Gram shook her head.

"Cassandra, do you know what's going on?" Dom asked.

Cass nodded. "Sort of," she said.

Nonno had caught his breath. He reached across the table and picked up Gram's hand. "I've been thinking about this moment for years," he said. "Wondering if it would ever be possible." Then he stood, with one hand leaning on the table, bent over, and tried to kiss Gram on the lips.

Quick as lightning, quicker than Cass knew she could move, Gram wrenched her head away, so all Nonno was left with was air.

"How could you," she said through her tears.

Luca looked at Cass, his eyes wide.

"What's going on?" he said.

But no one was ready to answer.

Chapter 22

SERRALUNGA D'ALBA, ITALY
Then

By the early afternoon, Giovanna was confident in her ability to dip a wine bottle in molten wax, lift it, and spin it enough for the wax to solidify. Eloisa and Gilberto, the couple dipping bottles with her and Vincenzo, ran the bakery in town and had supplied the pastries and bread the conte was serving. They had already disappeared to make sure all the loaves made it to the table. Vincenzo took the opportunity to press his hand against the small of Giovanna's back, making her want to melt right into him, when Bernardo came into the room.

"It's time to stop for lunch," he said.

Vincenzo stood and stretched his arms. Giovanna watched the muscles on his back shift under his shirt and shivered.

Federico came over. "It looks like I may lose you to the wine business," he joked. "I saw you spinning those bottles like you've been doing this your whole life."

Giovanna laughed and gave her father a quick hug and wondered if his words might one day prove prophetic.

"Are you ready to eat?" she asked him.

He nodded. "Let's go," he said, falling in line with one of the men he had been corking the bottles with all morning. "Alfonso," he said to the man, "this is my daughter, Giovanna." Then he turned to Giovanna. "Alfonso is in charge of the count's stables and of breeding and training the horses."

It seemed to Giovanna like the two men had gotten along well that morning. She was glad her father had found someone to talk to.

"Do you ride?" Alfonso asked her.

Giovanna shook her head. "I've never been on a horse," she said. "But I'd love to one day. They're so beautiful."

"I'd be honored to take you on your first horseback ride," Vincenzo said, coming up behind the trio. "Alfonso and I can teach you."

Giovanna tried not to read too much into anything, but that sentence felt more like a commitment than anything else Vincenzo had ever said to her. He let his gently swinging hand rub against her leg and she couldn't stop her smile from growing.

"That sounds wonderful," she said.

After lunch, Vincenzo went to help his father bring up a few bottles of the 1944 wine for everyone to taste, and her father was talking to his new friend Alfonso, so Giovanna decided to take a walk around the nearby part of the vineyard. She could see the grapes just starting to bud and reached out to touch them. After the years of fear and destruction, this day felt like a gift, something new, something beautiful.

Giovanna heard a twig crack behind her, and she turned. It was Vincenzo's sister, Chiara.

"Hello," Giovanna said, aware that she wanted to make a good impression.

"You know my brother's going to marry Isabella, right?" Chiara said to her as she walked closer. The silk scarf tied around her ponytail caught the breeze.

Chiara reminded Giovanna of the leader of a trio of girls she used to go to school with who made proclamations like that and then expected everyone to go along with them.

"That's what he'll do, if that's what he wants," Giovanna said.

Chiara shook her head. "You don't understand," she said. "That's what he'll do if it's what my father wants."

Giovanna shrugged. She didn't want to fight with Chiara. "You know your family better than I do," she answered.

It seemed that Chiara wanted to get a rise out of Giovanna and was frustrated that she wasn't getting it. "I've seen how you look at him," Chiara said. "Everyone can see it."

"Have you seen how he looks at me?" Giovanna answered, softly. "Can everyone see that, too?"

Chiara bit her lip, and her pause was truth enough. As was the fact that she'd sought Giovanna out to begin with. Everyone could see how Vincenzo looked at her.

"I think it may be time to go back and taste the wine," Giovanna added, when Chiara stayed quiet.

"Yes," Chiara said and turned on her heel. Giovanna trailed behind her, walking back to the group.

She believed completely in Vincenzo's feelings for her and hers for him. But after talking to Chiara, she couldn't help but wonder if she was being naïve. Even if his mother approved, would his father? In spite of Vincenzo's best intentions, in spite of her own, would this work out in the end?

Chapter 23

NEW YORK CITY, USA

Now

Nonno looked stunned, his arm on the table trembling. Luca went to him and helped him back into his seat. Cass was already next to her grandmother and said, "I think perhaps we should stop for today. Let's go, Gram," she said. "Dad."

And the three Fanellis left the kitchen and walked out of the apartment.

Once they were safely in the elevator, Dom said, "Could one of you please tell me what's going on?"

"I can," Gram said. "That man made me think he cared for me more than anyone in the world. And then he shattered my heart and never spoke to me again. How could he have . . ."

She wiped her hand across her lips.

Dom looked at his mother. He didn't look as shocked as Cass thought he would, but then again with three kids, two of whom were daredevil sons, he was good at projecting calm until he fully understood the situation.

"But you were crying before he tried to kiss you, Ma. What were you crying about?"

Gram closed her eyes. "Because I realized something," she said.

"Realized what?" Cass asked softly.

"I realized I never stopped loving him," Gram said.

Cass had no idea what to say next.

Chapter 24

GENOA, ITALY
Then

The Sunday after Giovanna and her father spent the day at the Della Rosa vineyard, they met Faustina and Betto outside the church before mass.

"Happy one-week anniversary," Giovanna said, smiling at them. She wasn't sure how Faustina was going to respond, since she'd been remarkably less than thrilled when Giovanna had told her a couple weeks ago about the planned trip to the Della Rosa vineyard.

"I don't understand why you and Papà are so taken with that family," she'd said. "They are the epitome of everything Betto and I have been working to change in our society."

Giovanna had sighed. "It's because we see them as people," she'd told her sister, "not as symbols. And they seem to be kind, generous people. Especially Vincenzo."

Faustina had narrowed her eyes. "Be careful around him. I know you find him intriguing, and I know he keeps coming to the shop to see you, but leave it at that, Giovanna."

Giovanna had swallowed hard when her sister said that. "I'll be careful," she promised, knowing full well she hadn't been careful at all.

"You are very chipper this morning," Faustina said.

Giovanna laughed. "I guess I'm in a good mood," she said just as Federico walked over.

"Was Giovanna telling you about our day yesterday?" he asked. He seemed happier than Giovanna had seen him in a while, too. Perhaps the mountain air had been good for both of them.

"She wasn't," Faustina said, shaking her head. "I was trying to forget that while I was coming back from my honeymoon, you spent the day on a count's estate." She said it like a joke, but Giovanna knew it wasn't.

Federico laughed. "It was a lovely day. I can't even tell you how long it's been since I was out in the country like that."

"Then maybe you should go to Saluzzo to visit Zio Enzo more often," Faustina suggested.

Giovanna knew that wasn't what her father had meant when he talked about how lovely the day was. There was something about the sunshine, the camaraderie, the opulence, the beauty all around them. But she also knew that she would have a hard time explaining that to Faustina. She bet her father would, too.

"Maybe," Federico said. "Come, it's time for mass. Let's find Betto and take our seats."

After the service Faustina and Betto came back with Federico and Giovanna for lunch. It was one of the few times that Giovanna had prepared a Sunday lunch all on her own, making sure the sausage was cooked through, the gnocchi were just firm enough, and the pesto wasn't too thin.

"We have some news," Betto said after Giovanna had served everyone a bowl.

When she heard those words, the first thing Giovanna wondered was whether her sister was pregnant. It would be so much fun to have a little baby in the family. Her cousin Guido, who lived in Saluzzo, had two little ones, and now Ilaria had a baby on the way, but she'd only seen them briefly at Faustina's wedding, and she wasn't sure when she would again.

"Betto's uncle agreed to sponsor us to immigrate to America," Faustina said.

Giovanna's breath caught in her throat.

Faustina had been talking about leaving Italy for America ever since the war ended, when many of their friends began conversations about starting over in the United States, moving to New York or Boston or Philadelphia and leaving the memories of the war behind them. Giovanna hadn't thought it would actually ever happen, though.

"Really?" she asked, trying to stay calm. "You're really going to go?"

Faustina nodded, a huge smile on her face, entirely oblivious to how her sister was feeling. "I think so! He told us what kind of paperwork we need to fill out and where we have to go to make it happen. Betto's going to work with him in his fruit business in New York City—he said he needs more family there he can trust. We'll live with him at first in Queens, and then maybe buy our own house one day. Could you even imagine?"

Giovanna couldn't imagine. Her head was reeling. "But . . . but what about us?" she said, including her father in the "us."

Betto smiled. "That's the other thing we wanted to ask you about," he said. "We would love for you to come with us. Zio Beppe said he can bring all four of us over."

Giovanna looked at her father. She couldn't read the expression on his face, but it wasn't a smile; it wasn't the happiness she saw yesterday in the vineyard.

There was silence around the table, everyone waiting to hear what he was going to say.

He cleared his throat. "That's such a generous offer," he finally said.

"So what do you think, Papà? Will you apply, too? And you, Giovannina?"

Giovanna thought of Vincenzo, of his arms around her, of their beautiful Saturdays together exploring the city and each other. She shook her head. "I don't want to leave," she said.

Faustina's face fell.

"I'm inclined to agree with your sister," Federico said. "I'm too old to start over. I have my shop, I have my customers, I have my church. And your mamma is here. I don't want to leave her alone. No one would visit her if I weren't here."

Giovanna could see Faustina's eyes getting teary. The huge grin she had earlier was gone, the joy in her face deflated.

"I thought this would be such a great opportunity for all of us," she said.

"It's a great opportunity for *you*," Giovanna said quietly. "You and Betto. And it's what you've wanted. You should take it. You should go. And Papà and I, we'll stay here. And we'll visit you and you can show us all the wonderful things in America. We'll eat hamburgers and dip potatoes in ketchup."

Faustina shook her head. "I wanted all of us to go. How can I leave you, Giovannina?"

"I'll be okay," Giovanna said, though her heart felt like it was cracking. How could she live without Faustina? Without talking to her and seeing her and getting angry with her and cooking meals with her and working in their father's shop together?

"Well," Betto said. "Maybe you two can think more about it."

Giovanna looked at her father, and he nodded, so she nodded.

"Of course," Federico said. "We'll think more about it."

But Giovanna knew his mind was made up. Hers was, too.

Chapter 25

GENOA, ITALY
Then

After they finished eating a tense lunch, Betto and Federico went to sit on the sofa, each with a section of the newspaper, and Giovanna and Faustina cleaned up the kitchen.

"So how was your first week as a married couple?" Giovanna asked, trying to warm things up between them. First with the vineyard, and now with America, Giovanna felt like she and Faustina were growing further and further apart. She wanted to bring them back together.

A tiny smile crossed Faustina's lips. "We had a very nice trip to Varazze. It would've been nicer in the summer, but we didn't leave our hotel very much anyway." She blushed, and Giovanna wanted to ask her so many things, but she listened instead. "And then coming back to our room in Betto's family's apartment . . . it'll take some getting used to. But I guess if all goes well, we won't be staying very long anyway." Her eyes got teary, and she wiped them with her shoulder, since her hands were now in the sudsy sink. "How did you and Papà do without me?"

"We did okay," Giovanna said. "I cooked too much pasta—I'm not used to cooking for two."

There were so many questions running through Giovanna's head. She wanted to ask her sister how it was, to be with someone like that. If it really did hurt. And what did she have to get used to? How was Betto's family different from theirs?

Faustina laughed. "If that's the worst that happened, then I guess you'll be fine."

"Well," Giovanna said. "I missed you."

Faustina didn't even bother drying her hands. She gave Giovanna a soapy hug and buried her face in her sister's curls. "I missed you, too."

The hug felt like it had so much more in it. Like her sister would keep hugging her if she could, forever, like she would hug her right onto a boat across the sea, right into the Port of New York City.

"So I know I said before that I was trying to forget what you and Papà were doing yesterday, but I would like to hear more about it," Faustina said, finally loosening her hug.

Maybe now was the time to admit everything, to tell her sister about what she and Vincenzo had been doing for the past two months. Maybe it would help Faustina understand why she didn't want to go to America. She knew Vincenzo wasn't who her sister wanted for her, but maybe she would understand their love and the hold it had on her. Giovanna took a breath, finished drying a dish, and placed it in the cupboard.

"We bottled the vineyard's 1944 vintage," she said. "It was a little party."

Faustina automatically handed her a glass to dry. It was the rhythm they'd had for years, washing and drying dishes. "I know you said you and Papà were invited because of the work we did on Vincenzo's clothing."

"Mm-hmm," Giovanna said.

There was a pause in the conversation.

"I just get the feeling there's something you're not telling me," Faustina said at last.

Giovanna dried the glass and put it away. If there was a time to tell her sister everything, it was now. Giovanna took a deep breath. "You know how Vincenzo keeps coming into the shop?"

"Yes," Faustina said. "With loose buttons. And pastries to say thank you for fixing the loose buttons. And that drawing of our shop." Faustina pulled her hands out of the sudsy sink water and looked at Giovanna.

Giovanna looked down at her shoes. "He's coming to see me," she said. "I think Papà suspects."

Faustina dried her hands and turned the water off. "Suspects what?" she said.

Giovanna sighed. "Suspects that Vincenzo and I have been . . . spending a lot of time together."

Faustina looked at Giovanna.

Giovanna looked at Faustina.

"What are you doing, Giovannina?" Faustina said. "People like him are what's wrong with Italian society. People like him are why Betto and I are going to America."

"People like him aren't all the same," Giovanna said, standing her ground, locking eyes with her sister. "Vincenzo is an individual the same way that you are, that I am. He's kind and sensitive and thoughtful. I've never met anyone else who makes me feel that just being who I am makes me wonderful."

Faustina shook her head. "You are on the wrong side of this," she said. "When the referendum passes, there will be no more counts or countesses. No more money from the townspeople paying taxes to support their noble way of life. That world is going to crumble. And if you spend more time with this man, you're going to have a front-row seat to it. I'm telling you, Giovannina, it's not going to be pretty."

Giovanna picked up a dripping-wet wineglass and wiped it with the dish towel. "That's not what Vincenzo thinks," she said.

Faustina closed her eyes, like she was trying to keep her temper in check. "But what do *you* think, Giovanna? After what you've heard on the radio, after the conversations we've had. Do you think he's right? Think about the direction the world has been going in. Think about what has happened in Italy over the past few years."

Giovanna shrugged. "I don't really know," she said. She'd thought she understood it when Faustina explained it to her before, but then she'd gotten to know Vincenzo and her whole worldview had shifted.

Faustina threw her arms up in the air. "Women have the right to vote in this election. You have to take it seriously! This choice will be, in part, yours. And mine, and everyone's."

Giovanna knew that, but she wasn't sure how she was going to vote. She knew what Faustina wanted, and she knew what Vincenzo wanted, but she had to figure out where she stood.

She wondered what would happen to Vincenzo if her sister was right, if enough people voted to abolish the monarchy. What if he lost his power—his promised power. She didn't know how that all worked, with taxes and land and lifestyle. Would he be happy as just an artist, just a winemaker?

Faustina's face was softer now. "It's not an easy decision for you, I know that," she said. "I know what falling in love feels like. But as for Vincenzo, no one likes to think their side is going to lose."

Giovanna smiled at her sister. Their mamma used to call Faustina *la bombetta* when she was small because she would explode and then fizzle like a little bomb. She was fizzling now. "So that's the same for you, too," Giovanna pointed out.

Faustina smiled back. "Will you promise me one thing?" she said.

"What is it?" Giovanna asked.

"Will you let me apply for you and Papà to come to America, too? You can decide not to go in the end, if you don't want to, but please let me put in the paperwork. None of us knows what the future will hold, and I want to have an insurance policy—for all of us."

Giovanna sighed. "I'll talk to Papà," she said. "I can promise we'll think about it."

Faustina nodded. "For now, that's enough."

Chapter 26

NEW YORK CITY, USA
Now

When they got to the street, Cass looked at her father and her grand-mother. "When in doubt," she prompted.

"Ice cream," her father answered.

It was something he did when she and her brothers were younger. When they were with him and something went wrong, someone got upset, whatever the situation, he would say, "When in doubt, ice cream." And the sweet dessert would somehow make things seem better, at least for a little while.

"This way," Cass said.

She led them both a block and a half to Mercer Playground and then sat them on a bench while she walked another block to get ice cream. It was artisanal, not the kind her dad used to get them at Friendly's when they were kids, but she knew the result would be the same. It would at least give them something else to focus on for a mo-ment, something enjoyable.

"I'll have a chocolate fudge brownie, a mint chip, and a cookies and cream," she said, ordering the old ice cream standbys.

They gave pint containers to her in a paper bag, and after picking up spoons and napkins, Cass started walking back, wondering how in the world she had gotten here. How her engagement weekend had ended up becoming a reunion for her grandmother and the first man she'd ever loved, the one she was still in love with. And how that person ended up being her fiancé's grandfather.

Cass had once read a novel where the same souls circled around each other for generations and generations. The two people were lovers in one iteration, best friends in the next, a parent and child in the next, and then lovers again. But no matter what, those souls would find each other because they were meant to be together.

In this moment, Cass couldn't help but wonder if there might have been a kernel of truth to that novel, if Gram's and Nonno's souls had been circling round each other in some cosmic kind of way. Were they meant to be together? Did their souls find each other because they had to and always would? Or . . . or was it her soul and Luca's that made this happen? Did their souls bring their grandparents back together?

Cass, her father, and her grandmother traded flavors back and forth quietly, each lost in thought. When the ice cream was gone, Gram said she was too tired to talk and wanted to go home to Long Island, so she and Cass waited while Dom got the car. Cass helped her grandmother in, hugged her tightly, and then walked back toward her and Luca's apartment.

She felt like the piece of fabric her grandmother had given her when she was seven to show her how to use a sewing machine. Cass had run it back and forth and back and forth under the needle, lines of stitches all wobbly and zigzagging across the felt. When she was done, the whole square had been haphazardly flattened with fuzz escaping in different patches. Cass had almost cried when she'd looked at the finished product, until Gram had magically fixed everything with an iron and a pair of scissors. She'd then found a small photo frame and put the fabric inside. "Look, Cassandra," she said. "You created art." Cass had taken it home and displayed it on the dresser in her bedroom for years. She had it in her office now, sitting on her desk for inspiration, reminding her that a change in perspective was often all you needed to turn a failure into a triumph.

When she got back home, the apartment was empty. Cass went to the kitchen and found the bottle of wine they'd been drinking last night still half full. She poured herself a glass and sat down on the couch.

I'm home, she texted Luca.

I'm on Sutton Place with my family, he texted back.

Cass closed her eyes and wondered how this all was going to play out. She honestly had no idea.

Chapter 27

GENOA, ITALY
Then

The next Saturday, Giovanna was back at Vincenzo's family's apartment. He handed her a purple silk gown when she walked through the door.

"A new dress?" she asked.

"A new painting," he said.

He'd come by the shop for a quick moment on Monday to tell Giovanna that he had a lot of meetings, that it would be hard to see her during the week, but that he couldn't wait to see her Saturday at his flat. She couldn't wait either. After being up with him in Alba, she felt like she knew him better, understood him better.

When she walked out of his sister's bedroom in the purple dress, she stepped into his arms. He ran his fingers along her collarbones, making her shiver.

"My mother thinks you're lovely," he whispered into her hair. "I think she'll be on our side."

Giovanna laid her head on his chest. "I thought she was lovely, too." Truthfully, the only person who hadn't been lovely was Chiara.

"Do you know what I kept thinking the whole time we were in the vineyard?" he asked, his fingers slowly running up her spine to the base of her neck.

"No," Giovanna whispered, "what were you thinking?"

He stroked her hair. "How when I'm the conte, I want you at my side. I want you to be my contessa."

"You do?" Giovanna said. She wasn't sure how to respond, wasn't sure if Vincenzo was speaking in dreams or realities.

"Giovanna," he whispered, looking into her eyes. "I want your warmth, your kindness, your openness, your honesty—you've changed me these past three months. You've tamped down my anger at the world, you've opened my eyes to the beauty, you've made me a better person. I love you."

Giovanna caught her breath. The voice inside her head was silenced. "You love me?"

"I've never loved anyone more," he answered, trailing his fingers along her cheek.

"I love you, too," she said, leaning against him. Her mind raced, though, wondering if his mother's support was enough, if he could stand up to his father with her alongside him, or if his father would cow them both. "I love you more than anyone else in the world." She'd been trying to hold back the feelings she had for him, the desire building deep in her body, the want that was threatening to consume her. She'd thought kisses would be enough, holding hands, picnicking at parks and talking and laughing. But it wasn't. She wanted so much more.

Their lips met, and they kissed with abandon, as if their confession—their admission—freed them. Vincenzo's hands slipped into the dress, and he cupped Giovanna's breasts in his palms. She let out a small sound of surprise.

"Is this good?" he asked.

"It's good," she answered, her heart racing. No one had ever touched her there before, and she could feel her body responding to it. She remembered the conversation she had with Faustina about Betto during the war. "We do everything but," Faustina had said. "Everything else . . . until we're married."

"What is everything else?" Giovanna had whispered to her sister, while they were both in their beds, their room illuminated by moonlight, waiting for Ilaria to sneak home from Aldo's house.

"Kissing," Faustina said, "touching."

"Touching . . . ?" Giovanna had said, asking an unspoken question.

"Touching . . . everywhere," Faustina had answered. "And . . . looking. There is something so incredible about looking. About being looked at." Faustina had smiled then, as if she had a sweet secret, the memory of which made her glow.

Giovanna wanted that glow, too. She wanted that smile on her face.

"Will you draw me?" Giovanna whispered, as Vincenzo's fingers made their way to her nipples.

"I have a whole sketchbook filled with drawings of you," he said. "I've even given you some."

"No," she said. "Not sketches like those. Not in a dress."

Vincenzo looked at her, his lips swollen from their kisses.

"Naked," she finished. "Will you draw me with nothing on?"

Vincenzo's face changed, his eyes closed. "You're going to kill me, tesoro. You think I'll be able to concentrate on drawing you when you have no clothing on?"

"I want to see how you see me," she said, shivering at the thought of it. "All of me. I want to see what I look like to you."

He rested his forehead against hers, kissed her softly. "I'll get my sketchbook," he said.

"One more thing," she called after him. "I want you to take off your clothes, too."

Giovanna couldn't believe she'd said that. Being with him made her bolder, braver.

"Your wish is my command," she heard him call from the other room.

And with that, she pulled the dress down, feeling the air on her skin, and stood in the puddle of purple silk, with just a pair of satin gloves on—and his mother's ring.

"Oh, Dio mio," Vincenzo whispered, when he walked back in the room, lifting his undershirt over his head, and stepping out of his paint-spattered pants.

Giovanna bit her lip.

Faustina was right about looking. There was something incredible about looking.

Giovanna had no idea how she'd ever look away from him again.

Chapter 28

NEW YORK CITY, USA
Now

The sun was starting to set when Luca finally made it back to the apartment. Cass was in their home office answering the emails she'd missed while she was out that day. She could hear her brother Nick saying, "Why are you doing work on a day you told them you weren't going to work?" just like he did when she used to go on vacation with her brothers and her parents, before all three of them settled down with their partners and her brothers had kids.

He was right, of course, but Cass had decided, when she chose to pursue a career in fashion, that she was always going to be the person in the room who worked the hardest, who answered the fastest, who went the extra mile. At first, she wanted to prove to her parents that she could make it in Manhattan, in corporate America. But then she did it for herself, to see how far she could go, how high she could stretch. She finally felt confident about where she was . . . but she still didn't want to drop any of the plates she had spinning, disappoint Samantha Li, the designer and CEO who was counting on her to make Daisy Lane huge in the United States. She knew she was good at her job, but she also knew there was a line of people who would be just as good waiting to take over if she faltered.

Cass was finishing up a response to the ad agency when she heard Luca's key in the door and then heard him call, "Stellina, dove sei?"

"In the office," she called back.

He came in looking . . . tired. "Hey," he said.

"Hey," she answered. "You okay?"

"Are you?" he asked.

She shrugged, resting her fingers on her keyboard and looking at him. "I have no idea."

He sighed and flopped down on the love seat. "Me neither," he said.

"Did you get more of the story?" she asked, closing her laptop. Her brain had been trying to fill in the missing details, but she couldn't piece a narrative together that made sense.

"Not much," Luca said. "He said that they dated when they were younger, and then got into a fight, and when he went back to apologize, she had already disappeared."

"Like she ghosted him?" Cass was still trying to find a story that fit. "But she was the one who seemed more upset. And if they dated for so long, wouldn't he know how to find her? Do you know what they fought about?"

Luca shook his head, his hair fluttering with the movement. "He didn't say. Something even stranger happened, though."

Cass couldn't think of anything stranger than her grandmother and Luca's grandfather having a history with each other. "What was it?" she asked.

"When we were leaving here to go back to my parents' place uptown, my grandfather asked me if I had a sketchbook and some charcoals he could borrow. Weird, right? But I gave them to him, and as soon as we got in the back of the car, he started sketching. Beautifully. I knew he'd designed the logo for the Della Rosa wines, but I hadn't realized he'd drawn it himself. It makes so much sense, now, why he was always encouraging my art and buying me paints and finding summer art programs in Italy for me to attend . . ."

"My grandmother said he painted her," Cass said, her brain clicking the information into place now. "I saw the painting when I was in Island Park. The way he captured the light was really wonderful."

Luca shook his head. "I asked him why I never knew he could draw like that, and he said that when his brother died during the war, the family needed him to take over the vineyards, and that was that. 'Basta,' he said. Enough. Can you believe that? He could draw that well and then . . . basta."

Cass moved from the desk chair to the love seat, next to Luca. "You're lucky things are different now," she said, trying to lighten the mood. "Or someone might force you into being a winemaker against your will."

Luca let out a small laugh. "I think that's what would've happened if my mom had her way."

Cass slid her arm around Luca's waist, tucking her hand in the back pocket of his jeans. It was something they connected about often—how they both felt like they didn't quite fit with their families, like they were off-center.

"Maybe you're more like your grandfather than you knew."

Luca smiled. "Maybe. Though I didn't get the feeling he became a winemaker entirely against his will," he said. "More like . . . he felt it was his responsibility. That he went where he was needed, if that makes sense."

Cass nodded. It did. And she would bet that Luca would make that same choice, if he felt his family needed him in the vineyard. "It's a shame he couldn't do both," she said.

Luca sighed. "I understand, though. Sometimes it's just easier to close a chapter completely."

Cass leaned her head against his shoulder, wondering what chapter he was thinking about in his own life, but feeling a little too emotionally drained to get into it. "What are the odds?" she said instead. That phrase had been on repeat in her brain all afternoon, between emails, when she thought about her gram and Nonno, and then Luca and herself. It was just so incredible that their families had a history together before the two of them were even born.

"Do you mean actually what are the odds?" Luca asked. "Because we could probably work it out. Is that a permutation or a combination? Something like 7.75 billion factorial divided by 7.75 billion minus two factorial multiplied by two factorial? With the two people being our grandparents?"

Cass laughed. She forgot sometimes that Luca was really good at math. He'd thought for a while about pursuing architecture because it combined the two things he was best at—art and mathematics—but when he took an architecture class, he missed the paint, the canvases, the stories and emotions. There were stories you could tell with buildings, but it wasn't quite the same.

"It's not a random event, though, right?" Cass said. "If you're calculating probability, then you need to know the likelihood of two people in the same city in the same age bracket in different socioeconomic circles meeting. And then do that with us, too. And then maybe multiply those numbers? I'm not sure. Do you have to take into account our likes and dislikes? Are there things in our backgrounds or personalities that make our families more likely to be drawn to one another? Does the fact that we're both Italian—or Italian American—increase the odds of us coming together?"

Luca twirled Cass's hair around his finger, coiling and uncoiling it. "Maybe," he said. "I guess we'd need a bit more data for our equation. But even without the data, I know that the odds are really, really small. Infinitesimal."

"Almost nonexistent," Cass said. "But it happened."

"Yeah," Luca said. "And forgetting about our grandparents and their drama for the time being, I'm glad it did."

Cass turned her face to Luca and gave him a kiss. And then she felt his hands against the cotton of her sweater, and she relaxed into him. In his arms, she felt enough.

"I love you," he whispered. "I love you the most of anyone, the most of anything."

"Yes," Cass said as he kissed the top of her head, loving to hear the refrain they both spoke to each other all the time. "I love you the most, too."

Even though their bed was only a room away, they curled up together on the too-small love seat, their bodies pressed to each other.

"This won't change us, will it?" Cass asked him. "No matter what happens, we are us?"

"Always," Luca said, pulling her in even closer. "Sempre."

Chapter 29

GENOA, ITALY
Then

After taking a long walk along the water holding hands, checking on the reconstruction at the port, and stopping for coffee, Giovanna and Vincenzo were back in his family's apartment. She was back in his mother's purple gown, the sun lighting the room through the window behind her.

"Just a few more touches, and I should be done for today," Vincenzo said.

She got up, holding the skirt carefully, and walked over to Vincenzo and his canvas. The way he lit her in the painting made her look otherworldly, like she was an angel or a saint, the glowing light behind her head reminiscent of the golden orbs she'd seen in Renaissance paintings.

"You're so talented," she told him. "I've never met anyone who could create art like you." She was amazed at how her hair looked like her hair, her eyes looked like her eyes, their color a mixture of green and gray and gold.

Vincenzo looked at her and smiled. "I love that about you," he said.

"Love what?" she asked.

"Love how open you are."

Giovanna laughed. "It's because I trust you," she said. "With my thoughts, with my opinions, with my heart."

Vincenzo dipped a thin paintbrush in white paint and added some tiny highlights to make her eyes look like they were sparkling.

"Well," he said when he was done. "I am one lucky man."

She rose up on her tiptoes and kissed his cheek. "I'm the lucky one," she said. "What are you going to call the painting?"

Just like paintings in museums, he titled each one.

"Giovannangela," he said.

She laughed. He saw her as an angel. He'd painted her as an angel.

He turned to her and put his paintbrush down. "I want to take you out tonight," he said. "To a dinner an old school friend of mine is having for his twenty-first birthday. Will you come?"

Until the weekend at the vineyard, Giovanna and Vincenzo's relationship had existed in a bubble, just the two of them, separate and apart from the rest of the world. But now she'd met his family, and she was going to meet more of his friends. This felt good, right, like the next step to making their relationship a reality. Though, there was still a prickle in the back of her mind: Chiara's declaration, Isabella's smile . . . but she trusted Vincenzo, she trusted his words, and she trusted his actions.

"I would love to," she said, wondering who these friends were, what they would think of her, if she'd be able to fit in. "Is this a fancy dinner?"

"I'll wear a suit," he said. "Do you want to see if there's anything my mother has here that you could wear?"

Giovanna shook her head, scrolling through her wardrobe in her mind. "I know exactly what I'll wear tonight," she said. Once Faustina's wedding dress was done, Giovanna had started working on some new clothing for herself, some dresses and skirts that made her feel more elegant, more mature.

"What's that?" Vincenzo asked.

"I've been making myself some new pieces," Giovanna told him. "And one of them is an emerald-green wrap dress that ties in a bow on the side." It was one she had copied from a page in *Grazia*, and she loved how it had come out.

"It sounds beautiful," Vincenzo said. "But truly, everything you wear looks beautiful on you. Do you make all of it?"

Giovanna nodded. "Sometimes Faustina helps," she said.

Vincenzo looked thoughtful. "You said the dress tonight is emerald green?"

Giovanna nodded.

"Then you should borrow this bracelet," he said, walking into his parents' bedroom and coming out with a gold filigree bracelet set with diamonds and emeralds. "I know it won't sparkle quite as much as you, but . . ."

Giovanna laughed. "That's a line if I've ever heard one." She took the bracelet he was offering and looked at it. She'd never seen so many diamonds in one place in her life. "I really couldn't borrow something like this." She tried to hand it back.

"I think my mother would be happy to lend it to you. And this way the whole night, even if we end up in different conversations, the weight on your wrist will remind you how much I love you."

Giovanna didn't know what to say, so instead she kissed him.

"Mm," he said. "You always taste so good."

He tasted so good to her, too. She wondered if they were somehow calibrated for each other. They were meant to kiss each other.

"Do you want me to draw you without any clothes on again?" he asked.

Giovanna shivered. She loved how that had felt, his eyes on her, focused on every private, intimate part of her.

"Yes," she said.

She stepped out of the dress and slowly took off her undergarments, looking up only when she was completely undressed. He was sliding his underpants off, and when he stood, she watched him grow while he took her in. She felt such power in making his body do that. It wasn't his choice, it happened because of the feelings that she stirred in him.

She'd never touched him there before, but she wanted to. She reached toward him.

"Giovanna?" he asked.

"Vincenzo," she answered.

He stepped closer and she swallowed. Then she knelt down, gently running her fingertips along the velvety softness of his skin.

"Mamma mia," he moaned.

The sound of his voice made her whole body shiver.

She felt it then, the desire to take him inside her, the desire to be so close to him that the two of them would become one, would unite. She wouldn't do it. She knew it was dangerous, that she could end up pregnant if she did, but she now understood why women wanted to. She understood the need that felt like it was somehow written into her blood, sewn into her muscles, and painted on her heart.

"I want so much of you," she told him, looking up, her fingertips still resting gently on him.

"I want so much of you, too," he said.

He reached down for her, and she stood, kissing him with her naked body pressed against his for the first time.

"Can I . . . can I touch you, too?" he whispered quietly.

Giovanna felt her body respond to that suggestion. "Yes," she answered.

His thumb traveled down from her navel and slid in between her legs, rubbing against a part of her body she didn't know was there, something seemingly magical that sent waves of pleasure spiraling through her.

"Sì, continua," she whispered. "Continua."

And he did, he kept stroking her there.

"You touch me, too," he said.

She reached down for him, her fingers matching his rhythm.

Soon the pleasure filled her whole self and her legs started to tremble. Vincenzo must've felt it, because he lowered both of them to the couch.

"Are you okay?" he asked.

Giovanna needed to catch her breath before she could answer. "Yes," she said. "I'm . . . more than okay." She was trying to understand what had just happened, the sensation that had just consumed her.

"Are you okay?" she asked.

"Wonderful," he answered.

She laid her head on his chest. "No one has ever . . . touched me like that," she said.

"Truth?" he asked.

"Yes?" she answered, not sure if he was asking if she was telling the truth, or asking if she wanted to hear the truth. "I mean, yes." The answer was the same to both.

"I've never touched anyone like that before."

She was surprised, not just because he was a man, but because he seemed so sure of himself.

"My cousin got me a magazine once," he said, blushing. "It had an article about how to . . . well . . . anyway, I read it over and over."

Giovanna laughed. "Did you do as well at school as you did after studying this magazine?" She wondered what he was like as a student. Was he outgoing? Shy? Did he do well on his exams? Ask his friends to help him in mathematics or Latin? It was funny that they didn't know that about each other. Their relationship was so—tight, so close in on tiny moments, just the two of them.

"I did okay," he said. "I might have done better if I hadn't been trying to draw my teachers during the lessons. Did you like school?" he asked.

Giovanna shrugged. "I guess," she said. "But a lot of the classes were difficult for me. I'm much better when I do things—sewing, cooking, even helping my father build a bookcase—than when I have to read about theories and figure out what writers mean in their stories. Faustina was good at school, though. Reading and theories and stories come easy to her. She wanted to apply to go to university, but my father couldn't spare her in the shop, and then when there was no shop, there was war. But school until I was sixteen was good enough for me."

The two of them sat for a moment, comfortable in their silence.

"I'm so glad my father decided to bring his clothing to your father's shop twenty-five years ago," Vincenzo said.

"I'm so glad that you decided to bring your clothing to my father's shop four months ago," Giovanna replied.

"I'm so glad you were the one behind the counter, and not your sister!" Vincenzo added.

"I'm usually behind the counter," Giovanna laughed. "I'm nicer."

Vincenzo laughed, too. "Well, I'm so glad you're nicer."

"I'm so glad you wanted to paint me."

"I'm so glad you let me."

The two of them curled up next to each other and Giovanna stroked Vincenzo's hair as his eyes closed. She started singing softly, a song her mother had used to put her to sleep as a child.

> *Stella, stellina.*
> *La notte s'avvicina.*
> *La fiamma traballa . . .*

> *Star, little star.*
> *The night arrives.*
> *The flame trembles . . .*

"Mmm," Vincenzo said. "I'd forgotten about that song. It's so pretty how you sing it."

"Thank you," she said, her fingertips brushing his hair away from his forehead. "It's how my mother used to sing it to me."

"We should sing it to our children one day."

Giovanna bent over and kissed him softly on the lips. "Yes," she said. "I'd love that."

She wondered if he was just daydreaming, or if he really did think about having children with her one day. She imagined their children growing up, like Vincenzo, in the Villa Della Rosa, with the same expectations—growing up as olive trees. Or maybe not. Maybe with the referendum, if the monarchy fell, there would come a different sort of freedom. The chance to be any tree they wanted to be.

Chapter 30

Luca and Cass spent the next week as go-betweens. Nonno wanted to talk to Gram. He asked if he could call her. Cass asked, and the message she relayed back was "No."

He asked if he could meet her for coffee, for dinner, for a glass of wine. The message Cass relayed back was "No, no, and no."

Finally, he brought by a series of drawings he'd made. Cass recognized the furniture in one of them: it was the sitting room in Nonno's apartment in Genoa. In it, he'd drawn a younger version of himself, crumpled to the ground in tears, a letter in his hand. Another was him, burying his father. A third was him, in a tailor shop with packed boxes piled against the counter, the ears of a stuffed rabbit poking out of his satchel. On the bottom of all the drawings, he'd written the same thing: *Tutto quello che non hai visto.*

All you did not see.

"Please," he said. "Will you give these to her?"

The lines and shading were a little clumsy, like he was out of practice and his hands weren't working quite the way they used to, but the images were clear enough. You could still see the talent in his fingers. Cass overnighted them to her parents' house, but not before she and Luca admired the drawings and wondered what it was Nonno was sharing with Gram, knowing she would understand the meaning even if they did not.

In the meantime, Cass and Luca's wedding plans were on hold.

"We have to fix this," Luca said, walking down the street next to Cass that Saturday, his fingers twined with hers. They had nowhere to go, nowhere to be; they were just out enjoying their SoHo neighborhood, wandering aimlessly, window-shopping as they went.

"I know," Cass said. "It feels wrong to move forward with anything until our grandparents can be in the same room as each other." She sighed and leaned her head against his shoulder.

"Oh, stellina," he said. "Do you need some ice cream?"

She squeezed his hand with hers. "I think I might," she said.

They changed direction, walking toward Van Leeuwen's.

"You know, my grandfather still wants to throw us an engagement party," he said.

"I know," Cass said. "I'll talk to my dad. Maybe he can get through to Gram. Or maybe I should go to Long Island for a few hours. Maybe I can figure out a way to smooth things over."

"Maybe we should both go," Luca said.

Cass liked the idea of having Luca there with her, but she wondered if it would be the right strategic move, with Gram the way she was.

"Let's think it through," she said.

Cass and Luca were walking so close to each other that when her phone started vibrating they both felt it.

They pulled out of the foot traffic on the sidewalk so she could see who was calling.

"My parents' house line," she told Luca, and picked up the phone. "Hello?"

"Cassandra?" It was Gram.

"Hi, Gram," she said. "What's going on?"

"I got Vincenzo's drawings just now. The mailman dropped off the envelope you sent."

Cass tilted the phone toward Luca so he could hear, too.

"I'm glad it arrived so quickly," she said. She wasn't sure what to say next.

"Tell him . . . tell him I'll talk to him," Gram said. "On the telephone."

Luca raised his hands up above his head in a silent victory cheer. Cass smiled at him.

"Okay, Gram, I will. I'm sure he'll want to call today. Is that okay?"

"Yes," Gram answered. "That's fine, Cassandra. Thank you. I'm going to go now."

"Okay," Cass said. "I love you."

"I love you, too, dear," she answered.

Before Cass could say another word, Luca was already dialing his grandfather's cell phone.

Cass wondered how the conversation would go, and what about the drawings made her grandmother change her mind.

Chapter 31

GENOA, ITALY
Then

On her way back home, Giovanna stopped by the local profumeria to see if there was any lipstick back on their shelves. Carmela was behind the counter—she was in Faustina's year at school and was engaged to Tommaso, one of Betto's friends who had been working with the Americans since the war had ended to salvage the shipwrecks at the port. Giovanna and Vincenzo watched the salvage crews sometimes, seeing what they found down there, wondering aloud who had been on those ships, what their plans for the future had been, whether the boat had gone down slowly, or quickly, with a big blast from the German U-boats that had been hiding off the coast of Liguria. The Italian members of the salvage crews were made up of a lot of sailors and dockworkers. It made Giovanna wonder if they thought *There but for the grace of God go I* every time they pulled a wreck from the sea.

But that wasn't what Giovanna was going to think about today. She was going to think about dinner. With Vincenzo. And his friends. He said they might even go to a jazz club afterward.

She checked the shelves where lipstick used to be stocked, but there wasn't any there.

"What are you looking for?" Carmela asked.

Giovanna turned. "Lipstick," she said. "I know there hasn't been much in ages, but I thought maybe . . ." She shrugged. She'd assumed there wouldn't be any, but it was still disappointing.

"Well, today is your lucky day," Carmela answered as she pulled out a tube of red lipstick from behind the counter.

Giovanna couldn't believe it. "Truly?"

Carmela nodded. "We got a small shipment yesterday, and I put a few behind the counter for special customers," she said, ringing Giovanna up. "I told Faustina she should have come to me before her wedding. Our shipments are starting to come a little more frequently, and I would have put some aside for her."

"Oh, Faustina didn't mind," Giovanna said. "She's used to making her own." There hadn't been makeup anywhere during the war. Some of the ingredients were needed for munitions, so all the girls at school started burning cork to use as mascara and lighting candles under china dishes so they could use the soot from the bottom as eye shadow. Boiled-down beetroot juice worked well for lipstick—it wasn't as red as the tube Giovanna was holding in her hands now, nor as creamy, but it stayed on longer. So at least there was a benefit. Faustina had worn all of that at her wedding, and she looked beautiful. It was what Giovanna had planned on wearing that night, until deciding to try her luck at the profumeria.

"You don't happen to have any mascara or eye shadow back there, too, do you?" Giovanna asked, even though she guessed the answer was no.

Carmela shook her head. "We haven't had a shipment of those in a few weeks, but I'd bet that means one will come soon. Do you want me to hold some aside for you?"

Giovanna nodded. "That would be wonderful. Thank you." Vincenzo might invite her to other parties, and it would be nice to have some real makeup to wear. If his access to coffee was any indication, his friends' girlfriends probably had access to makeup. Just like nylons, you could get some if you were willing to pay, if not in the regular way, then definitely on the black market.

Later that night, Giovanna was wearing her emerald green dress with beige leather T-strap pumps she'd gotten for Faustina's wedding, and she had on her new bright red lipstick. She pinned her hair up, her curls slightly tamed.

"I'm going to a dinner with Vincenzo," she told her father, who was listening to the news on the radio.

Federico stared at her for a moment. "When did you grow up on me?" he said finally.

Giovanna laughed. "This afternoon," she said.

Her father laughed, too, but she wasn't entirely joking. Her time with Vincenzo, the two of them naked, touching each other, made her feel older. Like she really had grown up this afternoon. And she had a feeling that the more time she spent with him, the more she would leave her past behind and become a grown woman. Of course, at twenty-one, many of her school friends were already married with a baby on their hip, but Giovanna's father's choices—and her own—had kept her away from so much during the war that she didn't feel that she had quite finished growing up. Not until Vincenzo. Not until he'd made her body thrill at his touch.

Not until he told her he loved her.

Chapter 32

GENOA, ITALY
Then

Vincenzo's friend Bruno was hosting the dinner for his birthday at a restaurant near the Chiesa di San Donato. The restaurant was opulent—the kind of place Giovanna's parents would have gone on their wedding anniversary—but not where Giovanna was used to eating. When she walked in on Vincenzo's arm, she couldn't help but admire the clothing the women were wearing and the jewelry that looked like the pieces in Vincenzo's parents' apartment safe, like the borrowed bracelet clasped securely on her left wrist. Even so, she felt self-conscious, but almost as if he knew, Vincenzo leaned down and whispered to her: "You're the most beautiful woman in this whole room."

She squeezed his arm in thanks and whispered back, "You're the most handsome man."

When Giovanna and Vincenzo arrived at the table, there were two empty seats waiting for them. Giovanna sat down next to Bruno's fiancée, Mariella, who Giovanna noted was wearing a dress that she had seen in one of her father's fashion magazines. It was one that she had tried to copy, actually, with ruching along the waist, which was incredibly difficult to sew so it lay right. In total there were six men and four women. Two of the men were there alone; all of the women were there with men. And all of them looked stunning.

"Giovanna!" Mariella said. "We've been begging to meet you. Vincenzo showed us one of his sketches of you last week, and Ernesto over there thought Vincenzo had created you, like Pygmalion. A woman who leapt out of a sketchbook. He's been calling you Galatea ever since."

Giovanna smiled. She had some vague notion of a Greek myth about a sculptor who had created a statue that came to life because he had fallen in love with her. They had studied Greek and Roman myths in school at some point before the war. "I promise I'm real," she said, wondering what else Ernesto and Mariella and all the rest had been saying about her.

"You've got to forgive Ernesto," Bruno said, leaning over Mariella. "He's studying ancient Greek and Latin at the university. And I think he is a bit jealous that our Vincenzo has found a beautiful woman in Genoa before he did."

Ernesto looked over the rim of his glass of liquor. "Stop maligning me," he said. "I'm not jealous. Just . . . incredulous."

Bruno shook his head.

Vincenzo, on the other side of Giovanna, whispered in her ear. "He's an ass. A loyal friend and a good person, but also an ass. Actually, a few of these gentlemen are asses. I apologize in advance for anything offensive they might say."

He grabbed her hand under the table and squeezed it. Giovanna squeezed back, but she was wondering why he spent time with these men if they were asses. Bruno seemed nice, though. And Mariella.

"So," Mariella said after the men got involved in a conversation about which one of them had actually climbed through Gregorio's sister's bedroom window on a dare when they were twelve and left a rose from the Villa Della Rosa on her bed. "Vincenzo told Bruno the two of you have been spending a lot of time together."

Giovanna nodded. "We have," she said, thinking about their afternoon, their plan to take a picnic to the Spianata dell'Acquasola the next day, his still-frequent trips to the shop with a loose button or a box of pastries so he could sneak in an afternoon kiss.

"Well," Mariella said. "I guess you'll get used to this group, then. Heaven knows I did." She took a sip from the glass of wine in front of her. "Oh! A Vernaccia di San Gimignano. Lovely. Gregorio must've ordered before we arrived. That's his favorite wine. I can't say I have any complaints."

Giovanna was amazed that Mariella was able to tell what kind of wine she was drinking after taking a sip from her glass. "How did you know?" she asked.

Mariella shrugged delicately. "My grandfather grows these grapes in his vineyard in Tuscany. So I can usually pick them out."

Her grandfather had a vineyard. Giovanna's grandfather in Saluzzo had a vegetable garden. And a fig tree. "Does everyone here have a family vineyard?" Giovanna asked. She hadn't meant to ask it out loud, but the thought seemed to jump from her brain to her mouth.

Mariella laughed. "I think about half of us," she said. "You know, Vincenzo was right. He said you were a breath of fresh air, and you absolutely are."

Giovanna was quiet for a moment. She guessed those words were meant as a compliment, but they felt a little like an insult, too. Giovanna was only a breath of fresh air because she wasn't like everyone else at the table. Then she heard Ernesto say, "We should ask her."

"Stop it," Vincenzo responded.

"No, really, I'm curious," Ernesto said. "Galatea, would you answer a question for us?"

"It's Giovanna," Vincenzo said. "Ernesto, I'm serious. Leave her alone."

Ernesto waved him away. "You'll answer, won't you?" he said to Giovanna.

She looked at Vincenzo.

"You don't have to," he said.

Everyone at the table was staring at her. She had no idea what the question was going to be, but it seemed like this was a test, and she had to pass it to really be considered part of the group. "I'll answer," she said. "What do you want to know?"

"We're talking about the referendum."

Giovanna nodded. She and her father had discussed it again earlier in the week—he had said he knew it was a little more complicated for Giovanna because of her . . . friendship with Vincenzo. That's how he said it. A pause before the word *friendship*, as if he was acknowledging that they both knew it was something more but were agreeing not to talk about it. She wondered if her . . . friendship with Vincenzo made it more complicated for her father, too.

"What about the referendum?" she asked.

"What do people like you think about it?"

Bruno smacked Ernesto on the back of the head. But it was too late. "People like me?" she asked. She couldn't believe he'd said that, but she would give him a chance to save face.

"You know," Ernesto said. "People who don't have money or titles. The plebeians of ancient Rome."

Giovanna felt her face get hot. Perhaps she shouldn't have given him that moment of grace. She didn't know what to say now, wasn't sure if there was anything she *could* say. Or at least anything she could say without telling Ernesto exactly what she thought of him and his question, which she wouldn't do. There was a long uncomfortable pause at the table.

Vincenzo stood up. "That's enough," he said. "Happy birthday, Bruno, but we have to go."

"Please don't," Bruno said.

Mariella put her hand on his. "Let them," she said.

He nodded. "Okay. I'll talk to you later this week," he said to Vincenzo.

Giovanna looked down at her emerald dress, the one she was so proud of. Now it felt wrong, off, cheap fabric masquerading as fashion.

Once they walked outside, Vincenzo said, "I'm so sorry. I'm so, so sorry, Giovanna. Ernesto is really an ass. I shouldn't have brought you."

He grabbed her hand and Giovanna held on to his tight. "No," she said. "If we're going to be together, we should go out to spend time with your friends. I just . . . wish you had different friends."

Vincenzo laughed.

"I'm not being funny," Giovanna said, giving voice to the realization she had as they walked from the room, Ernesto's eyes still on her. "They'll never accept me as one of them. They'll always see me as less than."

Vincenzo stopped on the sidewalk. "That's not true. Once you're my contessa, you'll have a higher status than almost all of them. They'll respect that."

"We live in different worlds," Giovanna said, her mind lingering on the words *once you're my contessa*. Could that really be possible? She still couldn't tell if he was speaking in dreams or realities.

"No," Vincenzo said, looking right at her. "We live in the same world, the same city even, just different neighborhoods. But people move neighborhoods all the time."

Giovanna reached up to kiss him. He was right, people did move neighborhoods. Maybe she could. Maybe it would all be fine in the end.

"Let's go get dinner," he said, running his finger along her cheek. "And then to a cabaret. We'll have more fun just the two of us anyway."

"Yes," she said, leaning her body against his. "We will."

"By the way," he added, looking down at her. "That dress is stunning."

Giovanna smiled. "Thank you," she said, a little bit of her confidence returning.

She linked her arm through his, and next to him, she felt beautiful once more.

Chapter 33

NEW YORK CITY, USA
Now

The next day, Nonno planned to take a black car to Island Park to meet with Gram at Bread & Circuses, a coffee shop that belonged to the grandson of Gram's first friend in America, Emilia Ricci. Nonno had called and asked Cass about Gram's favorite restaurants in the area. When she suggested the coffee shop and told him about her grandmother's connection to it, he agreed it was the perfect choice.

"You know," he said, "the first time I took Giovanna out, we had coffee. It was just after the war, and we'd missed coffee so. Or at least I had."

After they hung up, Cass shook her head in wonder. She was still having trouble wrapping her mind around her grandmother dating Nonno. And it was even harder to think of her as a young Italian woman named Giovanna. In Cass's memory, she had always been named Joanna, always been married to Pop, always been her grandmother. For a moment Cass wondered whether she would have grandchildren in the future, and if she did, whether they'd recognize her life right now. Would her current self seem just as much of a stranger to them as Gram's past self was to her? It was something she knew she would keep thinking about in the empty corners of her mind.

Chapter 34

"Are you as nervous to hear about today's meeting as I am?" Luca asked Cass that evening.

She had just gotten home from an afternoon with Kiley, and Luca handed her a glass of wine as she kicked off her high heels.

"I was nervous this morning," she said. "But I think if it was terrible, we would have heard by now."

"Good point," Luca said, sipping his wine and sitting down at the kitchen table.

"What are you going to do about the Jupiter and Juno painting?" she asked him, sitting by his side.

He shrugged. "Well, if the conversation went well and they're okay with it, I'll move forward with them sitting one last time together. If not . . . I'll do them one at a time. Not ideal, but workable."

"But you'll keep the painting in the show." Cass wondered how Gram and Nonno felt about being in a painting together now.

"I was planning to. Unless they tell me not to . . . and, if not, I'll find two other people to sit for it, I guess. I don't want to lose the parents of the pantheon. Or grandparents, I should say. It would be a hole in the show."

Cass sighed. "This really all got so complicated," she said.

"It's wild, isn't it?" Luca said. "I keep trying to imagine them back then, what they were like, what the world was like, how they came together . . ."

"I hope they tell us all the details one day." Cass had been trying to imagine it, too, but knew nothing she could imagine would be more intriguing than the real story.

Luca's phone buzzed and he pulled it out of his pocket. "Nonno," he said.

He answered it, holding the phone up to his ear. Cass strained to hear Nonno's muffled voice coming through the speaker. He was speaking Italian, though, and between that and the fact that the phone was against Luca's ear and not hers, she couldn't really follow the conversation.

He hung up after a minute or so, then turned to Cass. "So Nonno didn't say much, but he said that both the conversation and the coffee were better than he expected them to be."

Cass laughed at that. "Well, that's a backhanded coffee compliment if I've ever heard one."

Luca paused for a moment. Then he smiled and shook his head ruefully. "I think he meant it as an actual compliment. Anyway, I'm glad the conversation went okay. He said your grandmother agreed to come to the engagement party he'd like to throw us."

Cass let out a breath. "Well, that's a relief," she said.

"And we move forward," Luca said. "Forza e coraggio che la vita è un passaggio!"

"Yes," Cass said. "Strength and courage indeed."

Luca took her hand. "I'm glad we're on this ride together."

Cass squeezed his hand with hers. "Me too," she said. "Me too."

Chapter 35

GENOA, ITALY
Then

At the shop on Monday, Giovanna and Faustina were sitting in the back room. Faustina was running the bottom of a skirt through a sewing machine to shorten it, and Giovanna was repairing some lace on the bodice of a dress by hand.

"How are things going with your count?" Faustina asked.

"He's not a count yet," Giovanna said, concentrating on her stitches, making sure they blended with the pattern in the lace. "And I don't really know if he's mine."

"Well, then how are things going with the not-yet-a-count who may or may not be yours?"

Giovanna laughed. But then she stopped sewing and looked at her sister. "He's wonderful," she said. "He's interesting and thoughtful and caring and he loves me. He said he loves me, Faustina. He makes me feel more . . . more . . . everything. Like I'm prettier and funnier and smarter when I'm with him. And I love him, too."

"I hear a 'but' coming," Faustina said, finishing off the hem of the skirt.

Giovanna sighed. "But his sister was awful to me, and his friends were, too. We walked out of a dinner this weekend. We had a lovely time afterward, just the two of us, but . . . I don't know if I'll ever fit into his world."

Faustina was quiet for a moment. "This is why we have to vote to end the nobility," she said. "We have to vote for equality in Italy, so our worlds get closer together."

Giovanna put the lace down on the table in front of her. "No matter what happens with the referendum, I don't know if it will change what's in people's hearts and minds," Giovanna said. "Laws and feelings are two different things entirely."

"Perhaps not now, but in the future. It can be like it is in America."

Giovanna wondered not for the first time whether her sister's idea of America was too good to be true. There still were people there with more money and less, still people who were treated differently because of their religion or their skin color or where their family was from. There had to be. That was what happened with people. They found others with whom they could find common ground, then made a group. Giovanna had even seen it at school—girls who all liked film or athletics or cooking or mathematics became little groups, separating themselves from the others. And she saw it over the weekend at dinner—Vincenzo's friends saw themselves as part of a group that she wasn't in. The most extreme version was the basis of Hitler's war—separating out people he didn't think were perfect enough, Aryan enough.

"Even if the monarchy is voted down, you'll still leave?" she asked Faustina. She'd been hoping that maybe if Italy became more what Faustina wanted it to be, she would stay.

Faustina sighed. "Yes, even then," she said. "Betto and I want the opportunities we'll have with his uncle. You should come, too. You and Papà."

Giovanna was quiet, reflecting on what it truly would be like to live across an ocean from her sister. Faustina was quiet, too. They both picked up their work again and continued in companionable silence, both lost in their own minds.

"I have something to confess," Faustina said after a while. "I already applied for you. For you and Papà to come to America with us. You can make up your mind last minute, but the lawyer said it was better to apply for all of us together. So I did. I hope you really will consider it."

Giovanna smiled at her sister. She wasn't surprised at all. "I'll consider it," she said. "And I'll talk to Papà, too. But on one condition."

Faustina nodded, "Okay, what's that?"

"That if the monarchy goes down, you'll consider staying. Really consider it."

Faustina put her hand out and reached toward her sister. "Deal," she said.

Giovanna reached her hand out and clasped Faustina's in hers. "Deal," she echoed.

No matter what happened, Giovanna knew that in two weeks, after June 2, their world would not be the same.

Chapter 36

Nonno had rented out a rooftop restaurant, Nina's Nest, on top of the Gregory Hotel near the South Street Seaport. The Gregory family had had Della Rosa wine on their menu for years, and Nina Gregory was good friends with Alessandra—the two of them were in a book club together, one that Alessandra had actually invited Cass to join— so Cass wasn't surprised that this was the place Alessandra and Nonno chose. He'd invited their families, a short list of Cass and Luca's close friends, and the entire New York office of the Della Rosa d'Alba company, along with all of their business contacts in the area.

"Is this party for him or for us?" Cass had half joked to Luca when they went over the list together on their living room couch.

"Oh, it's entirely for him," Luca said, laughing a little. "An engagement is good for business. So is a party!"

"And?" Cass asked. There was something in his voice that felt like he was hiding something.

He sighed. "And . . . I feel like . . . if I can't contribute to the family business like my sister does, the least I can do is let them throw me a party that helps the company out."

"Throw us," Cass corrected.

He kissed her forehead. "Yes, throw us. That's what I meant."

She leaned against his shoulder. "We don't have to invite all these people to the wedding, do we?" she asked. She hadn't mentioned her father's offer to pay for a wedding for them on Long Island yet. There had been so much going on, so much drama, that it never quite seemed the right time. But wherever they had their wedding, she didn't necessarily want all these strangers there.

"I doubt they'd all travel to Italy even if we did invite them," Luca said.

Cass put down the coffee she was holding. "Wait a minute," she said. "We never talked about getting married in Italy."

"Oh!" Luca said, putting his coffee next to hers. "I'm sorry, I'd just assumed. Everyone in my family has gotten married in our family's chapel in Alba. I—I mean—you love Italy."

There were so many family traditions. Cass hadn't realized that at first, but they kept popping up. And some, like the calpestamento, were fun. But she didn't like when their life seemed dictated by what some count chose to do hundreds of years before.

"Is that what you want?" Cass asked him, picking her mug back up and feeling the warmth through the ceramic. "Not just because it's what your family does, but because it's what you'd choose, given the options?"

Luca sighed. "It's hard," he said, "to differentiate. Do I want it because I want it, or do I want it because the way I've been raised made me want it?"

"So you want it," Cass answered, resting the cup on the coffee table again after taking a sip. "Either way, you want it."

Luca nodded. "I always imagined that was where I'd get married. Whenever I dreamed of a wedding, even if I knew nothing else, I knew it would be in Italy, in our chapel, and in the orchards behind our villa. We'd drink the vintages the family saves for special occasions. And we'd have the chefs from the restaurants in town make all the food for our guests."

Cass was quiet for a moment. She had never thought about what her wedding would look like, just what she would wear. It was funny how different people's minds worked. She felt, though, like they should be making this decision together, that he should say to her, *Would you like to get married at my family's chapel in Italy?* And she should say, *Let's think about that. What are our other options? Let's make a list of pros and cons.* Or was this how compromises go? When someone really wanted something, you just let them have it. He could have Italy, and she could have her dress. But what about her brothers? Asking them to take off work, to fly their families halfway across the world?

"I don't know if my family can afford the trip," she said, slowly twirling a lock of hair around her finger.

"We can pay for it," he answered automatically.

Cass shook her head, setting the hair free. "They'd never take it." Then she thought about her father's offer. "My dad said he and Mom have saved up money for my wedding—they've been saving since I was a child. Maybe we could ask them to use that to pay for everyone to come and to stay in a hotel and all of that."

"They've been saving since you were a child?" Luca asked.

"Since I was born, actually," Cass said. "When my dad told me, it made me cry. Especially because he was apologetic that he didn't have enough to throw us a New York City wedding."

She wondered how often her parents wished she'd made different choices, had different dreams, lived a life more like theirs. She felt their confusion at times—as if they were questioning how their little girl could have turned into this woman who made decisions so foreign to them.

"Well," Luca said. "Using that money to get your family to Italy sounds like the perfect thing to have been saving up for."

Cass nodded, but she still felt uneasy. First with the guest list to the engagement party and now this, it felt like their wedding was turning into his family's wedding, not a joining of the two of them.

"Let's talk more about it later," Cass said. "I do love Italy. And both my parents have extended family there, too. So maybe I could spin it as a chance to see family again—we haven't been since Nick graduated from high school. If that's really what you want, I'm sure we can figure something out."

But Cass wasn't entirely sure how they would do that.

Chapter 37

GENOA, ITALY
Then

The next Saturday, Giovanna was standing in front of one of the lion statues at the Cattedrale di San Lorenzo. She ran her fingers against its carved mane, amazed that a sculptor had been able to create such movement from stone.

She heard footsteps behind her and turned. Somehow she'd become so attuned to the weight of his steps, the pace of his strides, that she knew Vincenzo was coming just from hearing his footfalls.

"Why did you want to meet here?" Giovanna asked when Vincenzo came up next to her, sliding his hand in hers.

He kissed her on both cheeks and said, "Bruno told me that the British navy shelled this cathedral five years ago, but the bomb never exploded. I wanted to see for myself."

The city had been rebuilding, but so much had been destroyed that Giovanna figured it would take years, if not decades, for La Superba to return to her former glory.

"It makes you really wonder about God, doesn't it?" Giovanna said softly, looking up at the church in front of her. "He protected his church but allowed the war to happen."

She wondered when, if ever, she'd stop thinking about the war, stop realizing new ways it had changed her, shaken her faith not only in humanity but in religion as well.

"Maybe it was all he could do," Vincenzo said. "With so many people following in the path of fallen angels, he only had so much power. Save a building here, protect a family there."

Giovanna had never thought about it that way. She'd believed what she was taught to believe but had trouble—initially after her mother died and family members told her that God had taken her home, and then especially after the war—really understanding why God would do things or let things happen. Why take a young mother home, when her daughters still needed her on earth? When her husband still loved her? Why destroy the lives of so many? Torture so many? Had God forsaken everyone who had been sent to death camps in Germany and Poland? Giovanna tried not to read the stories, but something compelled her to bear witness.

"You don't agree?" he asked gently.

Giovanna shrugged. "I've been confused about God for a long time. Ever since my mother . . ."

Vincenzo squeezed her hand. "I understand," he said softly. "It's hard to put your faith in a God who takes away people we love."

Giovanna nodded, relieved she didn't have to explain more. She squeezed his hand back.

"It's okay," he said. "I would be angry at God for that, too. I was angry about Leonardo. Still am angry about Leonardo. But . . . I'm grateful that he brought us together."

Giovanna smiled. She hadn't thought about that. "Yes," she said. "I'm grateful for that, too."

Vincenzo wrapped his arm around her shoulders in a one-sided hug. "So let's go thank him."

"Yes, let's," Giovanna said, a small smile still on her face.

The two of them walked into the church, genuflected at the door, and crossed themselves. Giovanna watched Vincenzo walk to a pew and kneel, his mouth moving in prayer. She walked to a pew across from his and knelt down as well. She closed her eyes and started reciting the Hail Mary softly.

Ave Maria, gratia plena
Dominus tecum.

She told Mary all she was grateful for, and then she talked about her fears, her worries, her hopes. When she was done, Giovanna repeated the Hail Mary and then opened her eyes. She saw that Vincenzo had gotten up and was now standing in front of a column near the door to the church. His hand was on it, his fingers rubbing against something in the stone, the way hers had been rubbing against the lion's mane.

She walked over to him. "What's that?" she asked quietly, trying not to startle him.

"A sleeping dog," he answered, taking his fingers away to show her the carving in the column. "When we came here as children, my grandfather showed it to me and Leonardo. He said the story is that one of the sculptors had a dog who died while he was working on this column, and he loved him so much that he wanted to memorialize him, so he carved him into the stone."

Giovanna reached out and touched the sleeping dog, just at the height of her eyes. "Do you know the dog's name?" she asked.

Vincenzo shook his head. "When I was younger, I imagined it was Nebbiolo, like our dog back then."

Giovanna laughed. "Nebbiolo like nebbia? Like fog?"

Vincenzo shook his head and laughed, too. "No, Nebbiolo like the grapes."

Of course. "Winemakers through and through," she said.

"Through and through," Vincenzo echoed. "Except for the part of me that understands the sculptor. That understands the desire to create art to memorialize. To show love and devotion. To say what you can't with words."

"Is that why you keep drawing and painting me?" Giovanna asked, teasing.

"Yes," he answered simply, his face serious.

The air between them was still for a moment. If they had been alone, she knew he would have pulled her to him and kissed her.

Instead, he took her hand and said, "Let's see if we can find the bomb."

She wove her fingers between his, and they started to walk, but all she could think about was the bomb that now lived in her heart. And how destroyed she would be if their relationship ever exploded.

Chapter 38

NEW YORK CITY, USA
Now

When Cass walked into the engagement party at Nina's Nest, she stopped for a moment to take in the room. It was filled with maroon and white flowers—the colors of the Della Rosa family crest. When Nonno was in town a year ago, he had taken her and Luca out to brunch at the Garden Room in the Gregory Hotel near Central Park, and Cass had been in awe of the flowers there. Nina had stopped by their table to say hello. When Cass complimented the flowers, Nina told them how she still loved to watch the room transform whenever the florists came with new bouquets. Cass would have loved to see this room transform, going from a blank, empty space to bursting with life and color.

"It takes your breath away, doesn't it?" Luca said.

Cass nodded.

"Humans can create beauty, but we can't rival Mother Nature," he added.

A waiter with a tray of wineglasses filled with Franciacorta came by. Cass and Luca each took a glass. "I can't believe Nonno is letting them serve someone else's wine at this party," she said as Alessandra and her husband, Ryan, walked up next to them.

"I convinced him he had to serve something sparkling to celebrate," Alessandra said, taking a glass for herself and handing a second to Ryan. "He finally relented, but only if it was the sparkling wine from his friend Cristiano's vineyard."

Luca took a sip. "Not a bad choice," he said. "Is Cristiano really still running things?"

Alessandra shook her head. "His granddaughter took over a couple of years ago." She took a sip of the wine and let out a soft "mm" of appreciation. "There are lots of things about Nonno to question," she added, "but his taste in wine is not one of them."

Cass laughed. She felt lucky that she really liked Luca's sister. She was just as intelligent as Marina but a more relaxed, warmer version. Alessandra and Ryan had been married for a year before Cass and Luca got together—they'd met in business school, after which Ryan had leveraged his family connections and started a hedge fund with two of their classmates, and Alessandra went into her family's business.

"I heard Nonno's been restoring the paintings in the chapel for your wedding," Ryan said. "He told us that if his artist grandson is getting married there, the art has to look its best."

"Does that mean you and Alessandra only got second-best art?" Cass asked him with a laugh.

"I'm afraid so," Ryan said. "Their cousin Serena, too. Now we know who the favorite grandchild really is. It was a toss-up for a while, but clearly Luca won out."

Alessandra shook her head. "You're always starting something, aren't you."

"With you, yes, always," he said.

Alessandra rolled her eyes and kissed him on the cheek.

Luca slid his arm around Cass and smiled at his sister and brother-in-law. "We need to see you two more often," he said. "You're better than a television show."

"Cute," Alessandra said.

There was a bit of a commotion at the door, and all four of them turned to see Cass's family walking in.

"Are those your brothers?" Alessandra asked.

Cass nodded. Nick and Chris were both wearing black pants and button-down shirts. A blue-and-white-striped one for Nick and a mint green one for Chris. Their dark hair was freshly cut, and Nick had trimmed his beard close.

"I see good looks run in the family," she said.

"Husband right here," Ryan replied in mock indignation.

"In your family, too," Alessandra told him, squeezing his arm.

It looked like Jenna had blown out Dina's hair—and Cass's mom's, too—and had given herself a loose French braid.

"I'm going to go say hi," Cass said, heading toward them. She'd had her own hair blown out for the party—long and sleek with waves at the bottom.

Luca turned to follow her.

"We're going to chase after the pass-around hors d'oeuvres waiters," Ryan said. "See you later."

Alessandra elbowed him. "We are not," she said, suppressing a laugh.

By the time Cass and Luca made it over to her family, the Franciacorta waiter had already been and gone. So they all had an impromptu toast to the bride and groom.

"Cent'anni," Gram said, wishing them both a hundred years of health and happiness. It was a toast Cass's grandfather used to make, and it had replaced Gram's usual *salute* in recent years.

Cass let out a sigh of relief and hugged her grandmother tight. "I'm so glad you're okay with Luca's family now," she whispered into her grandmother's ear.

"You're happy, Cassandra," Gram whispered back. "Vincenzo reminded me how important that is. When I was with him . . . we were so happy."

Cass looked at her grandmother. She wondered if she'd ever get the whole story about what happened when they were together.

Once Nonno arrived, the party felt like it began in earnest. He was holding court at one of the tables, all of the guests going to pay their respects.

"Are they gonna kiss his ring?" Nick asked, coming up next to Cassandra at the bar.

Cass laughed at her brother's words because the same thing had occurred to her. "He looks every inch the count, doesn't he?"

Nick shook his head. "I know Dad always called you his princess growing up, but don't you think this is taking it a little too far?"

"Even if the nobility were still a legal thing in Italy," Cass said, "Luca wouldn't inherit the title. It would go to his uncle Giorgio, and then Giorgio's son, Fabrizio."

"Still," Nick said. He took a sip of the Della Rosa wine in his hand. "Also, what's the deal with no liquor?"

Cass shrugged. "He owns a vineyard. His party, his choice."

"Good thing he's not throwing you a wedding!" Nick said. "Dad said he saved up a lot—but that he's worried you'll want to get married in New York City. I told him not to worry; you'd understand."

Cass swallowed. Nonno wasn't throwing them a wedding, but if they got married at his vineyard, at his family home, in his family chapel, he might as well be. And what to tell her father . . .

"We may get married in Italy," she told Nick. "It could be a fun trip, like when we went there to celebrate your high school graduation."

He gave her a look, the kind he had given her when she told him she was studying abroad, taking a fancy internship instead of life-guarding for the summer, dating the grandson of a count.

"What, America's not good enough for you?"

"It's not that," she said.

"What about all our cousins? And Mom and Dad's friends? You're making them fly to Italy?" He rubbed his hand across his beard. "You know Dad will never say it, but you're gonna break his heart with this wedding."

Cass took a deep breath.

"What if he uses the money he saved to fly everyone over," Cass suggested, realizing as she said it how silly it sounded.

"So he can host a plane flight instead of a wedding? And you think his friends would accept that? Hell, I'd hate to accept it."

Cass and Nick weren't speaking that loudly, but their mom, Christine, had some sort of radar for when her kids argued, and she walked over to them with Dina, Nick's wife.

"What's going on over here?" she asked.

Cass smiled at her mom. "You look great," she said.

"Gram helped me pick out the dress," Christine told her. "And then convinced me it needed to be taken in at the waist."

Cass laughed. "It fits perfectly," she said. The dress was a beautiful sapphire blue with a tailored skirt and a looser top; it looked almost like a two-piece.

"Have you decided what colors you want everyone to wear for the wedding?" Dina asked. For Dina's wedding to Nick, Cass and the other bridesmaids had worn a butter-yellow one-shouldered chiffon gown.

"I haven't even thought about it yet," Cass answered.

"Yeah," Nick said, "she's too busy planning a wedding in Italy."

Cass whipped her head around to stare at him.

"Is that true, Cassandra?" her mother asked.

"We're not planning anything yet," Cass answered softly, "but it's what Luca really wants."

"I see," her mom said.

All four of them went quiet.

Cass looked up and saw Luca talking to Nina Gregory. He caught Cass's eye and waved her over.

"I should go say hi," Cass said apologetically. "That's the Nina of Nina's Nest. She's one of Alessandra's friends."

"Of course she is," Nick said.

"We don't want to hold you back," her mom said quietly. "Go."

Luca waved again.

Cass went. But as she looked at her family over her shoulder, her mother's words played in her head. Was that how her mother saw things? Cass being held back by her family? Cass might have seen it that way once, but now . . . now they felt more like her anchor to who she was, to the parts of her that she wouldn't want to change, no matter what.

Chapter 39

GENOA, ITALY
Then

Giovanna wasn't going to see Vincenzo the day before the referendum voting began. His parents were coming down to Genoa, and he was going to spend time with them.

"After the vote is over," he said as they sat on their bench in Piazza San Matteo together, "I'll talk to my father about us."

"Then I will, too," she told him. "After the referendum, we can plan the rest of our lives together."

He wrapped his arm around her and she leaned her head against his shoulder.

They hadn't really talked much about the referendum—Giovanna had been nervous about bringing it up after the way his friends had acted at dinner, and perhaps Vincenzo felt the same way. Or perhaps, even with everything they both shared, they were worried that they didn't share the same feelings about this. Regardless, it was something they talked around, even now.

"The outcome will make a big difference to your family?" she asked.

She felt him let out a big breath. "Only if the republic wins."

"Right," she said, thinking about everything he'd shared with her about his family, his life, his dreams. What would happen to them if everything changed?

Vincenzo looked at his pocket watch. "I should go," he said, "to meet my parents."

He gave Giovanna a kiss on the cheek.

"You know," he said, "this vote will decide our future."

"That sounds so ominous," Giovanna said.

"Not ominous," Vincenzo answered. "But serious. This vote has the potential to change everything."

If the nobility was abolished, Giovanna wondered if that would bring her and Vincenzo closer together or further apart. She wasn't quite sure, but she knew that his words, his feelings, their future would inform her own choices, her own decisions. As far as she was concerned, Vincenzo had already changed everything—for her, at least.

That night, with the radio on low, Giovanna thought and thought about their future. And her future. And Faustina's future. And her father's. She thought about what they both had said to her about making up her own mind, deciding what she thought was best not just for her but for Italy. She thought, too, about the promise Faustina had made her. If the monarchy was abolished, she would think about staying. Giovanna knew that thinking about something didn't mean you would do it. She'd told Faustina she would think about going to America, but she wasn't planning to do that, either. Still, thinking about it meant there was a chance. A loose stitch that let you rip the seam easily.

And then there was Vincenzo. Her and Vincenzo. She knew his family would have to change a lot if the monarchy was abolished. But they had their vineyards, they had their properties, and Vincenzo was setting up an export business for their wine. Even without their title and the position and money it afforded them, she figured they would be fine. And though she knew Vincenzo and his family wanted the monarchy to stay, she wondered whether, if it was abolished, Vincenzo would have more freedom. The future generations of his family would have more freedom—to choose what they wanted to do, who they wanted to be with, where they wanted to live. If those future generations were her children and grandchildren, she wanted that freedom for them.

Faustina told her how wonderful it was that women were able to vote in this referendum. She imagined that their mother would have felt the same way—half of the country finally having a say in what happened, being able to use their minds and hearts to shape the future. And it was wonderful—and something Giovanna wanted to take seriously. She appreciated the gravity of the opportunity she now had. The whole country now had.

Giovanna tossed and turned all night trying to make up her mind. Part of her almost wished that women hadn't been given the right to vote, so she wouldn't have to make this decision. The rest of her knew that was silly, but that didn't mean the decision was easy. By the time Giovanna fell asleep, when the only thing on the radio was static, she had finally decided how she was going to vote.

The next morning, after church, Giovanna and her father walked to the voting booth.

"Oh!" her father said, peering across the piazza. "It's the conte!"

Though there were many contes, the only one who meant anything to their family was Vincenzo's father. Giovanna squinted into the sun and saw him, along with Vincenzo and his mother—and Isabella and her family—all walking together.

Vincenzo was walking right next to Isabella, the two of them trailing behind their parents, their heads bent toward each other, Isabella's hand on his arm. It was the same position that Vincenzo walked in with her. Giovanna felt like her breath had been stolen, like the time when she was eight, visiting her grandparents in Saluzzo, and she fell off the stone wall surrounding their yard, tumbling nearly two meters to the ground. It had taken her a moment, lying there, staring at the sky, to feel like she could breathe again.

"We should say hello," her father said.

Giovanna put her hand on his arm. "No, Papà. Stop." It was all she could do to keep down the communion wafer that had just dissolved on her tongue. "Let's go vote."

And for the first time ever, that was what she did.

Chapter 40

GENOA, ITALY
Then

Giovanna sat in her bedroom tearing the stitches out of the emerald dress she'd made. The ruching was wrong. And the neckline wasn't flattering.

She felt tears dripping off her chin and wiped them away. She was so stupid. She kept playing Chiara's words over in her mind, distilling their meaning: *He'll marry who our father wants him to marry.* How could Giovanna have ever thought that what she had with Vincenzo would last?

There was a knock on the bedroom door. "Papà?" she called out.

"It's me," Faustina said, opening the door. "Papà said something happened today, he's not sure what, and that you had locked yourself in the bedroom."

Giovanna broke down in tears. "I saw Vincenzo with Isabella, his sister's friend; their heads were bent toward each other, and her hand was on his arm."

Faustina wrapped her arms around her sister. "I can't believe I'm defending him here, but their families are friends, Giovannina. They could have just been out walking."

"But why was he touching her? And why wouldn't he tell me that he was going to see her? His sister said he's going to marry Isabella. What if she's right?"

Giovanna laid her head in her sister's lap and let Faustina stroke her hair.

"She might be right," Faustina said. "But she also might not be. Vincenzo is his own man."

Giovanna sat up slowly. "Is he, though? Or is he his family's man?"

It was a question Giovanna thought she'd known the answer to, but now she wasn't so sure.

"Listen," Faustina said. "I know you care a lot about him, but if he lets his parents tell him who to marry, he's not the right person for you."

Giovanna wiped her eyes. Her sister was right, but that wouldn't stop her heart from breaking.

"Let's talk about the men in America," Faustina said. "You know, I heard so many young men come to America alone looking for women to marry that you have your pick. It's like walking into a confectioner's shop, looking at all the sweets, and choosing your favorite one."

Giovanna smiled through her tears. "To hear you talk, America is better than heaven."

"Maybe it is!" Faustina shrugged.

"Nowhere is perfect," Giovanna said. "Italy is our home."

"Family is our home," Faustina said. "No matter where we are."

Giovanna started crying all over again because she'd thought Vincenzo was going to be her family, and she was realizing that might not be the case after all.

Faustina wrapped her sister in her arms and held her close. "It will be okay," she said. "One day we'll look back on today from far in the future, and none of this will matter. We'll be happy, we'll have families of our own, and no one will care about whether Vincenzo Della Rosa walked down the street with Isabella whatever-her-name-is."

Giovanna loved that about Faustina—the way she could pull back, look at the larger picture, take a wide perspective on things. Giovanna got too stuck in her feelings, in the immediacy of life, to take a wider look. But now, as she did, she could still see two lives—one where she kept working in her father's shop and found a different man to love and another where things worked out with Vincenzo.

"You know," she told her sister, "I voted to end the monarchy."

Faustina smiled. "I knew you would, once you asked me if I would consider staying if the monarchy was abolished."

"That's not the only reason," Giovanna told her. "But . . . will you still consider staying if it is?"

Faustina nodded. "I'll keep my word. But would you think differently about coming if you're not going to have a future with Vincenzo?"

That was a question Giovanna hadn't considered.

Chapter 41

"What if we have two weddings?" Cass asked Luca. They were in his studio, where Luca was taking photographs of the paintings he'd finished so far to send to Mauro, who owned the gallery that often showed his art in Milan. They were planning to take this collection and wanted to see some of the images.

"You want to get married twice?" Luca was moving the painting of Cassandra so it was more evenly lit.

Cass sighed. "Not really, but I want to make everyone happy. And my mom is so upset by the idea of a wedding in Italy that her friends won't be able to come to. And my brothers are grumbling about taking that much time away from work . . . I thought maybe we could have a wedding for my family and their friends on Long Island, and then one for your family and friends in Italy."

Luca stopped fiddling with the painting and looked at her. "Isn't the whole point of this that we're bringing two families together?"

"I guess," Cass said. "But if we're bringing them together, maybe we shouldn't get married in Italy."

Luca closed his eyes. "I thought you were okay with a wedding in Italy."

"I thought I was," Cass said. "But . . . that was before I knew how much it made a difference to my mom. How much it would hurt my dad." She wanted to give her parents the wedding they had dreamed she would have.

"But we're the ones getting married," Luca said. "Not your parents."

"I know, I know," Cass answered. "But my family is part of me, and I won't be happy if what we do makes them unhappy. And . . . I feel like I owe them this."

"I could say the same thing to you," Luca said. "Not getting married in Italy would make my parents—and my grandfather—unhappy."

"Right," Cass said. "That's why I was thinking two weddings. One here, one in Italy."

Luca massaged his temples and then looked at Cass. "Is that really what you want?"

She shrugged. "I can't think of any other option that would work."

He put his arm around her shoulder and dropped a kiss on top of her head. "Let's think some more," he said. "Two weddings feels like a path toward separation, not unity. What if we got married in between? Like . . . in London? Or on a boat?"

"I don't think that's any better as far as travel is concerned. I'll keep thinking."

And she would, but she wasn't sure if she'd come up with another choice. Maybe they should just elope. Disappoint everyone's family equally, and then have two parties once they were already married. That was probably an even worse idea.

"Would you mind standing over there?" Luca asked, pointing to the other side of the painting. "I think you're casting a shadow on yourself."

Cass laughed and walked to the other side of the portrait. She always found Luca's finished work amazing. She looked so exactly like herself, but better. Her skin was smoother, her hair fuller, her eyes a sparkling gold.

"It's like you painted me with an Instagram filter on," she told him.

"I painted you how I see you," he answered.

Cass understood what he meant. People changed depending on who was looking at them, on what feelings they brought with them. Often, when she was creating an ad campaign, she would think, *Whose heart do I want to touch, and how would that audience see this image?* With that filter in her mind, she would change the scene, what the focus was. In the upcoming holiday-launch campaign, they went for different images to appeal to the different audiences. A grandchild throwing their arms around a grandmother, parents and children walking together through a neighborhood filled with holiday lights, an extended family opening presents on FaceTime. Each meant to touch a different audience, to draw them in to the brand.

Cass shook her head to bring herself back to the moment. She looked at the painting of Minerva, Luca's mother behind an ornate desk, the sun bright in a window behind her, a phone cradled against her shoulder, her hands on a laptop keyboard, and her eyes elsewhere. Luca had painted sharp edges in her cheekbones but warmth in her eyes. She wondered if that was how he saw his mother when he was growing up, always in the middle of work, of too many things, but warmth in her eyes when she looked at him.

Was what people said about men marrying their mothers true? Was she another version of Marina? Would her kids see her the same way? Always working, always attached to her phone, always answering email in her downtime? That was something else to think about—but they had the wedding to figure out first.

"Mauro might want the exhibit next month," Luca said. "An artist he had booked pulled out, and I think I can finish in time. So if you can come, too, maybe we could go and look at my grandfather's villa, as, you know, part of thinking about our wedding."

Cass nodded. "Sure," she said. "I'll talk to Samantha about working from Italy for a week or two. As long as I keep U.S. hours, I'm sure it'll be fine. And if we're there, we'd probably go to your grandfather's villa anyway, right?"

"We would," Luca said.

Asking Samantha about working from Italy made Cass think about the conversation they'd had the other day in the office. Sam was wondering about expanding the brand into Italy and had asked Cass what she thought.

"Would you ever want to move back?" Cass asked him. Ever since the idea of getting married in Italy had come up, she'd been thinking more about her year abroad. She'd felt like she found herself there. Like she was connected to the country and its history in a way that was different from her relationship with America. She was American, for sure, but while she was in Florence, she kept thinking that if her grandparents and great-grandparents had made different choices, she'd have grown up in Italy instead.

It was funny; for all she'd wanted to leave Island Park, leave the closeness of the neighborhood, being in Italy made her feel as comfortable as she did growing up in her Italian-American community on Long Island—her last name was average, her religion dominant. When she went to college, she realized that the rest of America wasn't Island Park. And if she wanted to step outside the world she knew, the world she grew up in, she would always feel different. But that wasn't the case in Italy. It was like the entire country was her community.

But, of course, her family wasn't there. Her parents, her brothers, her grandmother. That was the most difficult part about her year abroad—being so far from them, in a different time zone, with reference points they hadn't experienced at all.

"Forever?" he answered.

"Or just for a while," she said.

He picked up the painting of his sister on a Vespa, modern-day Diana on the hunt.

"Maybe," he said. "Is this you thinking out loud, or is there a reason you're asking?"

"Samantha was talking about expanding Daisy Lane into Italy. And it got me thinking that I could ask to work with the team there to launch it, if she does. And maybe she'd let me."

"Lots of *if*s," he said.

"Lots of *if*s," Cass agreed. "But it could be exciting. Like another junior year abroad, except maybe longer, and with you."

"Should I point out," Luca said, coming over and putting his arms around her, "that you're iffy about a wedding in Italy, but talking about moving there entirely? How will your parents feel about that?"

Cass sighed. "I think they would miss me, of course, but they'd be okay with the move because they're not really involved in that decision—they haven't been saving, been dreaming about where we live. It doesn't have anything to do with their friends or my brothers. And they were already okay with me living there once, you know?"

She rested her head on Luca's shoulder.

"I do know," he said. "I do."

"Life seems to get more complicated the older I get."

"It does get more complicated. Once you step out of the world you were born into, once you establish your own path, once you realize your actions affect others, it's hard."

"It reminds me," Cass said, "of something Chris told me when Milo was born. He said he had to stand up for his baby, even if it was something other people didn't want to hear. It was when my mom wanted him to bring Milo to a huge family Christmas party when he was only a few weeks old, and Chris said no. It made me pause, because I realized how uncomfortable I was standing up for what I wanted when I didn't have someone supporting me. It's why I always appreciated having Nick on my side, or Gram. They always gave me the strength to stand up for myself."

"Have you talked to them about our wedding?" Luca asked.

Cass nodded. "Sort of. Nick was worried about me hurting our parents. I haven't spoken to Gram. And honestly, I haven't spoken to Nick about it after that one conversation, either, mostly because I'm not sure what to say."

"Maybe you should start there," Luca said. "Figure out what you would say to him. And then you and I should talk about it. Because I know what I want, but I can't really tell what you want exactly, and until you know, it's hard to have this conversation."

Cass nodded. He was right.

"Thank you," she said, laying her head on his chest.

"For what?" he asked.

"For being you," she said.

He wrapped his arms around her, tight.

"Come, stellina," he said. "Let's go look at some stars."

It was something they had done on an early date, something that Luca said always put things in perspective. So they took the elevator up to the roof, climbed through the emergency exit, and sat together, looking at the stars above them, holding hands, just two small specks in an ever-expanding universe.

Chapter 42

GENOA, ITALY
Then

The day after the voting ended, Faustina's ear was tuned to the radio while she and Giovanna worked together to sew beads back onto Signora Grieco's gown.

"Where do you think she's going to wear this?" Faustina asked.

Giovanna shrugged. "Ask Papà," she said. "He spoke to her when she brought it in. Maybe she told him."

Faustina looked at her sister critically. "You have to talk to Vincenzo," she said. "You need to find out what was going on."

Giovanna had been afraid to call his parents' apartment or even stop by. She wished she had taken down Mariella's telephone number or address when they'd gone to Bruno's birthday party. Maybe she could have reached him that way. But the fact that she was afraid to show up if his parents were there told her a lot.

"I'm hoping he'll come by," she said. The referendum vote was over now, so maybe he actually had told them about her. Or maybe he was telling them right that very moment.

Giovanna waited for Vincenzo while Faustina waited for the results of the vote. All day, and to no avail. The next morning, Giovanna found an envelope slid under the door addressed to her in Vincenzo's elegant handwriting. Inside was a quickly drawn sketch of Vincenzo sitting with his father, going over some sort of book or ledger. A message, she figured, that the conte was still in town, and Vincenzo couldn't get away. Giovanna's heart ached for him—and ached to talk to him. But he didn't come that day either. Nor did the results of the vote.

Finally, on June 5, just as Giovanna and Faustina were starting to close up the shop for the day, Giuseppe Romita, the minister of the interior, came on the radio and announced there were more than twelve million votes to abolish the monarchy, and only ten million to keep it. The Italian republic was born!

Faustina was glowing. "Our votes counted!" she said. "I wonder if the result would've been the same without women voting."

It was a good question. Giovanna smiled at her sister. "So," she said. "Are you going to stay in Italy now?"

Faustina smiled back. "I promised I'd consider it, and I will. I'll talk to Betto tonight."

Soon after the results were announced, Betto came running into the back of the shop and gave Faustina a hug, spinning her around. "Can you believe we won?" he said. "Italy's going to be a republic! We have to go celebrate!"

Faustina stood up. "You want to come?" she asked Giovanna.

Giovanna shook her head. "Maybe Vincenzo will come by, now that the results are in." At least she hoped he would. She didn't know how much longer her heart could take waiting for him.

"Are you ready to go home?" Federico asked Giovanna an hour later. The sun was about to set, the shop was clean, and the customers had all gone.

"A few more minutes," she told him. "Why don't you go up without me, and I'll be there soon."

He nodded. "I can get dinner started," he said.

"Thanks," Giovanna answered.

She straightened the pens on the counter. Swept some stray pins from the floor. None of this really needed doing, but she wanted to keep herself busy, so if Vincenzo showed up, it wouldn't look like she'd been waiting for him. The longer it took him, the angrier she got. He could have at least telephoned her. That one sketch two days ago wasn't enough. Not nearly.

Just as she was about to give up, she heard a knock on the door to the shop. She turned around and saw Vincenzo with his hands in his pockets and went over to let him in.

"Hey," she said, stepping aside so he could walk into the space.

"Did you hear the results?" he said.

Giovanna nodded, waiting for his apology for staying away for so long, and at the same time, wanting to hold him close. She missed him. She missed being next to him, having her head on his chest, her lips pressed against his.

"My father still can't believe it." He sat down on the platform customers stood on when Federico measured their pants and skirts to be shortened. "Bruno says he was being absurd to even think it was possible to avoid a republic—that we've been heading in this direction for years. But my father thought the support in the south might carry us through."

"Don't you think it might be better for everyone, though, to have a republic?" Giovanna said. "To have more representation? More of a say in what happens?" Even though she hadn't been as excited about women voting as Faustina was, there was a thrill in knowing she'd played a role in deciding Italy's future.

Vincenzo shook his head. "You don't understand."

Giovanna was hurt. "Understand what?" she asked. So much of their trust was built on sharing, on understanding, on compassion and empathy. How could he say she didn't understand now?

"You're just—you don't know what it means to have your future stolen from you."

Giovanna could envision Faustina rolling her eyes at this. "You still have your family's property. You still have your family's name. Their connections. From how I see it, your family's got a great future."

He shook his head again. "Like I said, you don't understand."

Giovanna was frustrated. She'd spent all week waiting to see him, to talk to him, to hear what he had to say, and now this? "Who does?" Giovanna asked. "Isabella?"

He looked at her. "Jealousy's not a good look on you, Giovanna."

Tears filled her eyes. "I saw you with her," she said. "You looked . . . closer than you led me to believe."

"I can't deal with this right now," he said.

"With what?" Giovanna said. "With me? I thought you wanted to marry me. Isn't that what you said? You wanted us to be together forever? Have children together? That you love me? Did you even tell your parents about us after the referendum, like you said you would?"

Vincenzo was quiet. He ran his fingers through his thick brown hair. "How did you vote?" he asked.

Now it was Giovanna's turn to remain silent.

"I asked you a question," Vincenzo said.

"I asked you one first," Giovanna replied.

"That means you voted for the republic. Ernesto was right. You aren't like us."

"You said Ernesto was an ass. Why are you behaving like him?"

Giovanna felt the blood rushing through her body, heating up her face and her temper.

"I was walking with Isabella because she's the woman my father wants me to marry, the one I mentioned to you weeks ago. But you already knew that, didn't you? Chiara told you at the vineyard."

"She did," Giovanna said, his admission not hurting as much as she'd expected it might, because it was information she already knew. But she was disappointed nonetheless. "I told her you made your own choices, though."

"You do, too."

"What do you mean?"

"You chose a republic over us. You didn't care about our future at all. That tells me everything I need to know about you."

"I do care about us! I can vote for a republic but still care about us. I actually thought a republic might be better for—"

"No," he said, cutting her off. "You *can't* vote for a republic and still care about us. In my family, family comes first. Before anything else. Before each of us individually, before our country, before . . . everything. You made it clear my family doesn't come first for you."

"But why should it?" Giovanna spat back. "You won't even tell your father you love me."

"I had to find a way to prove to him that you were worthy of joining our family. But it turns out you're not."

Giovanna felt like she'd been slapped. With every ounce of strength she had, she willed herself not to cry and said, "What makes you think you're worthy of joining mine? In my family, we love people even when they disagree with us. You, apparently, don't."

"That's not true," he said.

"It's not? You're acting like I should be grateful that you've deigned to talk to me. That I should give up my family and my principles for you, just because you want me to."

Vincenzo was quiet for a moment. "Ernesto really was right. Why did I ever think I could marry the daughter of a tailor?"

Giovanna couldn't stop her tears now—of hurt, of anger, of frustration. "Get out," she said. He stayed where he was. So she said, louder, "I said leave."

And, with one last look over his shoulder, he did.

Chapter 43

GENOA, ITALY
Then

Giovanna went into the back room of the tailor shop, crumpled down onto a bolt of fabric, and sobbed. She felt so stupid, so betrayed. Like this person she had gotten to know—fallen in love with—wasn't even real. Like he'd been pretending. Pretending he loved her, pretending he wanted to be with her, pretending there was a future for them when there clearly was not. He'd never respected her, never believed the two of them were equals. He'd probably never even intended to tell his father about her. She was some sort of fling before he settled down, a fairy tale he was playing at. How could she have believed otherwise?

Unbidden, the memories of him kissing her, touching her, twirling her around in the park, making her feel such intense joy flooded her mind. How could he have faked that? But he must've. He must've to have been able to say those awful things to her, to have cut her so deeply.

She heard the phone ringing at the counter, and for a moment, no matter how painful his words were, her heart leapt, thinking it was Vincenzo, telling her it was all a mistake and he didn't mean any of what he said. But then she realized it was probably her father, wondering what was keeping her.

She pulled herself up off the fabric, wiping her eyes and taking slow, steady breaths.

"Pronto," she said, holding the phone to her ear. But it wasn't her father on the other end, it was Faustina.

"Papà said you haven't come home yet," she said.

Giovanna tried to keep her voice steady, but she heard it waver as she said, "I'll be home soon."

"What happened?" Faustina asked.

Giovanna started crying again. "I'm never seeing Vincenzo again," she said. And even as terrible as he had been, that sentence made Giovanna feel physically ill. He was the only man she'd ever kissed with passion, the only man she'd wanted to reveal all of herself to, the only man who had ever made her body feel sensations she never believed truly existed. The only man she'd ever loved. And she wanted to be with him. But not the real him, apparently. She wanted the person she had imagined he was. The man she wanted him to be.

"Okay, okay," Faustina said. "You need to go home. I'll meet you there after Betto and I finish eating, how about that?"

"Okay," Giovanna answered, her breath catching in her throat.

As she walked up the stairs to their flat above the shop, her mind wouldn't let her stop thinking about Vincenzo. Her city had become their city, she realized. The street she'd walked on thousands of times had become the one they went down the first time they took a walk together. The bench in the piazza had become the bench they sat on to talk. The profumeria she'd visited her whole life had become the place where she bought lipstick to go to meet his friends. She should have known that night this would never work.

When she got upstairs, she found that her father had heated up the risotto she'd made the day before and set the table. A bottle of red wine was open. Thankfully, it wasn't one of the bottles the conte had given them when they finished bottling the 1944 vintage. Giovanna didn't think she could handle that right then. But wine would be welcome.

"Faustina told me what happened," her father said.

Giovanna nodded. "Is it okay if we don't talk about it?" she said. "How about instead you tell me a story I don't know about Mamma."

"Okay." Federico smiled sadly and sat down at the table. He poured them both some wine. Giovanna sat and served the risotto.

"Have I ever told you about the day we left Saluzzo?" he asked.

Giovanna shook her head.

Federico took a sip of wine. "Your mamma's cousin, Luciano, knew the man who owned this shop before me. You wouldn't remember him, but he was an old man with no family, no one to take over when he was gone. When he got ill, Luciano suggested that your mamma and I come to Genoa so I could take over for him here. I was afraid to come—Genoa's so big. I liked Saluzzo, I liked the mountains and the fresh air and the people I'd known since I was small. But your mamma loved it here. She was like your sister—always thinking, always trying to change things, and she knew that I'd have more opportunities in Genoa, not just waiting to take over half of the small shop my father had in Saluzzo. So we came. The first day here, we left our things at Luciano's and your mamma said we had to visit the Cimitero Monumentale di Staglieno. It was one of the first places she had ever visited in Genoa when she was a young girl, and she became fascinated with one of the statues there—a woman named Caterina Campodonico. She was a nut seller who saved all her money to be buried in this elegant, extravagant cemetery. And the statue she had created for herself after she died was of her selling nuts. Your mother thought it was wonderful—that this woman was so proud of who she was, what she did, and didn't create a new image of herself after she'd earned enough money to be buried with the city's wealthy citizens. She wanted to be remembered for all eternity exactly the way she was. Anyway, your mother wanted to visit the statue and tell Caterina that we had moved here. And that's when she said to me: 'I want to be remembered, too, after I die. I want to make a difference in someone's life.' And she did, you know. She made a huge difference in mine, but that's not what I mean. When all our work was done at the shop, she took the scraps home, and when she had enough she would sew a simple dress, a shirt, a pair of pants. She would make what she could, in whatever size she could, and leave them at the church for anyone in need. Once you girls came along, she didn't have as much time anymore, but even now I'll sometimes see a child running around in one of her dresses—usually patched or altered in some way, but she made a difference to so many families, even if they don't know it."

When her father finished talking, Giovanna felt calm. Stories about her mother always made her feel that way, as if her spirit came back, just briefly, to wrap Giovanna in a warm embrace, the way she did when she was alive, when simply breathing next to her mother made Giovanna feel at peace.

"I forgot Mamma was the one who made you come here," she said. "Did you ever think of going back to Saluzzo after she died?"

Federico took a sip of wine. "I did," he said. "My parents, your mother's father, our siblings and cousins—we have so much family there. I thought it would be easier. But your grandfather and uncle still had the tailor shop. It was just barely supporting them—there wasn't space for me, too. And here, we had loyal customers. Faustina loved school. And I knew you would be happy no matter where we were. So I stayed. Then the war came, and Saluzzo seemed like a safer place to be for a few years, but until your nonno decides to retire, there's no work for me there, even if I wanted to go back. But one day I will."

Giovanna and Federico had been living just the two of them since Faustina's wedding, but their conversations revolved more around the shop, the groceries, meals, and day-to-day life. She decided she had to ask her father questions more often, hear his stories, learn about his hopes for the future.

"That's what you want?" she said.

"Eventually," he said. "That's where I want to live the end of my life."

"But, Papà, you're only forty-six. You have a lot of living to do before then."

"I feel much older," he said.

"Now that Faustina and I are grown, you should find another wife," Giovanna told him. She couldn't believe they hadn't had a conversation like this before.

"No one will ever compare to your mamma," he said. "She and I knew each other our whole lives. I used to chase her around the schoolyard, make faces at her during mass." He sighed.

Giovanna shrugged. "Then don't compare, Papà. Find someone totally different. How about . . . Signora Grieco? Her husband died in the war. She talks to you a lot more than the other women who come into the shop. I think she likes you."

Federico was quiet for a moment, really and truly considering the idea. Giovanna could see his emotions changing, the way he was holding his mouth, his jaw, the tension releasing there. "Not her," he said finally, "but maybe someone. Someday."

Giovanna had just lifted her fork to her mouth when Faustina and Betto burst through the front door. Giovanna had been expecting Faustina to come, but was surprised Betto was here, too.

"You'll never guess what just happened," Faustina said.

"Our paperwork got approved for America!" Betto said, before Giovanna or Federico could guess. "For all four of us!"

Giovanna looked at her father. He looked back at her. Then he turned to Betto and Faustina. "Come," he said. "Have a drink. Let's toast to that."

Faustina grabbed two wineglasses and sat with Betto at the table, holding them steady while Federico filled them with Chianti.

"To our future," she said.

"To our future," they all echoed.

Especially after listening to her father's dreams, Giovanna wasn't sure what that future would be.

Chapter 44

LONG ISLAND, USA
Now

By early November, Nonno had returned to Italy and Cass and Luca were no closer to figuring out when and where they were going to get married. When Cass let herself acknowledge what she actually wanted, she knew she could be happy getting married in Italy, in a historic chapel, in a beautiful vineyard that meant so much to Luca. But that knowledge felt at war with her desire to make her parents happy, to do something for her own family that was connected to places that were meaningful to them. And then she felt stuck. Luca was being patient. "You need to listen to your heart, stellina. I know in my heart I want to get married in Italy. What other options sound good to you?"

But while Cass could come up with some beautiful restaurants on the beach that were close to her childhood home, that didn't feel quite right either.

In the meantime, Luca was spending the first weekend in November finishing up one of the final paintings in the series, and now he was under a deadline because Mauro was going to show the exhibit at his gallery in Milan in three weeks. Cass decided it would be a good time to go see her grandmother. Maybe even try to get her advice about the wedding.

When she got to the house, she found her father out front wrapping their fig trees in burlap for the winter. He gave her a hug, but she could feel the tension between them, the tension that had been there with both her parents since the engagement party.

"How are you doing?" she asked him.

"Good," he said. "But listen, before you go see Gram. She's been at a bunch of doctors' appointments this week. She's been having some trouble breathing, hasn't been able to walk very far without sitting down for a rest. We thought initially it might be her lungs, but it's looking like it's her heart. They changed her blood pressure medication, which hopefully will help. But . . . I just wanted you to know."

Cass felt the blood drain from her face. "Is it serious?" she asked. She couldn't believe he'd dropped that on her like that, with no warning. *We thought initially it might be her lungs, but it's looking like it's her heart.*

Her father wiped his hand across his forehead. "She's ninety-two, Cassandra. Everything's serious."

Cass nodded and tried to ignore the panicked beating of her own heart. The nausea she felt at this news.

"She's inside?" Cass asked.

He nodded. "Your mother's taking Aria to a birthday party. Nick got called in to a job and Dina has Nico at his peewee football game."

Sometimes Cass longed to be in her parents' lives the same way Nick and his family were. Constant contact, coming to help at the last minute. Her parents functioned as a unit with Nick and his family in a way that they didn't with Cass. She was extra, a guest, really. She knew it was her doing, her choice to move away, to get a job in New York City and throw herself into her life there. But sometimes it made her lonely. She felt it now, acutely. The choices she'd made, the distance between them. It was why she was so torn about her wedding.

"Gram!" she called, when she walked into the house.

"In here, Cassandra." She heard Gram's voice come back from the living room.

Normally Gram would've gotten up to greet her at the door. It was what she'd done last month. But obviously things had changed since then. Cass wondered if seeing Vincenzo had done this to her and immediately felt guilty. But then she realized that was silly. Broken hearts didn't literally break people's hearts.

Cass sat down next to her grandmother. "How are you feeling?" she asked.

"Old," her grandmother said. "I'm feeling old."

"Well, you look beautiful," Cass said. And her grandmother did, as always. She was dressed in a cream sweater and a pair of brown pants that hit her ankles in the perfect spot. Cass often stuck to dresses because she didn't want to have to get pants tailored to fit her the way they should. Shorten the bottom, take in the waist. It made a difference if you tailored the clothing yourself, exactly to size.

Her grandmother smiled.

"Luca finished the painting," Cass said. "Would you like to see it?"

In the end, Gram and Nonno had agreed to be in the painting together, but Gram asked not to sit with him again. So Luca did the rest from memory and photographs and one quick FaceTime where he wanted to look more closely at the shape of the curls in Gram's hair.

"I would love to," Gram said, putting on the reading glasses that were folded next to her on the couch.

Cass pulled the painting up on her phone. It was one of her favorites of the series so far. Luca had painted the most wistful expressions on Gram's and Nonno's faces. And after a few different attempts, he'd decided to paint them holding hands. It looked like the two of them were each other's life preservers—like they were keeping each other afloat, giving each other strength to face each new day.

"Oh, it's lovely," Gram breathed, wiping a stray tear from the corner of her eye. "Your Luca is more talented than his grandfather."

"He's also had more training," Cass said. She wondered what Nonno might have done with the kind of encouragement and support he had given Luca.

Gram nodded. "I was sorry to hear that Vincenzo had given up his art."

Cass wondered if now was the time to ask her. What exactly had happened? What had the two of them talked about last month? Were they still in touch now? But she didn't want to pry. And she wasn't sure what to say. "Luca's paintings are going to be shown at a gallery in Milan," Cass told her. "He and I are going to fly there for the opening in a few weeks."

"You're going to Italy in a few weeks?" Gram asked.

Cass nodded.

"I wonder . . ." Gram started, but then stopped.

"Wonder what?" Cass asked. She looked closely at her grandmother's face. Wanted to make sure she'd always remember every inch of it. The little creases on the edges of her eyes, the tiny mole on her cheek, the cupid's-bow shape of her lips.

"Wonder if . . . if I could come with you. I'd like to see Italy again before I die." Gram said it matter-of-factly, like she knew this was going to happen in the not-too-distant future and had accepted it.

"Oh, Gram! You're not dying any time soon," Cass said.

"Every moment I have these days seems like a gift," Gram told her, patting Cass's hand. "Every moment I spend with you is an even bigger gift."

Cass knew she should talk to Luca about Gram's request before responding. It might change their plans—where they stayed, what they did—but how could she say no? "We'd love to have you come with us, Gram."

"Truly?" Gram asked, her eyes sparkling like Cass remembered from when she was younger.

"Truly," Cass answered. "Is there anywhere in particular you'd like to see?"

"Genoa," she said. "Saluzzo. And . . . Serralunga d'Alba."

Cass was surprised by the last one, but perhaps she shouldn't have been, not after everything Nonno's visit had brought back to the surface. "Okay," she said. "We can do that. Luca has to stay in Milan for a few days, but you and I can go to Piemonte and Liguria. Or we can wait for him and all three of us can go together."

Gram nodded. "Your father won't like it."

Cass thought about it. "You're probably right. He won't."

"It's a good thing I can buy my own ticket, then," Gram said with a laugh.

"Good thing," Cass said, smiling. She knew that she and Luca were traveling first class and figured she could upgrade her grandmother to a first-class seat, too.

"Can you find my purse, Cassandra? Let's do this now, before I lose the nerve." *Before I lose the nerve*, Cass thought. Her father for sure wouldn't be happy with this, and the last thing she needed to do was drive a deeper wedge between the two of them. But Gram seemed happier than she'd been in ages. So Cass found Gram's purse, took out her credit card, and bought her a ticket on the same flight to Milan she and Luca had already booked, and then she used her miles to upgrade her grandmother to the seat across the aisle.

"There you go," she said when she clicked the last button. "One first-class ticket to Italy for Mrs. Joanna Fanelli."

Gram laughed. "I feel almost giddy!" she said. "Did you know that I've only been back three times in the last seventy years? Once to introduce your grandfather to the family there. Once to bury my father. And once on a big family vacation after your grandfather and I retired, a couple of years before you were born. When I left, I never thought I would be back so infrequently."

Cass imagined what that must've been like, leaving home so young and hardly ever going back.

"You had Aunt Faustina here with you, though," she said.

Gram nodded. "I did. I wouldn't have stayed if it weren't for her and Betto."

"Would you have . . . gone back for Nonno?" Cass asked softly.

Gram was quiet.

Cass tried again from a different angle. "Are you glad you two had a chance to talk before he went back?"

"I am," Gram said. "There was a lot I didn't know."

Cass wondered whether what he had shared changed her grandmother's perspective on what had happened those many years ago. "What did he say?" Cass asked.

Gram took a deep breath and closed her eyes, as if remembering the moment. Then she opened them again. "There are a few things you have to know to understand the time Vincenzo and I spent to-gether," she said. "The first is that our courtship was in the months leading up to the vote on the institutional referendum to end the monarchy in Italy. And the second is that Vincenzo and I were on opposite sides of that vote. That's what we ended up fighting about the last time we spoke, and it got ugly. Really ugly. I said things I regret-ted, but what he said was worse."

Cass nodded but stayed quiet, worried that if she said anything, her grandmother would stop talking.

"So the drawings he sent me were to show me what else had hap-pened. That there was more to the story than I knew."

Cass nodded again, but her grandmother had stopped talking this time, so she added, "And what didn't you know?"

Gram fiddled with the clasp on her watch. "A lot," she said. "But the long story short is that Vincenzo said he'd been wanting to make this right for seventy years. And that he'd never stopped thinking about me."

Cass wanted the long story, not the short one. But this was at least something. She couldn't wait to tell Luca what she'd learned. "That sounds romantic, Gram," Cass said.

Gram patted Cassandra's leg.

"Come," she said. "I'm having trouble figuring out the new coffee machine Christopher dropped off last week. It has these pods, he called them, and far too many buttons. Do I push the big cup or the small cup?"

Cass smiled. It seemed like her grandmother was done sharing for the moment.

"I got you covered," Cass said, helping her grandmother off the couch. "It's the big cup, if you want American-style coffee. The small cup if you want Italian-style coffee."

"Let's go with Italian," Gram said. "We have to practice, right?"

"Assolutamente," Cass answered.

She wondered what would happen on their trip to Italy. Whether being there would loosen Gram's tongue even more. And whether the reason she wanted to go to Serralunga d'Alba was that she had some things she'd been waiting seventy years to say, too.

Chapter 45

GENOA, ITALY
Then

Betto had left, and Giovanna and Faustina were back in their old room together.

"You should come," Faustina was saying while she was sitting on the bed, brushing her sister's hair.

"Papà won't come," Giovanna answered. "And I can't leave him alone."

Faustina put the brush down. "Papà had his life, he made his choices, he can go back to Saluzzo if he wants. But you, Giovannina, you have a whole life ahead of you. There's so much you can do and be and experience. Come for a year. If you hate it after a year, you can come back. We'll keep the money for your return passage in a box and make sure not to spend it, just in case."

Giovanna thought about that. A year wasn't so long. Maybe she needed a change, a chance to see new things, and—if she was honest—an ocean between her and Vincenzo wouldn't be the worst thing. At least it would stop her from looking at every place they'd walked, everywhere they'd spent time, every store she associated with him, and feeling her broken heart all over again. The truth was, the decision would be easy now if it weren't for her father.

"And if Papà's too lonely, I can come back?" Giovanna asked. "Even if I don't hate it?"

Faustina divided half of Giovanna's hair into three sections. "If you decide for any reason after a year that you want to come back, you can," she said as she started to braid.

Giovanna remembered the days and weeks after their mother died, when Faustina brushed her hair every night with a brush dipped in water, the way their mother did, and then braided it to tame her curls.

"Christmas," Giovanna said. "I'll give it from now to Christmas. And then I can come back, if I want. For Christmas."

Faustina wrapped a rubber band around the bottom of Giovanna's braid. "Half a year," she said.

"Half a year," Giovanna agreed. "I think that's a good compromise between a year and not at all."

Faustina laughed. "When did you become a negotiator?" She started a second braid.

Giovanna shrugged. This part of her, the part where she was un-afraid to push back, to say what she wanted and what she needed, had been revealed by Vincenzo.

Tears filled her eyes again just thinking about him, and about how stupid she was to ever think he would actually marry her. She wiped at the teardrop that leaked out of the corner of her eye.

She felt Faustina's fingers pause in their braid.

"You know," Faustina said, "Betto told me his cousin in America is a year older than you. If you're not interested in him, I bet he has lots of friends."

Giovanna laughed.

"I'm serious," Faustina said. "Maybe by Christmas you won't want to come back to Italy, because you'll have found someone there you won't want to leave."

Even though Giovanna couldn't imagine feeling about someone else the way she did about Vincenzo, she did like that idea.

"I guess I have to practice my English," she said, now finding something else to worry about. Giovanna wasn't good at school, the way Faustina was. It took her longer to learn to read, and it wasn't until her father suggested she hold a piece of paper underneath the line she was reading that she was able to focus on the words enough to really make sense of them. She found spelling difficult enough in Italian, but in English, forget it. That language made no sense.

"Don't worry," Faustina said. "A lot of people in America speak Italian. And learning a language by using it is a lot different from learning it in a classroom." She ended the second braid and wrapped another rubber band around it. "Besides, you'll have me to help."

Giovanna smiled. That was the best part about having Faustina as a sister. She was always there to help, if Giovanna let her.

Chapter 46

The night after his fight with his father, after his fight with Giovanna, Vincenzo woke to the sound of his mother screaming. "He's not breathing! He's not breathing!"

Before he even understood the words, before he even checked the time, he felt the panic in her voice and went running. "I'm coming, Mamma!" he shouted as he threw off the blanket and raced down the hall.

By the time he got to his mother's side, he knew that his father was gone. The conte's face was entirely still. His chest wasn't rising and falling. His skin was waxy and pale.

"He's cold, Vincenzino, he's cold," his mother said through her tears.

Vincenzo wrapped his arms around her, and she wrapped hers around him.

All Vincenzo could think was that this referendum had killed his father. And maybe he had, too.

Chapter 47

Giovanna spent the next two weeks saying goodbye to Italy. All three Ferreros went to Saluzzo. While Federico spoke to his brother and father, and Faustina helped their grandmother prepare lunch, Giovanna took a walk through the town on her own, taking in the buildings and the mountain views. The town looked much the same as it always had. Ilaria told her that some members of the Jewish community had returned, but far fewer than there had been. Many had been killed, and the rest were trying to leave—to go to Palestine, America, Australia. It seemed like so many people were leaving. She wondered how many of them were going on walks like she was—walks to remember: the market in the town square, the castello that had once been the home of the Marquis of Saluzzo and then was a prison, the Duomo, and the Chiesa di San Giovanni, which she and Mamma had always visited when she was younger. Mamma had said she felt like the church needed some extra love, since it had been eclipsed in importance by the Duomo when it was built.

Even if she was away for only six months, she would need these memories to keep her grounded, to keep her heart full. When she hugged her grandparents, when she kissed Ilaria on both cheeks and wished her a safe and easy delivery of her baby this summer, when she squeezed Guido's children tight, she wondered how much would change between now and the next time she saw them. How she would change.

Back in Genoa, she visited the friends who were left there. She walked through the harbor and watched the salvage teams at work. She visited the parks and breathed in all the Italian flowers. She walked at night under an Italian sky filled with stars. And then she went to her mother's grave.

"Mamma," she said. "I know it's been a while since I visited you here. I prefer to think of you watching us from above, not closed up in a box. Since you've been watching, you probably know that I'm leaving. Faustina and Betto and I. I talked with Papà about it for a long time, and he said I should go. I should take the kind of risk the two of you took, leaving Saluzzo and coming here. And I can always come home again.

"Remember when I was six years old, and we went on a trip to Varazze in August? Faustina went running into the waves, and I stayed with you and Papà on the towel watching.

"'Go,' you said to me. 'Look how your sister is brave!'

"And then Papà said, 'Her sister is fearless. There's a difference. Bravery is being afraid and doing something in spite of your fear.' And then he turned to me and said, 'Can you be brave, little one?'

"And I went and had the most wonderful day running in the waves with Faustina. Papà reminded me of that day. He said maybe America would be like that. So I am going. I am going to be brave. If I don't like it, I can come back. I'll keep wearing bright colors for you, though. Even when I leave Italy, I know you'll be able to find me."

Giovanna walked home, up and down Genoa's hills. She was coming to terms with the fact that she really was going to leave. At first she'd harbored hope that Vincenzo would come by the shop the Monday following the referendum, just as he usually did. Would apologize. Would show her he didn't really mean it. And she would stay. But the more time that went by without hearing from him, the more she tried to harden her heart. Tried to prepare for her voyage. She'd thought a few times about sending him a letter to tell him she was leaving, but if he didn't care enough about her to make things right, why would he care that she was gone?

By the time their friends showed up at a bar near the port to send her, Faustina, and Betto off in good spirits, Giovanna stopped expecting that Vincenzo would walk through the door.

Mostly.

Chapter 48

"So you're really taking Gram to Italy?" Nick said.

"That's the plan," Cass answered.

Nick was in Manhattan because his friend was rewiring an old brownstone and wanted another set of eyes on the project. When he told Cass he was in her borough, she immediately cleared her schedule so they could have lunch. Time alone with her brother was rare these days, and she didn't want to give up the opportunity.

"And you really haven't decided about your wedding yet?"

They were eating at JG Melon at Nick's request. Cass had taken him there for burgers once, and he had proclaimed them the best he'd ever eaten.

"We really haven't," Cass said, dipping a French fry in ketchup.

He shook his head. "You know you're making Mom crazy. Dad, too."

Cass licked the ketchup off the fry.

"I forgot you do that," Nick said. "You're so weird."

Cass put the fry in her mouth. "Luca likes it," she told her brother. "He says it's unique."

"He's weird, too," Nick said, dipping his own fry in ketchup.

"I don't mean to make them crazy," Cass said. "I just want . . . I want everyone to be happy. Gram, Dad, Mom, you, Luca. And I'm kind of paralyzed trying to make that happen."

Nick reached across the table with his napkin. "You have a little ketchup on your . . ."

"I do?" Cass wiped her nose with her own napkin. No ketchup came off.

"Nah," Nick said. "You don't. I just wanted to make you smile."

Cass laughed. "Thank you," she said.

Nick took another bite of his burger. After he swallowed he said, "Listen. I hate that I'm saying this, because I think it may cause even more trouble, but this is the start of your life with Luca. You've gotta pick something that you and he are both comfortable with. Everyone else will adjust."

"Easy for you to say," Cass said. "All your choices always seem to be what everyone else wants anyway."

Nick put down his burger. "Not totally true. Dad got mad when I didn't buy an American-made car because Dina really wanted that huge Mazda that everyone else in the neighborhood is driving."

"He was being unreasonable," Cass said. She still didn't totally understand why her dad was so annoyed about that.

"He didn't think so," Nick said. "No one ever thinks they're the one being unreasonable."

Cass picked up another French fry. "True," she said. "So you'd come if I got married in Italy?"

Nick wiped his mouth. "I'd grumble about it, but I'd come. Hell, Cass, I'd come if you got married in Antarctica."

"Elephant shoes," she told him, like she did when she was little and he said she couldn't just run around telling him she loved him in front of his friends.

"Elephant shoes to you, too," he answered.

And something relaxed inside her knowing that Nick was on her side. In the end, he'd be there for her, even if she got married in Antarctica.

Chapter 49

THE ATLANTIC OCEAN
Then

Giovanna couldn't get the image out of her mind: Papà, on the dock, dressed in his finest suit and hat, waving a handkerchief at his daughters until he became a tiny dot of movement, then a speck, then nothing at all as the *Conte di Savoia*—a ship with a name that was so ironic Giovanna had to laugh when Faustina booked their tickets—picked up speed into the open water. She had wondered, in the depths of her heart, in the place she'd tried to lock up tight, whether Vincenzo might have heard she was leaving, would come to the port to say goodbye, to apologize, to tell her he was wrong, to ask her to stay, but he hadn't. It had just been Papà, waving and waving and waving until he disappeared.

Faustina and Betto had gone belowdecks, but Giovanna couldn't make herself move from the railing; she couldn't leave until the very last bit of Italy evaporated into the horizon. She felt like she had left so much of herself there. Her father, her mother, her childhood . . . She was going to start fresh, begin again in a new country.

Sitting down on a bench near the railing, Giovanna unzipped her bag. Just one suitcase of necessities for the journey, but inside were the drawings and paintings of her that Vincenzo had made. Making sure no one was around, she pulled out the pencil drawing he'd done of her without her clothing on. Her chin was raised, and the way he had drawn her eyes made her look seductive, as if she were inviting the viewer to come touch her. She ran her fingers over the lines of her body and then got up and tossed the drawing overboard. She watched it flutter down to the cresting waves and then dip under until it disappeared, like her father's waving hand, like the last glimpse of her country.

There was another sketch of her in a dress that Giovanna cast overboard. And one more of just her face, lit by the afternoon sun. She remembered when he drew that, while they were sitting outside in the Spianata dell'Acquasola. He had wanted to sketch the carousel, and she wanted to spend time with him. It was the most beautiful day—warm and bright with the scent of freesia floating by on the breeze.

"I'm jealous of the sun," he'd said.

"Why?" she'd asked, feeling it warm on her face.

"Because it's kissing you," he'd said.

She'd laughed and he said, "Like that! Don't move!" And he'd taken his sketchbook and pencil from his pocket.

Looking at the drawing, she could feel the day, the sun on her skin, the wind in her hair, the thrum of Vincenzo's presence vibrating throughout her body. She didn't want to be able to feel it anymore. Didn't want these memories of him to keep resurfacing every time she looked at his art, every time she saw herself through his eyes.

With tears on her cheeks, she cast it into the wind.

Giovanna wiped her eyes and then bent over to take the painting out of her bag. The canvas was wrapped in one of her dresses both to protect it and to hide it. But before she could unwrap it and cast it into the water, too, a shadow fell across her face. She looked up to see what had blocked the sun, but it wasn't a what, it was a who. A woman who looked about her age, dressed in the same kind of simple traveling dress Giovanna herself was wearing, a sweater layered on top. Her hair was parted in the center and pinned back, like photographs Giovanna had seen of Vivien Leigh.

"I couldn't help but notice you were alone up here, like me," the woman said. "Did you marry an American soldier, too? My husband is waiting for me in New York City."

Giovanna shook her head as she stood up. "No," she said. "My sister and her husband are belowdecks. They convinced me I should come with them to America to start over."

"Start over?" the woman said with her eyebrow raised. "Well, that sounds intriguing! I'm Emilia Ricci. Come," she added, quickly zipping and then lifting Giovanna's bag, "there's less of a chance to get wet if we sit a bit farther from the railing."

Giovanna smiled. Emilia seemed so warm, so happy. Just talking to her lifted Giovanna's spirits. "I'm Giovanna," she said. "Giovanna Ferrero."

"A pleasure." Emilia sat them down on a bench looking west. "So, why do you need to start over? And please don't leave out the juicy details. I love a good story."

Would she actually tell Emilia her story? "How about you tell me yours first," Giovanna said. "I want to hear about your American soldier."

Emilia clasped her hands behind her head and sighed. "If you insist," she said with a smile. Then she leaned back against the bench. "I noticed Tony because of his uniform, but fell in love with him because of his freckles."

Giovanna settled in to listen to Emilia's story, wondering if she might one day fall in love with an American man because of his freckles.

She thought back to the painting still in her suitcase. Maybe it should stay there. Proof of her story. Proof of the person she had been before, even if that proof stayed tucked away where she wouldn't see it, wouldn't even remember to look.

Chapter 50

GENOA, ITALY
Then

After he'd buried his father, after he'd discovered the true extent of the financial hardship his family would be in once the creditors came after them for the money his father had borrowed to keep the vineyards productive during the war, after he'd tried so hard to stay away from her, he knew the only way he could move forward was with Giovanna at his side. She made him feel strong, she made him feel safe, she listened to his secrets and kept them close.

The last conversation—argument really—he'd had with his father was about Giovanna. After the monarchy had been voted out, his father explained that without their title, without the financial protection that came with it, they wouldn't be able to keep their house or their vineyards or their apartment unless Vincenzo married well, married into money to pay back the creditors. And then they would have to build their vineyards into a true business—and a successful one. After his father said all of that, Chiara decided to tell him about Vincenzo and Giovanna. She hadn't known the details but had looked through one of Vincenzo's sketchbooks when he left it in his bedroom, and she had known enough.

The words they'd exchanged were ugly, born of anger and fear. And his father had made him a deal: if he went to Giovanna, if she had voted for the monarchy, they would figure out another way to get the money. But if not, Vincenzo would agree to stop seeing her and would get serious about Isabella. And so Vincenzo had gone to Giovanna and learned she hadn't voted for the monarchy. The harsh words he rained down on her came from his devastation and what felt, at the time, like a betrayal. Of course, she had been voting her conscience, as she should, but that wasn't how he'd felt that week, when it seemed like his family was about to lose everything, when it seemed like he was about to lose everything.

But now, a month later, he knew he had to go back to Genoa to see her. He had thought about sending her a drawing, or even a letter, but there was too much to say. He had to apologize and see if she would take him back. He missed her. He needed her. And maybe if Chiara married a wealthy businessman, Vincenzo could partner with him on the wine business, own the vineyards together. Maybe Chiara's future husband could even buy the apartment in Genoa so that it stayed in the family, or at least stayed with Chiara.

It was moments like this when Vincenzo wished more than anything that Leonardo had lived, that the two brothers were in this together, trying to figure out their family's complicated future. Instead, he spoke to his mother; he told her that he would figure it all out, but that he needed Giovanna.

"Then go to her," his mother said.

With that blessing, he went to the Ferreros' tailor shop, the rabbit Giovanna had sewn for him tucked into his satchel. He pushed his way through the door, remembering how Giovanna had looked behind the counter when he first met her, bathed in light. But now her father was at the counter. Vincenzo saw her dimples in his cheeks.

"Hello, signor," Vincenzo said.

He expected the smile he usually got from Signor Ferrero, but there was no warmth in his face now. "Is there something I can help you with?" he asked.

Vincenzo swallowed. "I, um, I was wondering if I could speak to Giovanna," he said.

"I'm afraid she's not here," he said.

Vincenzo looked around and saw most of the shop in boxes.

"Are you moving?" he asked.

"I'm selling the shop," Federico told him. "And then moving home to help my brother in his shop in Saluzzo. Our father decided it was time to retire."

Vincenzo had heard of the mountain town from Giovanna, but he'd never been there himself. He wondered if it was as quiet and close-knit as Alba. That was one of the best and worst things about Genoa—you could do what you wanted without the eyes of a whole village on you.

"Has Giovanna already gone?" he asked, still looking around the store for her, wondering if she was behind the curtain doing some work.

"Giovanna and her sister left for America two weeks ago," he said.

Vincenzo felt panic rise in his chest. How could she be gone?

"I've been in Alba," Vincenzo said, trying to keep his voice steady, "sorting out some family matters. My father . . . my father died. When will they be back?"

"I'm sorry for your loss," Signor Ferrero said. "Your father was a good man."

Vincenzo murmured his thanks, the pro forma thing he'd been doing for the past month, waiting for the answer to his question about Giovanna's return.

"As far as my daughters, I don't know if they're coming back at all," he said. "This move may be for good."

Vincenzo swallowed hard, trying to quell his panic. He needed Giovanna, the way she not only listened but heard, the way she told him he never had to hide his emotions around her, the way, with her, he felt like he could be his true self, his best self. And he had to apologize. She had accused him of acting like Ernesto, and she was right. He felt terrible about it. "Is there an address where I can write to her?" he asked.

Signor Ferrero's typically warm hazel eyes turned hard. "I think you've said enough to my daughter."

Vincenzo felt the words like a slap across the face. "I understand, signor," he finally said. "Would you . . . would you tell her I came by? Next time you write to her? If she wants to write to me . . . I . . . there's a lot I have to say."

The tailor gave a noncommittal shrug. Vincenzo hoped fervently that he would. And that Giovanna would respond. Because he realized now that he had no other way to contact her. He didn't know what city she was in. And didn't know anyone he could ask.

It didn't seem fair, to lose so much all at once.

Vincenzo went back to his family's flat, held the stuffed rabbit, and sobbed, for all he'd lost and all he would have to face now, alone.

Chapter 51

THE ATLANTIC OCEAN
Then

After sixteen days at sea, sixteen days playing shuffleboard with Emilia and practicing English with Faustina and wondering if she'd made the right decision in leaving Italy, the crew of the *Conte di Savoia* called everyone out on deck for their first glimpse of New York Harbor.

Giovanna stood next to Faustina, who was next to Betto. The sun was caressing their faces as the Statue of Liberty came into view, tall and majestic, keeping watch over the harbor.

"Give me your tired, your poor," Faustina whispered, quoting the English poem she had told Giovanna was on the base of the Statue of Liberty—written by a woman! "Your huddled masses yearning to breathe free, / The wretched refuse of your teeming shore. / Send these, the homeless, tempest-tost to me, / I lift my lamp beside the golden door!"

Giovanna didn't understand all the English words, but her sister had told her what the poem meant: that even if you had nothing, even if you felt like nothing, America would welcome you.

"Grazie," Giovanna said to the statue, quietly at first. Then: "Grazie!" she shouted. Faustina laughed and repeated, "Grazie!" Then a few other people, and a few more, until it felt like the whole ship was shouting thank you to the lady with the lamp.

Faustina squeezed Giovanna's hand. "I have a really good feeling about this," she said. "I predict you'll be in love with this country before you even start thinking about Christmas."

Giovanna wasn't quite so certain.

Chapter 52

Cass and Luca were out at Stefano's winery in Brooklyn, listening to a musician Stefano swore would blow up any day now. The keyboardist was playing her heart out, singing a song about the dark night of her soul, when Cass's phone started buzzing in her handbag. It stopped and started again. Then stopped and started a third time.

"Excuse me," she said to Luca when the song ended and the room started applauding. "Someone's stalking my phone." When this happened, it was either her family or work—or once in a while Kiley—and regardless of who was calling, it meant something wonderful or terrible had happened and she had to pick up.

She pulled the phone out of her bag as she walked to the vestibule by the door and saw a missed call from her dad and three from her brother Chris.

She called him back without checking to see if he'd left a voice mail. "What's wrong?" she asked when he picked up.

"Gram's in the hospital," he said. "Why the hell didn't you pick up your phone?"

Cass leaned against the wall. "Sorry, we were out at a music thing. What happened? Is she okay?"

Her heart was racing, and she wished she had brought her drink with her.

"She fainted when she got up from dinner tonight, and Dad called 911. She came to pretty quickly, but they checked her in for the night because her blood pressure was through the roof."

Cass felt her own blood pressure skyrocket. "But she's okay now?"

"I mean, I guess so," Chris said. "She's awake and talking and acting like her usual self, if that's what you mean. She's at the hospital, though."

"Right," Cass said. "They don't keep you there if you're totally fine."

"Right," Chris echoed.

There was a pause.

"Which hospital?" Cass asked.

"Saint Francis," he said. "The heart one. That's where Dad asked the ambulance to go, and since she was stable, they agreed."

A wave of applause rose and fell behind Cass, and she covered the mouthpiece for a moment.

"Got it," Cass said when the applause subsided. "Will she be there for a while?"

"I don't know," Chris answered; she could hear his feet squeaking on the floor. He was pacing while he was talking—something he'd done on the phone since he was a teenager. She remembered the sound of his footsteps back and forth and back and forth in the up-stairs hallway of their house. "But visiting hours are twelve noon to eight p.m. Dad said to expect she'll still be there tomorrow afternoon for visitors, if you want to go see her."

"Of course," Cass said. "I'll be there tomorrow."

"Good," he said.

Cass didn't like the tone of her brother's voice. "What's that supposed to mean?" she said.

"Nothing," he said. "Just glad you can make it here from Manhattan."

"I always—" she said, but then stopped. It wasn't worth getting into now, here. And she knew that no matter what she said, Chris would feel like her parents did. Like her choice to live a different kind of life meant she rejected their choices. It wasn't true, but that didn't matter. "Thanks for letting me know. Maybe I'll see you tomorrow."

"Yeah," he said. "Let me know what time you're coming."

They both said goodbye and Cass took a moment to compose herself before she walked back into the show.

She wondered if this meant that Gram wouldn't make it to Italy. They were supposed to leave in two weeks. What if she'd just lost her chance to see her homeland one last time before she died?

Chapter 53

QUEENS, USA
Then

Giovanna sat on the New York City subway train trying to take up as little space as possible. Her arms were pressed against her body, her purse on her lap, both hands clutching the leather. Genoa was a big city with a lot of people, but it was nothing compared to New York City. There were about half a million people who lived in Genoa, Faustina had told her. New York City had about seven and a half million. Giovanna had trouble wrapping her mind around it. This city was like fifteen Genoas of people. Fifteen!

Through Emilia's husband's connections, Giovanna had gotten a job in the garment district in Manhattan, sewing beads onto wedding dresses in exquisitely intricate patterns. She missed the variety she had when she was working in her father's shop, but she liked what she was doing and she was good at it, which her boss had already noticed only a month into the job. Two other women who worked in the large sewing room were Italian, too, from the area around Napoli, and the three of them took their lunch breaks together.

Between them and Emilia, Giovanna already had a little group of friends in New York, a closer group than she'd had since before the war.

Betto was enjoying his job working for his uncle's fruit delivery service, getting up before dawn to go to the docks, where shipments of fruit from different providers would get sorted onto his uncle's trucks and delivered to grocers and restaurants before they opened for the day. And Faustina had gotten it in her head that she was going to become a teacher. She was studying English every day so she could apply to Queens College for a university degree.

"Can you believe it?" she'd said to Giovanna. "Everything feels possible here. Isn't it wonderful?"

And Giovanna did understand what Faustina meant. There was an energy about America—or at least about New York City—that felt electric, contagious. When she got out of the subway to walk to work, she could feel the pulse of the city, the rushed excitement, the infinite possibilities.

But she missed Italy, too. She missed her father. She missed her job. She missed everyone speaking her language. She missed the familiarity of the food, the streets, the sounds. Here, even the sirens on the ambulances sounded different. And it was amazing how many different places people were from. At home, almost everyone was from somewhere in Italy. Here there were people from Asia, Africa, South America, all of Europe. Betto called it a melting pot, but Giovanna thought of it as a quilt, with different patches from all over the world forming this mash-up of a unified whole that was entirely different from all of its parts.

Here, it was as if she had to learn to navigate an entirely new world—with new rules, new norms, new expectations. Sometimes it was too hard. Sometimes the homesickness broke her. And in those moments, to her shame, she found herself thinking of Vincenzo. Thinking of his apartment, his body, his kisses, the way being in his arms felt like another definition of home. The life she'd imagined with him, living in his villa, dancing with him at parties, walking together through the vineyard, being his muse. It was all so different from the life she was living now.

Maria, one of the women Giovanna worked with, said her fiancé had a friend who was looking to be introduced to a nice woman, so she and Maria were going on a double date soon. Giovanna wondered if being with someone else would ever feel the way being with Vincenzo did. She couldn't imagine it would. But she was hopeful that one day she'd meet someone else who made her happy—perhaps in a different way, but happy nonetheless.

Perhaps Maria's fiancé's friend would be that person.

Or, perhaps not.

Chapter 54

Cass showed up at Gram's hospital room at twelve noon with a silk robe she'd bought on the walk from her apartment to the subway. She wasn't sure what foods were good for her grandmother to eat now, and Luca told her that sometimes flowers weren't allowed for heart patients either. She wanted to bring something, though, and as she window-shopped her way to the station, she remembered Jenna complaining about having to wear hospital gowns after giving birth to Milo. With her love of beautiful clothing, Cass thought her grandmother might have a similar distaste for them.

She knocked on the hospital room door before she walked in and found her grandmother alone. There was a pulse oximeter on her finger and some wires attached to a box the size of a cell phone that Cass assumed was monitoring Gram's heart. Her hair was squashed sideways, but otherwise she seemed okay. She was watching *Say Yes to the Dress* on the television.

"Cassandra!" Gram said, looking toward the door. "Can you believe all of this? Just for a little fainting spell?"

Cass sat down on Gram's bed. "Well," she said. "Everyone's worried about you."

The woman on TV chose a dress. "Oh good," Gram said to the TV. "That was the one I'd been hoping you'd pick. It flatters your figure." She turned the television off with the remote next to her bed.

"Did you make dresses like those?" Cass asked her.

Gram shook her head. "Those were lace. The ones I made were always beaded. That was my job—sewing on all the tiny beads. But I didn't do it for long. Only a few years, until your father was born. That's when Pop got his construction job and we all moved to Island Park. I stayed home after that."

Cass took off her coat and pulled the guest chair closer to Gram's bed. "Is that what you wanted?" she asked. Cass had been thinking more about jobs recently, particularly for women, ever since her realization when looking at Luca's painting of Marina as Minerva. It's a privilege not to have to work—one that was much more prevalent sixty years ago than now. Cass's mother worked, but she did it from home. She was a Dictaphone typist. Lawyers and doctors, mostly, would send her recordings of their notes and she would type them up and send them back. When Cass thought of her mother during her childhood, she always pictured her with headphones on, her fingers flying across the keys, while Cass sat next to her doing her homework. There was something nice about that, working next to her mom, feeling that solidarity. She wondered if she saw the world differently because her mom worked—if Luca did. Cass imagined it probably did form both of their perspectives on society, on what women could do or should do.

Gram adjusted herself in bed. "It's what was expected," she said. "And even though your great-aunt went against expectations, back then it was what I wanted. But if I were part of your generation, I think it would have been different. Perhaps I would have been different."

If she had been born in her grandmother's generation, Cass wondered, would she have been different?

"Would you have kept making wedding dresses?" Cass asked.

Gram shook her head, her curls rubbing against the pillow. "I would've wanted to become a clothing designer. Everyone always said I made the best-looking dresses in town. I designed and sewed them for Mrs. Ricci and her daughters—for holidays or for weddings, that sort of thing. And for myself, too, and your great-aunt Faustina, and her daughter, Anne. She and Mrs. Ricci both encouraged me to open my own shop for bespoke dresses, but it never seemed like the right time."

"I loved the dresses you made me when I was a kid," Cass said.

"My only granddaughter." Gram patted her hand. "Can you believe it? Two sons and six grandsons to get to you."

Cass laughed. "Glad everyone kept trying," she said.

She lifted up the bag she brought her grandmother. "In case you weren't happy with the hospital attire, I brought you this."

Gram took the bag and opened it, pulling out a red silk robe with bell sleeves. "Oh, Cassandra," she said. "This is lovely. How did you know just what to bring to lift my spirits?"

Cass shrugged. "I guess I know you well." Though the truth was, she only knew what her grandmother let her know. There was so much more to Gram than Cass ever imagined, and she couldn't believe she was just discovering it now.

"Will you help me put it on? I hate that the back on this hospital gown doesn't close properly."

As Cass was helping her grandmother into the robe, slipping the pulse oximeter off her finger briefly, her father walked into the room.

"Should you be doing that?" he asked.

With Gram's arm through the armhole, Cass slipped it right back on. "It was only off for two seconds," she said. "I don't think it was a problem."

Her dad nodded, but she could tell he was worried about Gram. Cass understood. She was his mother.

The doctor came in a few minutes behind her father.

"Well," he said, "good news, Mrs. Fanelli. Your blood pressure seems to be under control again. As we've discussed, you do have cardiomyopathy, which isn't uncommon at your age. Your heart muscle is weak, and will eventually get weaker, but I've changed the dosages of your medications again, and I think it's fine for you to go home today."

Cass didn't like that word, *cardiomyopathy*. She made a note in her head to look it up later. But Gram was apparently focused on the beginning and end of the doctor's statement, not the middle.

"Oh, that's wonderful news, Doctor," she said. "Thank you."

Cass and her father exchanged a look.

"Do you have any questions for me?" the doctor asked. "Otherwise, I'll have the discharge nurse come and go over everything with you."

"Just one question," Gram said. "Is it safe for me to travel to Italy with my granddaughter and her fiancé in two weeks?" She looked at Cass and smiled.

The doctor slipped his pen into his pocket. "As safe as anything," he said. "I always tell my patients to get up and walk around a few times on the plane to keep your circulation going—and get yourself a pair of compression socks to wear. Make sure you take your medication and be reasonable about what you can do. But otherwise, I don't see any reason you can't go." He turned to Cass. "Are you the grand-daughter going to Italy?"

Cass nodded.

"Nothing too strenuous, okay?"

Cass nodded again. "Of course."

"Great. I'll send the discharge nurse in so she can get your paper-work sorted. We've adjusted your blood pressure medication, so make sure to pick up the new prescription."

"We will," Cass's father said.

The doctor left, and then Dom turned to Cass and Gram. "Mom," he said. "You're not going to Italy. Cassandra, you're not taking her. I didn't like this idea from the start, and after this, no way."

Cass waited to see what her grandmother would say. She would support her, even if it meant upsetting her father again.

"Dom," Gram said softly. "I'm afraid this isn't your decision. The doctor said it's safe. And I'd like to go to Italy again. There are some things I'd like to do there. Some people I'd like to see. As long as Cassandra and Luca will take me, I'm going." She turned to Cass. "Are you still okay with that? Will Luca be?"

"I am, and I'm sure he will be, too," Cass answered. She'd been slightly worried when she told him about telling Gram she could join their trip, but he'd been happy about it. "Maybe she and Nonno will have some more time to reconnect," he'd said. Cass had laughed, but she'd been wondering ever since what would happen when the two of them saw each other again.

"Wonderful," Gram said. "Then it's set."

Cass's father's face was red, but he didn't say anything. He clearly wasn't happy, but it also seemed he knew that Gram was right. This wasn't his choice. It was hers.

"There will be more to this conversation later, Cassandra," he said. Cass nodded. "Sure, Dad."

Whatever he asked her to do, she would do. She just wanted to make her grandmother's desire to go to her homeland again a reality. It seemed like a fair trade for bringing her long-ago heartbreak to the surface this close to the end of her life.

On her way out of the hospital, Cass stopped at the chapel. There was a man sitting in one of the pews, alternately crying and praying. To her left, in front of a glowing stained-glass window was a table of candles. Cass crossed herself and picked up a match from the box. She lit it from one of the already glowing flames, then touched it to an unlit wick, whispering, "Please heal my grandmother. Please keep her safe. And please . . . please let her see her home one more time before she dies. Amen."

Cass pulled the Immaculate Heart of Mary out from under her sweater and kissed it. Then she wiped the tears from her eyes and started her trip back to Manhattan.

Chapter 55

The air was getting colder. Giovanna had just experienced her first American Thanksgiving, a holiday filled with food and family and friends who felt like family. They went around the table, everyone saying something they were thankful for, and Giovanna had said, "Everyone sitting here." Now Christmas was fast approaching, and with it, Giovanna's self-imposed deadline. The time she would choose what her future would hold.

"Have you decided?" Faustina asked her that Sunday night, looking up from her schoolbooks, spread out on the table in front of her.

Giovanna had been exchanging letters with her father. He seemed happy back in Saluzzo, enjoying the time with his brother and parents and nieces and nephews. While he missed her—and Faustina—he didn't need her there. He encouraged her to stay, in fact, said that it would give him peace of mind knowing that his daughters were together, watching out for each other. And she liked her new friends, her new job, the new foods and new landscapes. The only thing giving her pause was the thought of Vincenzo. She couldn't get him out of her mind. And she knew she had to. She knew, deep in her heart, that he was her past, not her future.

She took a deep breath. "I'm going to stay," Giovanna told her sister.

Faustina threw her arms around Giovanna. "I hoped that was going to be your answer," she said.

That night, in bed, Giovanna took a piece of linen writing paper, rested it on a book, and carefully wrote a letter. It was something she had to do so that she could move on.

Dear Vincenzo,

> *I hope this letter finds you well. I think of you often. Every time I try to tell my heart to say goodbye to you, it rebels. I am writing this letter so my heart knows, so my mind knows, so my soul knows: Goodbye.*

> *Your Giovanna*

She looked at how she'd signed it. No matter how badly he hurt her, a part of her would always be his. But it didn't matter. There was an ocean between them. And she was going to keep it that way. She didn't add a return address.

Chapter 56

Cassandra was focused on her phone as she walked into her apartment after work, mindlessly shrugging herself out of her coat and kicking off her heels.

"Ahem."

She heard Luca clear his throat and looked up from the email she was reading. "Oh!" she said. "Hi."

Sometimes she had trouble making the brain shift from work to home. All the thoughts about the marketing data, ad testing, demographics had to recede so the topics she talked about with Luca could surface.

"Who did what today at the office?" Luca asked with a smile. His hands were stained with paint, and there was a deep-blue smudge on his forearm. "Where is that beautiful brain of yours?"

Cass smiled. "We were testing a few potential ads and were surprised by the results." She shook her head. "Nothing that can't wait until tomorrow, though. The world won't end on account of an ad test."

Luca opened his arms and Cass walked into his embrace, resting her head on his chest. "How was your day?" she asked.

"Well," he said. "I finished the last brushstroke on the last painting in the show," he said.

She leaned back so she could see his face. "You did? Congratulations!" She rose up on her tiptoes to kiss him on the lips. "Can I see?"

"Of course," he answered. "But I think my art is best enjoyed with a glass of wine." He already had a bottle of Della Rosa wine uncorked on the counter, breathing, and poured them each a glass. "Shall we?" he said.

Cass followed him through the apartment into his studio. The paintings lined the walls, each one slightly taller than she was. She loved seeing his shows when they were complete, how they came together with a shared palette.

"It's all the colors from your proposal!" she said, realizing as her eyes traveled around the room.

Luca nodded, clearly delighted she'd noticed.

"These are breathtaking," she said, walking closer to the first painting in the lineup but making sure to stay far enough away that they were safe from her glass of wine. It was interesting because while she saw the faces and postures of different family members, the paintings clearly weren't them. Cass imagined it would be the same way if you were close to someone who was an actor. You recognize them, but also you don't.

She walked from painting to painting, making comments about things she liked—the lift of his sister's eyebrow, the way he drew his father's hair, the look in his mother's eye. Stefano was painted as Bacchus, which seemed quite fitting. And Izzy, Alessandra's little daughter, was painted in triplicate as the three Graces, performing in tutus at a ballet recital. The eighth and final painting showed a child asleep in a crib, a pink and gray rocking horse in the background, and two parents holding hands in the foreground, watching over the sleeping child.

As she got closer, Cass thought she recognized her profile and Luca's, too. "What's this one, Lu?" she asked.

"It's called *Fortuna*," he answered.

Cass scrolled through Roman mythology in her mind. Fortuna was Venus's daughter with Mercury.

"Is she . . . ours?" Cass said, not sure how else to ask it. "Are you Mercury?"

Luca nodded. "The painting of our grandparents felt unfinished until I added a little baby asleep in one of the photo frames. And once I did, I knew she was ours. And that she was Fortuna. Our Fortuna. And she needed her own painting."

Cass put her wine down on Luca's drafting table and walked closer to the painting. The baby's nose looked just like Cass's, and she had Luca's curling eyelashes.

"We have to figure out our wedding," Cass said, her own eyelashes wet.

"I know," Luca answered, wrapping her in his arms and pressing his lips against the part in her hair. "We do."

"But how can we make everyone happy?" she asked him, her voice muffled by his sweater.

"Maybe," he said, laying his cheek on her head, "we can't. And we have to accept that."

"What if I can't accept that?" Cass whispered. "And what if what makes you happy isn't what makes me happy?"

Luca held her, but he didn't answer her question.

Chapter 57

OVER THE ATLANTIC OCEAN

Now

They had reshuffled their seats so that Gram and Cassandra were sitting next to each other on the plane, and Luca was in the single middle section seat across the aisle from them. Cass had been worried that in the end her grandmother might not be able to make this trip, but Gram was determined and spent the two weeks between her quick hospital stay and their flight building up her strength, walking slowly back and forth across the small living room in her apartment. Even so, she needed a wheelchair in the airport, and Cass realized she'd probably need one to do any sightseeing in Italy, too. When she mentioned that to Luca, he told her not to worry and he would have it all sorted by the time they landed. She kissed him, so grateful that he was by her side for this.

The first-class flight attendant, a young Italian man, had been taken with Gram from the moment she got on the plane, calling her Nonna. He came by now to clear their dinner trays.

"Nonna," he said to her, "is there anything else I can get you? Another drink? An extra pillow?"

Gram smiled. "Thank you, Riccardo. I think I have everything I need, though." She patted Cass's hand. "My granddaughter is taking wonderful care of me."

Cass smiled at her. "Doing my best," she said.

Once Riccardo left, the cabin lights were dimmed.

"Are you tired?" Gram asked Cass.

Cass shook her head. "Not really. I have trouble sleeping on planes, even when the seats lie flat." She looked over at Luca, who was already curled up under the airplane blanket, his eye shade on.

"I keep thinking about the boat I took to America," Gram said. "It took us more than two weeks. Can you believe that? And now we'll be in Italy in eight hours."

It wasn't something Cass often thought about—the way in which travel was different than it had been seventy years ago. But now that she was thinking about it, she wondered what would be next. By the time she was in her nineties, would there be flying cars? Commercial planes going at supersonic speeds? Would a trip in a rocket to the moon be commonplace? It was amazing to think about the technological advances her grandmother had lived through.

"Will you tell me a story about the boat?" Cass asked. "I don't know anything about your trip over."

"There's not much to tell," Gram said, resettling herself on the airplane pillow.

"There's always a story," Cass answered.

Gram thought for a moment. "Well," she said. "You know I met Mrs. Ricci on the boat."

Cass nodded.

"She was my salvation when we came to America, truly. Her husband was waiting for her here, and as luck would have it, we were both going to live in Queens, in New York. I guess it wasn't truly luck—there was a big Italian American community in Queens back then. Your great-aunt Faustina was so happy to be in America, and Uncle Betto was working hard at his uncle's business, and I felt a bit adrift. You understand, I'd never left Italy before, never spent more than a night or two away from my father. And Vincenzo and I had just ended things. I wanted to start over, but I was homesick and heartbroken.

"Mrs. Ricci was homesick, too. And neither of us spoke English very well. So we stuck together. Her husband helped me get a job in the garment district and then decided his friend from grade school should teach me and Mrs. Ricci English. Well, I think it was a bit of a setup because—"

"Is that how you met Pop?" Cass asked. She'd always known that Gram and Pop had met through Mr. Ricci, but she'd never asked how.

Gram nodded.

"I knew he was good friends with Mr. Ricci from when they were kids, but I had no idea he taught you English!" Cass said.

Gram laughed. "I was a terrible student in school—just like Chris, it was hard for me to read. My father was like that, too. He taught me to put a piece of paper under the words I was reading to stay focused on them, and it helped sometimes, but it was never easy. I was so relieved when your father and uncle didn't have the same difficulties. Thank goodness your brother was able to get more help than I did."

There was so much Cass was learning about her grandmother. She knew Gram didn't like to read, and that Pop was always the one who read bedtime stories to her out loud when she stayed at their house, but she'd figured it was because English was Gram's second language. She hadn't realized there was more to it.

"You have dyslexia, Gram?" Cass asked. That was what her brother had been diagnosed with in elementary school.

"I assume so," she said. "No one ever gave me an official diagnosis, but I assume so."

"Did that make learning English even more difficult?" Cass asked.

"Your grandfather was very patient," Gram answered. "He would take me out—for coffee, for ice cream, to the store, and he would supply the words for me when I faltered. One day, when I was feeling a bit discouraged, he brought me to the kitchen at the restaurant he and his brothers owned, opened up a gallon of ice cream that was in the freezer, and we stood on the side of the kitchen while I pretended to order ice cream from him over and over until I got it right. Then we shared an ice cream sundae together."

Cass laughed. "Is that when you fell in love with him?" she asked.

Gram smiled. "It was when I knew that if he asked me to marry him, I would say yes."

"Your English is perfect now, though," Cass said.

"I've been here a long time, Cassandra," Gram said. "The great majority of my life."

Cass thought about that. It was more than half a century since her grandmother had left Italy. "Luca says Italy still feels like home to him," she said. "How long did it feel like home to you?"

Gram shrugged. "Your Luca is different. He spent every summer there as a child, he went back for holidays. He always had one foot in each country. It's a different kind of immigration."

Cass looked over at him; he was lying on his back, and she could see the gentle rise and fall of his chest. He was sleeping so peacefully. She thought of the painting he'd made of their future child, sleeping just the same way, and her whole self felt soft.

"Luca wants to get married in Italy," she said to Gram.

"So I've heard," Gram said.

"It's not what my parents want." Cass hadn't found the time to talk to her grandmother about this yet, but she should have.

"Sometimes it's more important to do what you want." There was a faraway look in her eyes.

"Are you thinking about something in particular?" Cass asked.

Gram nodded, a small smile on her face. "I was thinking about Vincenzo. We've been talking, you know."

"You have?" Cass asked. She wasn't completely surprised, but this was the first Gram had mentioned it. "Often?"

"Often enough," Gram said. "He apologized so many times for the way things ended between us, the way he let his father's opinion sway his own. And he told me about things that had happened in his family right after he and I fought that I hadn't been aware of. He had tried to apologize then, too."

"And what did you say?" Cass asked. The airplane was humming softly, giving the conversation an almost dreamlike quality.

"I told him I forgave him. I told him it was too long to hold on to hurt, especially when there was still love there."

Cass looked at her grandmother, her snow-white hair curling softly against her cheeks. "You really still love him?" Cass asked.

"A piece of me has always loved him," Gram said. "But we were talking about you. About your wedding to your Luca."

Cass nodded. "Right," she said. "What should I do?"

"What do you want to do?" Gram asked. Everyone kept asking her this. She'd been asking herself, too. And her answer was always the same, and was always impossible.

"I want to make everyone happy," she said.

Jill Santopolo

Gram patted her hand. "If that's your goal, you will always be disappointed," she said.

Cass closed her eyes for a moment to stop the tears of frustration she knew would come.

"Let's turn off the lights, principessa," her grandmother said, "and see if we can get some sleep."

Soon Gram was breathing quietly beside Cass, but Cass was still awake, turning the problem over and over in her head. No matter how she looked at this situation, she couldn't figure out a solution.

Chapter 58

The gallery had sent a car to pick them up at the airport in Milan and take them straight to the Principe di Savoia hotel. Gram started laughing when she heard the hotel's name.

"What is it?" Luca asked as he helped her out of the wheelchair.

"Just seems fitting that the conte's great-grandson is taking me to a hotel named for the last Italian royal family, is all," she said.

Cass smiled.

"You know," Luca said, "my grandfather told me the vote was close. Nearly half of Italy wanted to keep things the way they were."

"Cass's great-aunt Faustina would point out the word *nearly* in that sentence," Gram said, still laughing a bit.

When they checked in at the hotel, the concierge smiled at Gram and said, "I hope you enjoy your surprise!"

"What's that about?" Cass asked Luca as they left the reception desk.

"No idea," he said, shrugging. "Maybe my grandfather sent over a bottle of wine?"

The three of them walked through the elegant lobby with carved entryways and marble walls and took the elevator up to their suite. Cass always forgot, until she came back to Europe, how grand the continent was. Even though so many areas had been bombed during the war, so much of the beautiful architecture survived—the sculpture, the carvings, the ornamentation. In the United States, buildings from the 1700s were incredibly old. In Italy, you could go back centuries before that. It was a different order of magnitude here.

Luca opened the hotel suite door and took a quick step back. "Someone's in there," he said softly. "Are you sure this is the right room number?"

At the sound of the door, the person in the room turned. "Ciao, Luca," he said.

"Nonno?" Luca asked, switching into Italian. "I thought we weren't going to see you until tomorrow. Wait— Are you Gram's surprise?"

Cass and Gram followed Luca into the room.

"I am," Nonno said with a small laugh. "I'm sorry for not calling first, but seventy-plus years is long enough to wait. I couldn't wait a moment more. Especially not after the conversations Giovanna and I have been having."

A moment more for what? Cass was trying to find solid ground in the conversation as she went back to close the door now that they were all in the room.

Nonno turned to Gram, who was still standing, her hands resting on the back of the wing-backed chair that separated the two of them.

"I'm not sure if this is what you hoped would happen when you told me you were coming to Italy, but it's the first thing I thought of. Please forgive me for not getting down on one knee, or waiting until the two of us were alone . . ." he said.

Cass turned back and looked at him. She knew what this sounded like, but her mind was having a hard time processing it. He walked closer to Gram and took one of her hands in his.

"Giovanna, would you marry me? I know we're old and neither one of us has much time left, but whatever time I do have, I would like to spend with you."

Cass looked at Luca and saw her shock mirrored on his face. If anyone had told her this was what would happen when they got to Italy, she wouldn't have believed them.

Gram still hadn't responded, so Cass took a step to the side to see her face. Her expression was unreadable.

"I should have asked you this seventy years ago," Nonno added. "But I was young and stupid and too wrapped up in pleasing my father and doing what I thought I needed to do to honor my family. But I want to make it right now, as much as I can. Better late, yes?"

Gram lifted her hand to her mouth and then put it back down on the chair. "I . . . I don't know what to say," she finally said. "I'd wanted to see you, I'd wanted to spend time with you, but I hadn't thought about this at all."

"Please say yes," Nonno answered. "Say you want to come home with me, say you want to be my contessa, say you want to make our dreams from more than half a century ago come true."

Gram looked at Cass, bewildered.

"You can take some time to think, Gram," Cass told her, not sure what her grandmother needed right now.

Gram shook her head, a resolute expression forming on her face. "I don't need time to think," she said and turned back to Nonno. "I accept."

Nonno stepped even closer and wrapped his arms around her. Then Gram lifted her face toward his. Cass thought she heard her grandmother whisper "bene" before he slowly and softly kissed her.

Cass felt tears in her eyes and watched them until Luca tugged her toward one of the bedrooms.

"Did you know?" Cass whispered to him as they shut the door to give their grandparents some space.

"Not at all," he whispered back. "This is crazy."

"I think it's sweet," Cass said.

Luca let out a breath. "I worry my family won't agree."

It took Cass a moment to figure out what he meant, and then she realized: the inheritance, the winery, the jewelry, the villa. There was a lot that came with being a Della Rosa d'Alba.

"It always comes down to money, doesn't it," Cass said quietly.

"Love or money," Luca said. "That's what motivates everything. It's just unfortunate when they collide."

Cass didn't want to think about that now. She didn't want to think about what her family would think either, what her father might say about his mother—his ill mother—moving halfway across the world. She just wanted to think about the joy she saw on her grandmother's face when she was in Nonno's arms.

Chapter 59

Cass and Luca left their grandparents in the hotel suite and headed into the city center to stop by the art gallery Luca was showing in. He wanted to make sure that the paintings had arrived in perfect condition. The canvases had been packed and shipped a few days earlier, and had cleared customs the day before Cass and Luca arrived. Tomorrow he would be there while they hung the show, which would open the following Monday.

As they walked through the city, the Duomo appeared majestic in front of them, and Cass couldn't help but think about all the other times she'd been in Milan, both with Luca and when she was a student in college, traveling around the country with her new study-abroad friends. There was one day when they'd all climbed the stairs to the top of the Duomo and sunbathed on the roof, soaking in the warmth.

"Come," she said, tugging him toward the church. "I want to climb to the roof."

"I have to meet Mauro in the gallery," he said, resisting.

"You didn't give him a time, right? So let's take a short diversion. Please?"

People swirled around them, talking into cell phones and with one another. The music of so many people speaking Italian at once crescendoed. "Pretty please?" she added. "With a kiss on top?"

Luca laughed. "Okay, okay, we'll go to the roof of the Duomo."

They bought their tickets and then climbed round and round in the staircase, their hands on the ancient stone, fingertips rubbing it smooth as so many millions of hands had done before them.

"Here we are," Luca said, coming out of the top of the staircase onto the roof. "Oh. Whoa."

He stepped aside so Cass could come out, too. She looked at the twirling spires and the intricate stonework. She looked at the blue, blue sky, and felt the desire to thank God for the world. "Benedic, anima mea, Domino," she said softly, "et omnia quæ intra me sunt nomini sancto ejus."

Then she turned to Luca and took his hand, leading him through the stone walkways to the top of the cathedral, onto the slightly angled, smooth area of roof.

"Now what?" he asked.

"Now we lie down."

And they did, the two of them, their heads next to each other, looking up into the expanse of sky.

"It's so peaceful up here," he said after a moment.

"Right?" she said. "It's one of my favorite memories of my junior year abroad."

"Not the Vespa rides or the dance clubs or the trips to the Amalfi coast?" Luca said.

"I liked those, too," Cass said. "But lying on top of the Duomo in Milan, staring into the heavens . . . it made me feel at peace."

She remembered herself as she was then, knowing she had to tell her father she didn't want to be a bookkeeper or return to the same town she grew up in, understanding that she didn't want her life to look like her older brothers' lives and had to figure out what it was she did want . . . it was a lot to handle. But then she and her roommates went to Milan and she lay on a roof and stared at the sky. A powerful feeling had washed over her then; she'd recited the Hail Mary and felt at peace. After that, she made the decisions she had to make, and knew they were all necessary and right.

She hoped this trip to the roof would give her the same clarity about her future, about her wedding to Luca, about her relationship with her family, about living in Italy again. She stared into the sky and breathed deeply. *Ave Maria*, she prayed silently, *gratia plena. Dominus tecum. Benedicta tu in mulieribus* . . .

No clarity came her way, but she felt heard. And she felt like the answers would come; all she had to do was open herself to them.

When they got back to the hotel after visiting the gallery, Gram and Nonno were waiting for them in the room.

"We're going to go to Alba," Nonno said.

Cass started to protest, but Gram held up her hand. "Vincenzo and I will take care of each other," she said. "We'll come back to Milan with Giorgio for the gallery opening next week, and then go back with him to Alba."

Nonno cleared his throat. "Giorgio and Fabrizio are getting ready to press the grapes to make Piemonte Moscato Passito this week—a new experiment Fabrizio wanted to try," he said. "I told Giovanna about the traditional engagement calpestamento, and since those grapes are being pressed now, she and I will have a chance to do it this weekend. We'd love for you to come."

Cass smiled and looked at Luca. He bit his lip at the memory.

"Okay," Luca said. "We'll see you in Alba this weekend and then at the opening."

Nonno nodded. "Very good. I'll call us a car to take us home. Would you mind ringing the concierge to bring down Giovanna's suitcase?"

"Sure." Luca picked up the room phone to make the call.

Cass walked over to her grandmother. "Are you sure about this?" she asked.

"Completely certain," her grandmother answered. Then she switched to Italian: "Sicurissima."

Cass hadn't noticed before how you used the same word in Italian for *sure*, *secure*, and *safe*. She wondered if that was why her grandmother switched languages, because she wanted to express all three.

"Good," Cass said, wrapping her grandmother in a hug. And she toasted her with the same words Gram had used to toast Cass and Luca's engagement, Pop's words. "Cent'anni."

"I certainly hope so, Cassandra," Gram said. "I certainly hope so."

Cass did, too.

Chapter 60

Cass and Luca arrived at Villa Della Rosa that weekend in a rented Maserati.

"Did I ever tell you my grandmother Isabella's family owned an automobile company?" he said as they got out of the car.

"I don't think so," Cass said, taking in the majesty of Luca's ancestral home.

"They got bought out by Fiat in the late 1940s," he said.

"So now we drive only Fiat-brand cars?" Cass asked, taking in this new information.

"Exactly," he said. "My cousin Fabrizio always jokes that the Della Rosa d'Alba family motto should be 'fedeltà e uva.'"

"Loyalty and grapes?" Cass said, laughing.

"Words to live by," Luca said, locking the car and taking Cass's hand.

They walked into the grand entry hall of the Villa Della Rosa and heard Zio Giorgio arguing with Nonno, their voices echoing.

"Papà, your mind is out like a balcony," Giorgio was saying. "Do we need to have your mental state evaluated by a doctor?"

"I'm fine," Nonno said. "Perfectly mentally fit. Just enjoying myself. And righting some wrongs from my past before I die."

"Should we go in?" Cass asked quietly.

Luca shook his head. "Let's give them a moment."

"Fabrizio set up the calpestamento," Giorgio said. "But I really don't like this."

"Your complaint has been noted," Nonno answered, the tone of his voice clearly ending the conversation.

There was a pause, and then they heard Giorgio's footsteps. A door closed a few seconds later.

"Now?" Cass asked.

Luca nodded. The two of them found Gram first, sitting in the parlor.

"You know I don't want anything from him," she said when Luca walked into the room.

"I'm sorry you had to hear that," Luca answered.

Nonno came into the room next, and he looked livid.

"Come sit," Gram said to him, patting the space next to her on the couch.

"I apologize for my son," he said. "He's clearly more concerned about money than about happiness."

Gram took his hand. "You know I don't care about the money. I just want to sit with you and enjoy being together the way we did at the Spianata dell'Acquasola, when you drew me laughing. Do you remember that day?"

"Of course," Nonno said, his face softening. "Of course. Do you still have that drawing, too?"

Gram shook her head. "I'm sorry, I don't," she said.

He put his hand on her cheek. "I'll draw you a new one," he said. "Please don't let what Giorgio just said hurt you. It doesn't matter what he thinks."

It looked like Gram was going to respond, but before she could, Nonno turned to Cass and Luca. "Would you mind helping Giovanna to the car? We'll drive down to the calpestamento now."

Luca nodded. "Happy to," he said.

"Are you sure this is safe?" Fabrizio asked when Nonno started climbing up the staircase into the barrel of grapes.

"Giovanna?" Nonno asked.

"Let's try it," she said.

So Fabrizio helped them both into the barrel and took a few pictures as they held on to each other, mashing the grapes beneath their feet, while Luca caught what was coming out of the spigot in a big bucket.

"I think that's enough," Gram said after a few minutes. "Have we made wine?"

Nonno laughed. "Not quite, but the children can finish it for us."

Fabrizio helped them out again, while Cass and Luca took off their shoes and wiped their feet with a damp cloth that was next to the barrel.

"Ready for another go?" Luca asked as he started climbing up.

"Always," Cass said, climbing up behind him.

"I got the bucket," Fabrizio called to them, and Cass and Luca started mashing, the grapes between their toes.

"How long does Moscato Passito take until it's ready to bottle?" Cass heard Gram ask Nonno. She listened for the reply.

"At least three years," Nonno answered.

Gram was quiet. Cass felt Luca's feet slow. He'd heard the conversation, too.

"What are you thinking about?" Nonno asked Gram.

"That I might not be here in three years," she answered. "Maybe not even one."

Cass tried to wipe her tears away, but a few of them dripped off her hand and into the must.

Somehow it seemed right that this barrel of wine would be flavored by tears.

Chapter 61

MILAN, ITALY
Now

"Who was that?" Cass asked when Luca hung up the phone. She was leaning close to the bathroom mirror, applying a second layer of mascara.

"My mother," he answered. "She's getting on a flight tonight. She thinks Nonno will listen to her, even if he won't listen to Giorgio."

The two of them were in the middle of getting ready for the show's opening, but his family was in full-blown crisis mode, trying to stop Nonno from marrying Gram.

"Can you explain again why this is such a big deal?" Cass asked.

Her dad and uncle were upset that Gram wanted to spend the last chapter of her life in Italy, away from them, but they weren't actively trying to stop things.

"Italian inheritance laws are different than in the U.S. There's a quota, and in this particular scenario, the wife is entitled to twenty-five percent of her husband's estate."

"Can't your grandfather write a will that says otherwise?" Cass asked. "My grandmother said she doesn't care about the money."

"The twenty-five percent is what she's entitled to with a will. Without one, it's thirty-three percent." Luca shook his head. "I don't see why they can't just spend this part of their lives together without getting married."

Cass picked up her tube of red lipstick. "They could," she said. "But that's not what they want." She applied it and turned to Luca. "Don't you think they should be able to do what they want in their nineties? Haven't they waited long enough?"

Luca sighed. "Is my shirt okay?"

Cass turned to look at him. She wanted to finish this conversation with him, but he had clearly decided he was done talking about their grandparents. And she understood—it was his big night professionally; he wanted to focus on that. So she looked at his outfit. He was wearing black tailored pants, a gray button-down shirt with the top two buttons undone, and a black leather blazer. She put two fingers in her mouth and wolf-whistled, like her brothers taught her when she was a kid, and then wiped the lipstick off her fingers with a tissue.

He smiled. "So it's good tucked in?"

Cass nodded. "Definitely. Did you bring a belt?"

Luca rummaged through his suitcase and held up three of them. "The thin black one?" he asked.

Cass nodded again.

"Good thing I have a fiancée who works in fashion," Luca said. "I'm so nervous tonight, I'd probably make some horrible clothing faux pas if you weren't here to stop me."

Cass walked over and gave him a long hug. "I'd kiss you, too, but I don't want the art critics to mention the lipstick on your lips when they talk about the show's opening. It's going to be great, though. I promise. Everyone who's seen your paintings loves them. Mauro said he already has interested buyers. There's no need to be nervous: you're Luca Bartolomei, world-renowned artist and generally phenomenal human."

He wrapped his arms around her and kissed the top of her head. "Thank you, stellina," he said. "I needed that."

Zio Giorgio and his wife, Zia Vanessa, both came to the show, along with Nonno and Gram, and a ton of other people that Cass didn't know. There was a bench near the wall where the Jupiter and Juno painting hung, and Nonno and Gram sat there soon after they arrived. Cass brought them some wine—from the Della Rosa d'Alba vineyards, of course—and a plate of olives, cheese, and bread.

Cass could have joined them, but she wanted to look at the art again, particularly the piece Luca had created of Fortuna, the baby he imagined was their future child. Luca's father had told them a story a few months ago about a great-great-grandmother of his who was a masca, a kind of shaman from Paroldo, a tiny town between Turin and Genoa. She had the power to cure illnesses, like the other masche. Cass wondered if some of that kind of black magic could have passed down to Luca, if he could have actually painted the future, their future.

She was contemplating this when an art critic found her and asked her if she was Venus.

"I am," she answered, but pointed the critic toward Nonno and Gram. "That's Jupiter and Juno," she said. "If you want to hear a wonderful story, ask them about what they realized when they came to sit for the painting."

The critic walked over, and Cass saw her join them on the bench. The three of them started talking.

Then Zia Vanessa came over to Cass and, with an eye on the older couple, said, "Since they're occupied right now, can we talk about this?"

"About . . . ?" Cass asked.

"About their marriage. It's clear your grandmother isn't well, and she should be back home with her family. I know Nonno loves her, but your parents must agree that this is silly."

Cass was taken aback, but at least with this argument, she did understand what Vanessa was saying. Still, she would defend her grandmother to the end.

"Is it ideal?" Cass said. "No. Would my father prefer she be home with them? Yes. But as my grandmother has reminded my father numerous times, there are some decisions that are hers alone to make. And if she wants to spend the rest of her life here, with Nonno, that's her choice, in the same way that it's his."

"Venus?" The art critic had come back.

"It's Cassandra," Cass said, turning to her. "Yes?"

"They told me to ask you to find someone in America who can take a photograph of the painting he did of her in the 1940s. I want to run a small feature on them within the larger review of this show."

Cass nodded. "I'm sure I can make that happen. Where should I send it?"

By the time Cass had exchanged information with the reviewer, Zia Vanessa had been pulled into a different conversation. Cass wondered if she'd come over on her own accord or at the request of Giorgio and Marina, as the family's least intimidating messenger, to try to convert Cass to their side.

She searched the room for Luca and found him leaning against the corner with a glass of wine in his hand, taking it all in. Seeing him standing like that made her so proud, so happy that he seemed happy.

As she went to join him, she realized that whatever happened with their grandparents would affect their families' feelings about each other forever. Would a marriage between Gram and Nonno put Cass's future with Luca in jeopardy, too?

It reminded her of a marketing campaign she once created where they showed how one small gift of a new sweater rippled out and out and out and had a huge effect on an entire community of people. Cass thought back to her moment on the roof of the Duomo with Luca.

Hail Mary, full of grace, she prayed, *please help me through this.*

Chapter 62

SERRALUNGA D'ALBA, ITALY
Now

At the end of the opening, Nonno asked Luca and Cass if they wanted to stay at the Villa Della Rosa over the weekend. Cass could see that Luca was on the fence, and she said, "We can check out the chapel, like you wanted."

Luca nodded. "Okay," he said.

They returned to the Villa Della Rosa that Friday afternoon. Gram was sitting out in the garden and welcomed them when they arrived. "I'm so glad you and Luca are here, Cassandra. Poor Vincenzo has had Giorgio and Marina both talking at him all morning."

Cass knew what Gram meant. Luca's uncle and mother had been calling Luca, too, giving updates. And then Alessandra had called. And Fabrizio, who had already spoken to his sister, Serena, and wanted to relay her thoughts as well. Cass couldn't believe how much energy Luca's family was spending on trying to stop Nonno from marrying Gram.

Cass crouched down to her grandmother's level as Luca went to bring their bags into the house. "Are you and Nonno sure you want to go through with this?" she asked. "Their family seems to be in a bit of turmoil."

Gram sighed. "I told Vincenzo I was fine either way," she said. "My joy is in being with him again. But Vincenzo insists. And the more they push against him, the more he's digging in. I think he feels a bit like he took his inheritance and his wife's inheritance and grew it all into something so much larger, so he gets to decide what he wants to do or not do with it now. He made his sacrifices for his family, and now he wants to choose for himself."

Cass understood why someone might feel that way. "Where's Nonno?" she asked, changing the subject.

"Inside," Gram said, "talking to Agnese about dinner. It's nice to have someone cook our meals, particularly at our age. Look what Vincenzo gave me last night."

She held up her arm and on her wrist was a stunning gold filigreed bracelet set with diamonds and emeralds. "It belonged to the wife of the very first count," she said. "It was a piece of his family's jewelry that Vincenzo lent me for an evening in 1946. He said he had never found himself able to give it to Isabella, that it always reminded him of me. Isn't it beautiful?"

"It is," Cass said, so glad that Nonno was able to make her grandmother smile like that. She couldn't imagine what it must be like for Gram to be living with one foot in her memories, watching her past and her future collide.

"Vincenzo wants to get married next weekend," she said. "In his family's chapel. You know I had imagined what that would be like when I was in my early twenties. If someone had told me then that it would take seventy years for that to happen, I would never have believed it."

Cass wondered what would happen in her life if she lived to her nineties and if her current self would be equally mind-blown.

"What about Dad and Uncle Freddy?" Cass asked. "Won't they want to see you get married?"

Gram smiled. "Vincenzo offered to fly them over, but it's such short notice. They can come for Christmas. And anyway, we don't really need an audience; we're doing this for ourselves. Vincenzo says it's to make things right, but it feels more to me like making things whole, like when you bring the fabric together to make a skirt and sew the seam up the back. This feels like my seam, like my life getting completed."

It was a beautiful image, the long line of a life coming together. It made it seem like nothing really ended, it could circle back over and over again. Maybe life wasn't a line, but a series of loops and spirals, where a year abroad in Italy during college turned into marrying an Italian man, where a prayer on the roof of the Duomo kept coming back, again and again.

"I'm glad it feels that way," Cass said. "It must bring you peace."

Gram nodded. "It does, in a way," she said. "It makes me feel like I was meant to live the life I've lived. And so was Vincenzo. He and I had such a lovely conversation last night over dinner. We were talking about dreams that we had fulfilled and those we hadn't, and I told him that I wished I could sew a dress that encapsulated my life, that would show all its layers to everyone I loved."

This was such an interesting idea. "What would it look like?" she asked her grandmother. "The dress of your life."

Gram smiled. "Well," she said, "it would be made of cotton. The fabric is easy and versatile. And it would have tiers—each layer of skirt would be slightly shorter than the one below it, and each layer would represent places and people I've cared about. There would be pockets to show the secrets I've kept. And a belt around the waist to show how I always held things together, no matter what was going on—when your pop lost the restaurant, when your uncle got divorced, when Faustina got sick."

Cass could see this dress. It was beautiful and elegant and unique and strong, just like Gram.

"What about the top?" Cass asked.

Gram blushed. "I joked with Vincenzo that it would be low-cut, because I've always liked feeling a little bit sexy."

Cass hadn't been expecting that and let out a laugh in surprise. "I love it," she said. "You should make it."

Gram shook her head. "It's too much work for me at this point. It would be more complicated than anything else I've ever made. I can see it in my mind's eye. That's enough."

Nonno and Luca walked out from the house.

"Agnese's cooking smells amazing," Luca said as he crossed the garden, bending to give Gram kisses on both her cheeks.

Nonno came a little more slowly, leaning on his cane. "Dinner is black truffle risotto with sausage," he told everyone.

"That sounds fantastic," Gram said.

"Absolutely fantastic," Cass echoed. She remembered Agnese's cooking from the last few times she'd been to the Villa Della Rosa and remembered it being better than most restaurants she'd been to.

Nonno sat down on the stone bench next to Gram. She leaned into him so naturally it looked like they'd been together forever.

Then Nonno patted his pocket, which was buzzing. "If it's Giorgio again . . ."

"You don't have to answer it," Gram said to him. "You can talk to him later."

"I should just get it over with," Nonno said. He fumbled in his pocket for the phone, but it stopped buzzing by the time he got it. "It wasn't Giorgio," he said. "But they left a message."

He pressed the button on his phone and held it to his ear. As he listened, his face got angrier and angrier. When he put the phone down, he looked furious.

"What is it?" Gram asked.

Nonno jammed the phone into his jacket pocket. "Giorgio must've gotten to Father Vitale. He said he has been praying on it and that he thinks we should go through a series of Pre-Cana conversations before we marry, that he's not comfortable marrying us next weekend. My son is . . ." He shook his head.

"I bet it was my mom's idea," Luca whispered to Cass.

Cass closed her eyes for a moment. Then she opened them and saw the look of sadness on her grandmother's face. The anger on Nonno's.

It just seemed wrong that the two of them had to fight his family on top of everything else they'd been through. She had to talk to Luca. They had to try to fix this. Or at least help Nonno and Gram find a way around it.

Chapter 63

Gram, Nonno, Cass, and Luca were all in the kitchen that afternoon, sitting at the large, tiled counter, drinking wine.

"Do you know the first thing my sister told me about Vincenzo?" Gram asked Cass and Luca.

They both shook their heads.

"Did you ever tell me this?" Vincenzo asked.

"No," Gram said. "But now that time has passed, it seems okay to share."

"What was it, Gram?" Cass asked.

"She said Vincenzo's father was a fascist—and then later she said he threw parties for Italian soldiers, even after they allied themselves with the Nazis." She turned to Nonno. "Is it true? I always wondered."

"It's true," he said, running his finger around the rim of his wineglass. "The king backed the fascists, my father backed the king. And then afterward, after my brother died in combat, my father kept supporting the Italian army. Then, when the Germans occupied Italy, when they were in charge . . . well, my father always tried to stay on the good side of whoever was in power. I'm not saying it was the right choice, and it's not the choice I would have made, but it was his choice."

Gram reached toward him, and he held her hand. "One night," she said, looking into Vincenzo's eyes, "after I was married to my husband Domenico, I told him how I regretted my actions during the war. How I regretted not doing more, like my sister did. I thought about what you and I had said, about our guilt and our sorrow during that time. He was a good man, my Nico. After I told him that, he started making a contribution, every year, to help people who had survived the camps, who were displaced after the war and needed new homes. And then, as years went on, it went to the survivors of other wars. Of course, it didn't change the past, but I hoped it helped the future."

Cass hadn't known that about her grandfather. She hadn't known that about her grandmother either, about how she felt during World War II. She never talked about it.

"My father did something similar," Nonno said. "He gave money to help rebuild one of the synagogues that was destroyed in Livorno. He never said it out loud, but I could tell he felt he was on the wrong side of history then. Everyone who was alive during the war has to grapple with the same question—what did you do then? And what can you do now?"

"If I inherit any of your estate," she said, rubbing her thumb against his hand, "I'll donate the money to refugees."

Vincenzo lifted her hand to his lips and kissed it. "I'll do that anyway," he said. "The last twenty-five percent of my estate, that's where it will go. Fifty percent to Giorgio and Marina, twenty-five percent to you—and then the last twenty-five percent, the disposable quota, I'll donate."

Cass looked up at Luca. He downed his glass of wine and reached for the bottle to pour another one. She imagined that this new revelation would not go over well with his family either.

Chapter 64

One of the things that struck Cass every time she and Luca slept in the villa was how everything seemed to be a family heirloom. They were sleeping in a hand-carved bed that had images of the Garden of Eden on it, complete with Adam and Eve with fig leaves covering the parts of their bodies that the church wouldn't want people to see.

"Adamo ed Eva," Luca said as he sat on the bed wearing boxer briefs and a T-shirt. He ran his fingers over the carving.

Cass watched his eyes, the set of his mouth, and something passed across his face. "You've come up with your next show," she said.

He looked at her for a moment and then laughed. "You know me too well." He scooted himself closer to her. "I want to do what I did for the Roman gods and goddesses, but with biblical stories. Adam and Eve, Mary Magdalene washing Jesus's feet, Noah's ark . . . there are so many. What would those stories look like today?"

Cass gave Luca a hug. "I love it," she said. "I bet Mauro will, too."

Luca leaned back against a pillow. "There's something about Italy," he said. "I come here and all of a sudden . . ." He mimed an explosion with his hands. "I came up with the idea for the last show when I was showing you Pompeii."

"I know," Cass said. "Maybe I *should* ask Sam about launching Daisy Lane in Italy. Maybe we should move here for a while."

Luca looked at her, as if he were trying to read her expression and not completely succeeding. "Are you serious about this? If you want it, we should do it."

Cass rummaged through her toiletries bag on her nightstand. "I don't know," she said. "It's a big decision."

"Like our wedding," he said.

"Right," Cass told him. "Like our wedding."

He shifted on the bed so he was looking right at her. "Is disappointing your parents the only thing holding you back from getting married in Italy?"

Cass nodded. It was. She loved Italy. She loved Nonno and his house. She loved that Gram was here now, too. She just kept thinking about her parents, about their friends, about all the money they'd saved. When Luca didn't respond right away, she said, "I'm going to brush my teeth."

The bedroom they were in had a sitting room in front of it, and beyond that was a hallway with a bathroom. There was a balcony by their bedroom window, too, which led to a window in the hallway. Luca told her that when he was a kid, he always asked to sleep in this room so he could walk out onto the balcony at night and wait there until Alessandra went to get ready for bed in the bathroom, and then he would pop into the hallway to scare her.

He did it once to Cass, the first time they stayed at the villa, and she'd been so surprised she squeezed the toothpaste tube in her hand hard enough that the toothpaste hit the ceiling.

"Be on the lookout for ghosts," Luca said after another moment, seeming to agree that the conversation about their future could be shelved for now.

Cass dropped a kiss on his forehead as she headed out the bedroom door, knowing at some point they would have to figure all of this out. And they'd have to talk more about their grandparents' marriage, too.

Just as Cass spit her toothpaste into the sink, her cell phone pinged. It was a text from her brother Nick, who had taken a few photos of the painting hanging in Gram's apartment.

Thank you, she wrote with one thumb while holding her toothbrush in the other hand.

Is everything ok over there? he asked. Dad is worried.

Cass sent back a thumbs-up, and then wrote Luca's grandfather treats Gram like a queen. His family is not happy about it, but I'm assuming they'll get over it.

At least she hoped they would . . .

Nick sent her a thumbs-up back. And then: Let us know if you need us, sis. Elephant shoes.

Cass sent back an emoji of an elephant and a pair of shoes. She remembered how he had taped the pictures she drew for him of elephants wearing shoes to his closet door, even though he was in high school when she was eight. She remembered how he'd found her an elephant charm to put on her keychain when she moved out to go to college. "So you always remember I've got your back," he said.

Her mom often told the story that when she was pregnant with Cass, Nick and Chris got into a fistfight because Chris wanted a little brother and Nick wanted a little sister. He had always been there for her. Even now, from across the Atlantic. And she loved him so much for it.

When she got back to the bedroom, Luca left to brush his teeth, and she forwarded the photo to the art critic. She got a quick response: Thank you for this! I mentioned the story to my editor, and he asked if I could send a photographer to watch them get married. It's supposed to be next weekend, yes? He thought it would be fun to run a feature on them. A human-interest piece, if they're okay with that.

She'd talk to Gram and Nonno tomorrow about how they wanted her to respond.

Luca came back into the room.

"Ready for bed?" he asked, lifting the quilt and sliding in.

"I want to be there for Gram and Nonno when they get married," she said. She'd been thinking about how Luca wanted to avoid the conversation the night of the gallery opening and hadn't brought it up again. How she knew that meant he didn't want to support their grandparents in this. How Nick's response felt so different. She was seeing a new side of Luca, one where money and family loyalty might outweigh love, and it was making her question him. Question whether he'd always be there for her.

Luca laid his head back on the pillow. "Please don't get involved," he said. "Let them do what they want to do, but please don't take sides."

Cass sat up straighter. "They need our support. When you were a kid and you wanted to study art, your grandfather helped you. It was because he told your mom it was okay that she didn't pressure you into joining the family business. And how many times did my grandmother help me when I was younger? Over and over and over. Now it's our turn to be there for them."

Luca shook his head. "Don't do it, Cass."

"Why aren't you standing up for them?" Cass asked, rustling the sheets as she moved.

Luca took a deep breath. "Maybe I agree with my family that them getting married at this age isn't necessary. That there are larger things to think about. That sometimes just wanting something doesn't make it right."

Cass sighed. "Of course. If you want to do something illegal or that will hurt someone else, that doesn't make it right. But their marriage will make them happy and it won't hurt anyone."

Luca rolled over. "It will hurt my family," he said. And then he turned the light off on his side of the bed.

Clearly, he was ending this conversation. Again. And it worried Cass. There were more and more of those these days. More and more conversations they didn't finish because they weren't quite on the same page and didn't know how to talk through that difference. Cass knew they had to figure out another way, because they were going to disagree throughout their life, throughout their marriage, and if they couldn't talk things through now, things would only get harder later.

Chapter 65

SERRALUNGA D'ALBA, ITALY
Now

The next morning Luca went back to Milan to spend some time with Mauro and find a quiet space to start sketches for his new show. At least that was what he said to Nonno and Gram, but he told Cass he was upset that she was supporting Gram and Nonno getting married, and that he didn't want to go against his family and be a part of this. She could stay if she wanted, but he was going back to Milan.

"I don't understand how we see this so differently," she said to him. It was disconcerting. At first it made her feel unsure of her decision, but then it made her feel even more unsure of his—and of him.

"Maybe we should talk some more before you go?" she said as she walked him to the car.

"Talk about what?" he said as he threw his bag in the back seat. "I know how you feel, and you know how I feel. When this is all over, we'll talk."

Cass had been thinking about what her grandmother had told her, that Vincenzo didn't propose to her when they'd first met because of his family. "I can't believe your family's opinion of my grandmother hasn't changed."

Luca looked at her as if he hadn't thought about that, as if he *would* think about that. "I'll see you in Milano next week?" he said.

Cass nodded. She walked back to the villa with dread in her stomach, but she couldn't imagine that her supporting their grandparents' love would be so trying to theirs.

That afternoon, after Nonno made a phone call to a priest he knew in Genoa who agreed to marry them, Cass took Gram shopping for a new dress, and she made a post-wedding reservation at Osteria da Gemma, the Michelin-starred restaurant in Barolo that was run by an incredible older woman who Nonno had been friendly with for years. They were known for bringing out course upon course for lunch—it took Cass and Luca three hours to finish the last time they were there. And they were so full they ended up skipping dinner that night.

Cass asked Gram if she wanted to invite her cousins' children and grandchildren from Saluzzo to the wedding, but Gram said no. "I would love to see them, but it feels funny to have Ilaria and Guido's children there when my own sons won't be."

Cass nodded.

"But there is one thing I'd like to do before I get married," Gram said to Cass. "Will you take me to see my parents' graves? In Genoa?"

"Of course!" Cass said.

The next day, Agnese's husband Danilo drove them in one of Vincenzo's cars and told them he'd wait in the city until they were ready to go home.

Cass pushed Gram in a wheelchair down a manicured path until they reached the proper plot. There were two headstones next to each other, dated thirty-four years apart.

"Didn't your father live in Saluzzo when he died?" Cass asked Gram.

She nodded. "He did," she said, "but he couldn't bear leaving my mother alone, so when she was buried, he asked for the plot next to her, too, saving it for whenever he needed it."

"He never remarried?" Cass asked, bending down to clean some fallen leaves from the plots.

"Never," Gram said. "He said he never found anyone else who he loved enough to spend his days with."

"We love hard in our family," Cass said, standing up and brushing her hands against her jeans. She was thinking about Luca. Thinking about how much she loved him, and simultaneously how disappointed she was in his response to all of this.

Gram sighed. "Can you push me a little closer?" she asked.

Cass obliged.

"Mamma," Gram said softly, "Papà, I just wanted you to know that I'm home. I've been away much longer than I ever thought, but my heart brought me back. I still feel guilty that I left you, Papà. I know you said it was okay, but I've carried that pain with me for years. Even with all the time and distance between us, I still miss you both. And Faustina. I often pick up the phone to call her, to tell her a funny story or share a worry or a fear, and then remember she's gone. It's been nearly twenty years now. Nearly twenty years that I'm the only one of us left. I hope the three of you are together, and that you're waiting for me. It would be so wonderful to see you again one day. I wish . . . I wish so much that you were here." Her breath started to shake, and Gram stopped talking.

Cass bent down to hug her grandmother, feeling Gram's tears mingling with hers as they pressed their cheeks together.

Gram took a deep breath. "Thank you for taking me here today," she said.

"Of course," Cass said, still not letting go. "Of course."

She refused to think about the time when the only way she'd be able to talk to her grandmother would be standing in a graveyard like this one, hoping her words were carried by the wind up to heaven.

Chapter 66

SERRALUNGA D'ALBA, ITALY

Now

"Let's talk about your wedding, too," Gram said the next morning, in the parlor at the Villa Della Rosa.

Cass had decided that after Nonno and Gram got married on Friday, she would go back to Milan, to Luca, and tell him they had to talk—really talk. It was the first time in their relationship she felt deeply disappointed in him, in who he was. And the way they would navigate this would mean a lot for their future. She didn't want to think about their wedding right now.

"Let's get yours taken care of first," she said.

"Well, how about we just talk about your dress, then?" Gram said. She'd been tired, so they were home, sitting in the parlor with Nonno. He was reading the newspaper while the two women were talking.

Cass smiled. "Okay," she said. "That's easy. I want it to look just like yours, just like the one you wore when you and Pop got married."

"You do?" Gram said.

Cass nodded. "I remember looking at that picture of you and Pop when I was little, the one that was framed on your mantelpiece, and thinking that you looked like a movie star. I always dreamed I would wear a dress like yours when I got married."

Gram reached over to Cass and squeezed her hand.

"I wish I could sew it for you," Gram said, "but I don't think I have another wedding dress in me. I can draw you a pattern, though, how about that?"

Nonno put down his newspaper. "Can I watch?" he asked.

"Of course, my love," Gram told him.

He sat down on her other side while Cass went to get a pencil and paper from Nonno's study.

Gram started sketching the full skirt, the lace trim. "Are you sure you want a V-neck top?" she said to Cass. "I hardly ever see you wear those."

It was true, Cass preferred a square neckline. She liked how it showed off her collarbones. "What do you think I'd look best in?" Cass asked.

Gram assessed her and then drew a boat neck on the top of the dress. She added in the three-quarter sleeves.

"Any other additions you'd like?" she asked.

Cass looked at the drawing of the dress, getting into the spirit. "Hmm," she said. "How about pockets?" Gram drew them in, little openings on either side of the full skirt. "And buttons up the back?"

"Perfect," Gram said, handing her the paper. "Now write down your measurements, and then leave this with me. I'll create something for you to bring to any seamstress you'd like."

Cass wrote down her bust size, her waist, her hips, and the measurement from the hollow of her throat to the floor. She'd been around designers often enough that she knew what to provide for a gown.

"You know," she said, "I'm only one of three women to get to wear a Giovanna Ferrero original to my wedding."

Gram laughed. "It's wonderful to be Giovanna again. I shouldn't have listened when Betto's uncle suggested I change my name to something that sounded more American." She turned to Nonno. "Yet another gift you've given me, Vincenzo."

Cass went into town to talk to the jeweler about wedding rings—asking him to engrave Gram's name and their wedding date inside Nonno's ring, and Nonno's name along with the date inside Gram's. Cass loved the Italian custom of having your beloved's name pressed next to your skin. She had planned to pick out these kinds of rings with Luca, but they had to have a wedding date before they could engrave it on a ring. He'd texted a few times since he went to Milan—to say that he found a great studio space, that he missed her, that he was thinking about going back to the roof of the Duomo. She hated that he wasn't here with her, here with their grandparents.

When Cass got back, she found Gram asleep on the couch and Nonno sketching her.

"Thank you for staying with us, Cassandra," Nonno said, looking up when she walked into the room. "It means a lot to your grandmother. And to me."

"I would do pretty much anything to see my grandmother happy," Cass answered.

"Me too, Cassandra," he said. "Me too."

Chapter 67

SERRALUNGA D'ALBA, ITALY
Now

That night, Cass was awoken by ambulance sirens that got louder and louder, closer and closer until she realized they were coming toward the Villa Della Rosa. She rushed out of her bed to the bedroom where her grandmother was sleeping—the room was connected to Vincenzo's by a doorway, which the two of them had been leaving open. Vincenzo was with her, a sweater over his pajamas and loafers on his feet.

"What happened?" Cassandra asked.

Her grandmother was breathing heavily. Cass propped another pillow behind her back, which seemed to help a little.

"I woke in the night and came to check on Giovanna," Nonno said. "And I heard how she was gasping for air. I woke her and she still was having trouble breathing, so I called the ambulance. I didn't want to risk anything, to risk losing her."

Cassandra put one arm around Nonno and then turned to her grandmother. "How are you feeling now?" she asked, noticing that Gram's face was pale.

"A bit better," she said between breaths. "I'm sure the doctors will be able to help."

The paramedics rang the doorbell and Cass flew down the stairs to let them in. They put an oxygen mask on Gram and helped her onto a stretcher.

"Would you like to ride with your wife?" one of the paramedics asked Nonno.

"Yes," he said. "But she's my fiancée."

The paramedic cocked his head for a moment, then nodded as Nonno picked up his cane and followed them out the bedroom door.

"I'll meet you at the hospital," Cass said.

As she threw a sweatshirt on over her T-shirt and pajama pants, Cass texted Luca. Gram is going to the hospital, she wrote. She's having trouble breathing.

The doctor who admitted Gram put her on oxygen and the nurse made sure the head of her bed was angled up to make breathing easier. After the flurry of attention, Gram fell asleep to the steady beeping of monitors. Nonno fell asleep in a chair at her bedside, his hand still on hers. Cass watched them for a long time, wondering what she should do now, wishing Luca were here with her, wishing Nick were here with her, wishing she hadn't googled *heart failure* and seen Gram's symptoms.

"Salve, Regina," Cass prayed, "Mater misericordiæ, vita, dulcedo, et spes nostra, salve. Ad te clamamus exsules filii Hevæ, ad te suspiramus, gementes et flentes in hac lacrimarum valle. Eia, ergo, advocata nostra, illos tuos misericordes oculos ad nos converte . . ." *Hail, holy Queen, Mother of Mercy, our life, our sweetness, and our hope. To thee do we cry, poor banished children of Eve; to thee do we send up our sighs, mourning and weeping in this valley of tears. Turn then, most gracious Advocate, thine eyes of mercy toward us.*

She prayed it over, and over, and over again until she, too, fell asleep.

Chapter 68

OSPEDALE DI ALBA, ITALY
Now

When Cass woke up the next morning, Gram and Nonno were already awake, already talking softly to each other. They were holding hands, and Cass wondered for a moment if they'd ever let go, or if they'd slept that way and woke that way, skin pressed to skin.

"Good morning," Cass said to them as she stretched, her back in knots from the hours folded into the hospital chair.

Her grandmother smiled at her and squeezed Nonno's hand. "Two of my favorite people here with me," she said softly.

"Your color looks a little better," Cass said to her. There was a slight pink to her cheeks and lips that hadn't been there the night before.

"I'm glad," Gram said, her voice still weak. "Or I would have asked you to go home for my rouge and lipstick."

Cass smiled. Things couldn't be as bad as she'd imagined last night if her grandmother was making jokes. She looked at her watch. It was still the middle of the night in New York. She knew she had to call her father, but the phone call could wait a few hours it seemed.

"I didn't sleep through the doctor, did I?" Cass asked.

Nonno shook his head. "The nurse said the doctor would be in soon. In the meantime, they brought this for breakfast."

Cass looked at the two packs of rusks, marmalade, and tea. "How about if I go find us some pastries?" she said.

"That would be lovely," Gram answered.

Cass came back with panini al cioccolato for all three of them and espresso for her and Nonno. She wasn't sure if Gram was allowed any. She walked in with a smile on her face, but that quickly changed when she saw Gram and Nonno both in tears.

"What happened?" she said.

Gram wiped her eyes first. "The doctor was in," she said. "My heart is failing, Cassandra. I don't have much longer."

Cass felt her own heart squeeze, tears rushing to her eyes. It couldn't be. It wasn't fair. There was so much for Gram to live for now. "How much longer *do* you have?"

"Days," Gram said. "Maybe weeks. Probably not months."

Cass bit her lip to keep from crying, but tears fell anyway. Her grandmother wouldn't be there to see her get married. Wouldn't be there to meet her future children. Wouldn't be there to talk to, or cook with . . .

"Oh, Gram," she said, reaching for her grandmother's hand and then wrapping her in a hug. She was trying to memorize the feeling of her grandmother's cheek against hers, the pressure of her arms around her back. "I love you so much," she said.

"I love you, too," Gram whispered to her. "Always have, always will."

Cass hugged her grandmother harder, hugged her for every time she would want to in the future and wouldn't be able to. Then she heard Nonno clear his throat.

"Giovanna," he said. "Let's get married today."

Cass loosened her hold on her grandmother, and Gram turned to look at Nonno. "Today?" she said.

"Today," he answered.

"But I'm dying," she said.

"We're all dying," he told her, reaching for her hand. "Every single one of us. From the minute we're born, we're dying. Please, I've been dreaming this dream for decades. Let me be your husband, Giovanna. Even if it's only for a moment, I want you to be my wife."

Gram held his one hand in both of hers. Tears were in his eyes.

"I want that, too," she whispered.

Chapter 69

OSPEDALE DI ALBA, ITALY

Now

Cass called her father to let him know what was going on. And then she drove back to Villa Della Rosa to get a bottle of wine and the family Bible, and she called the jeweler to see if he could rush the rings—and change the date. Once he heard what was happening, he was happy to do so. Before she headed back, she texted Luca that their grandparents were going to get married in the hospital. And then added a line from the reading she was going to give at the wedding, one that Gram and Nonno had chosen just yesterday: *Rimani nel mio amore. Remain in my love.* She hoped he would understand what she meant: both that love wasn't for people to pass judgment on, only God, and that she wanted their love to remain strong, too.

Back at the hospital, Nonno had found the hospital priest. Marriages weren't typically one of the services Father Francesco provided at the hospital, except in a case of *matrimonio in pericolo di vita*—marriage when life was in danger. After Nonno explained the situation, Father

Francesco agreed that Nonno and Gram's marriage fell into that category. They needed two witnesses, so Nonno asked one of the nurses to join them. Once Cass returned, they all sat in her grandmother's hospital room.

"Is anyone else coming?" Father Francesco asked.

Nonno shook his head.

Cass had been holding out hope that Luca would show up. But he still wasn't there—and hadn't responded to her text.

The priest cleared his throat. "Obviously, we're not having a full nuptial mass, but I believe your granddaughter is going to do a reading from John?"

Gram nodded, and Cass opened the Della Rosa family Bible. She turned to John 15:9 and read:

> *"As the Father loves me, so I also love you.*
> *Remain in my love.*
> *If you keep my commandments, you will remain in my love,*
> *just as I have kept my Father's commandments*
> *and remain in his love.*
> *I have told you this so that my joy may be in you*
> *and your joy may be complete.*
> *This is my commandment: love one another as I love you."*

Cass let out a breath. She wasn't used to reading aloud in Italian.

"Beautiful," Nonno said.

The priest nodded and then began the vows.

Cass could see the tears in Nonno's and Gram's eyes and felt them forming in her own. It just seemed so unfair, so colossally unfair that the two of them had found each other now, just to lose each other again. She tried to hold her tears back, but she couldn't. She cried for Gram, for Nonno, for all they had missed, all they would miss. And all that she would, too. And she cried for Luca, for the fact that he wasn't here, that her own heart felt bruised and broken, too.

Then she heard the door open and footsteps behind her. Cass turned to see Luca walking toward her. Her heart leapt, and she moved toward him. He put a finger to his lips and then slid his arm around her.

"You came," she said quietly, laying her head on his chest.

"I was already on the way when I got your text," he whispered softly into her hair. "When I woke up this morning to your text about Gram, it clarified a lot for me . . . I knew I was wrong. I should have been here with you. With them. Love and devotion are commanded by God. We shouldn't get in the way." Then he leaned down and softly kissed the top of Cass's head. "We shouldn't get in our own way either."

And he held her while they watched their grandparents exchange vows on her grandmother's deathbed.

Chapter 70

Giovanna Cassandra Ferrero Fanelli Della Rosa d'Alba died the next day. Her husband, Vincenzo, was by her side. He'd held her hand until the very end and wouldn't let go after she was gone.

"I'll see you soon," he kept saying. "I'll see you soon, my love."

Chapter 71

SERRALUNGA D'ALBA, ITALY
Now

Cass and Luca walked together through the vineyards after sunset, just as the sky began to fill with stars.

Cass's parents and uncle were on their way to Italy to bury Giovanna in the cemetery on the Della Rosa property. Nonno insisted, and when Cass explained what she had witnessed these past days—Nonno's love and devotion to Gram, and hers to him—they agreed to the idea.

"How is your family doing?" Luca asked. "How are you doing?"

"It's so hard to accept," Cass said, holding his hand tightly. "But I keep reminding myself that she lived a long life, a happy life, and knew so much love and joy, even in the last moments. My pop always toasted to a hundred years. She didn't quite make it, but she was close."

"I hope we live as long as our grandparents," he said. Then he turned to look at her. "And if we do, I'll apologize for just as long for leaving for Milano, for not supporting them, and for not being here when you needed me. If you want to get married on Long Island for your parents, we can. What matters is it's us, you and me. Whatever we do, my mom will get over it. Just like she got over me being an artist. It'll all be fine once we give her another grandchild anyway."

Cass pulled herself closer to Luca, so their shoulders touched as they walked. "I'm sorry, too, for not making a choice, not taking a stand. And thank you for saying that about our wedding. But I've been thinking maybe we should get married here. This place is special to you and your family, but it's also special to me and my family now. Gram is here." Her voice caught on the last sentence, and Luca took her in his arms.

"I was thinking about Fortuna," she whispered while he was holding her. She'd been thinking a lot about the future, about that painting he'd made.

"It's a pretty name, isn't it?" Luca answered.

"Can we add Giovanna in the middle?" Cass said. "Fortuna Giovanna Bartolomei?"

"It's even more beautiful that way," Luca said.

They were both quiet for a moment. "Do you think we'll actually have a daughter one day?" Cass asked.

"I have faith," he said, "in her and in us."

Epilogue

SERRALUNGA D'ALBA, ITALY

Vincenzo sat down on the stone bench he'd put next to Giovanna's grave. He visited her every day. Talked to her about whatever was on his mind. This last week in August, it was Cassandra and Luca's wedding.

"You would have loved it," he told Giovanna. "Cassandra looked beautiful. She had the dress you designed created for her, and it fit her perfectly, just as if you'd made it yourself. And she wore the diamond and emerald bracelet I'd given you. It made it feel, to me at least, like some piece of you was there with us. I remember you said that you liked to wear red so that your mother would be able to see you from heaven. I wore a red tie this past weekend. Did you see me? I danced with Cassandra and imagined I was dancing with you. Even though you weren't there in body, you were at their wedding in spirit. Cassandra spoke about you, Luca spoke about you. And I did, too, in the toast I made. We opened up the very last bottles of the 1944 vintage in our wine cellar; perhaps your hands had dipped them in wax."

Vincenzo was quiet, remembering that day more than seven decades ago, remembering how he felt so enamored with her, and so afraid of what those feelings would mean. He couldn't believe how long ago that was now. How long ago everything seemed these days.

He'd lived nearly a century. He'd seen war. He'd seen peace. He'd seen the dissolution of the monarchy and a government that changed over and over again. He'd seen a business grow and expand until it could take care of his whole family and hundreds of employees. He saw his grandson become the artist he never was. And he saw his love, his Giovanna, come back to him, just to be taken away months later.

He was glad they had married, glad she knew he had loved her then and loved her now, loved her enough to make her his. To make himself hers.

He'd been feeling tired all day.

Vincenzo Fabrizio Della Rosa d'Alba, the man who would have been conte, placed a rose on his wife's grave. Then he sat back down. He felt the setting sun on his face, the breeze in his hair, and closed his eyes. His breathing slowed.

He saw his Giovanna's beautiful face in front of him, bathed in the most stunning golden light.

"I told you I'd see you soon," he said.

Acknowledgments

I am so grateful to so many people on both sides of the Atlantic for helping make this book happen.

The seed of this story was planted in the summer of 2019 in Italy, when Cristina Prasso, my Italian publisher, suggested that I write a family story set in Italy. Not only did she start my mind spinning, but, in the nearly final version of this manuscript, she fact-checked my Italian history, Italian culture, and Italian language, and provided insightful and thoughtful feedback on the story and characters. She is this book's fairy godmother, and it truly would not exist without her. Cristina, grazie mille volte, dal profondo del mio cuore.

On that same trip, we spent time with my husband's Italian cousins, whose stories inspired Vincenzo's and Giovanna's. Angelica and Mario took us to the stunning vineyards of the Barolo region (and Osteria da Gemma) and told us about the 1946 institutional referendum, Donatella and Giuliano hosted us in Saluzzo, Carlotta and Francesca—and their wonderful children—took us on a tour of Saluzzo and shared the history of the town and their family with us, and Carlo and Carla shared more history and gave us a tour of the beautiful abbey that has been in their family for centuries. Nicoletta, Vittoria, Marco, Alberto, Giorgio, Ludovica, Maria, Valentina, Sara, and Luca gave us a delicious taste of Milano; Paola and Antonio showed us the stunning views of Cortina and shared stories about Italy's participation in both world wars; Alessandro and Giada introduced us to the mountains outside of Genoa; and Alberto and Elisa showed us the beauty of Varazze. I feel so lucky to have married into this sprawling, phenomenal family. Grazie a tutti per condividere le vostre case ei vostri cuori con me.

And a second thank-you to Carlotta for answering my random Italian questions on WhatsApp and for putting me in touch with professors and experts who helped in my research for this book. Graziella Romeo, Pierangelo Gentile, Carlo Ellena, and Livio Berardo: Grazie per la tua generositá e tempo. Lo apprezzo molto.

On this side of the Atlantic, a massive thank-you to my agent, Miriam Altshuler, and to my editor, Tara Singh Carlson. You both know how grateful I am to be on this literary journey with you. I am so thankful for your support, your friendship, and your thoughtful and heartfelt notes that made this book the strongest it could possibly be. You are my Juno and my Minerva, goddesses of protection and wisdom. I couldn't do any of this without you.

Thank you, too, to the rest of the team at PRH, Putnam, and DeFiore for all of your hard work on behalf of me and my books. Particular thank-yous to Leigh Butler, Tom Dussel, Ashley Di Dio, Reiko Davis, Tamara Kawar, Ivan Held, Sally Kim, Alexis Welby, Ashley Hewlett, Ellie Schaffer, Katie McKee, Ashley McClay, Brennin Cummings, Samantha Bryant, Ben Lee, Kelly Gildea, Emily Mileham, Maija Baldauf, Claire Sullivan, Amy Schneider, Erin Byrne, Tiffany Estreicher, Katie Punia, Anthony Ramondo, Vi-An Nguyen, and everyone else behind the scenes in the printing, binding, audio recording, shipping, and selling of my novels.

None of my books would be what they are without my trusted

writing group, who read these pages before anyone and gave me such helpful notes: Thank you, Marianna Baer, Daphne Benedis-Grab, Anna Godbersen, Anne Heltzel, Marie Rutkoski, and Eliot Schrefer. And thank you to sommelier Ilana Kresch, who schooled me on wine; cardiologist Dr. Seth Bender, who taught me about congestive heart failure; and my grandmother, Beverly Franklin, to whom this book is dedicated, for telling me what it was like to be a teenager in the 1940s. I so appreciate the time you all took answering my questions and reading my words. Thank you, too, to Talia Benamy and Sarah Fogelman for being early readers on this one and helping me polish the final draft. And thank you to all the writers whose books and articles I used for research. I've never read so much to prepare to write a book!

Another big thank-you to everyone whose support buoyed me during the writing of this book: Amanda Kaplan, Ellen Kaplan, and Carolina Proenca for taking such wonderful care of Miss Lollipop while I wrote; the Vikings, Philomels, and Flamingos, who inspire me every day; readers, writers, and booksellers, whose messages and posts and social media interactions make me smile on a daily basis; authors who so generously offered their blurbs and their time. I am so grateful for all of these various communities that keep me afloat.

And thank you times a million to my family and friends who have always kept me anchored: my mom, Beth Santopolo; my stepdad, David Turret; my sisters, Alison May and Suzanne Foger; my stepbrothers, Dan and Jason Turret; my grandmother, Beverly Franklin; my grandfather, Larry Franklin; my aunt Ellen Franklin Silver; my in-laws, Flavia and Dan Claster; my sister-in-law, Becky Claster; and all of the phenomenal people you have all brought into my life either by marrying or creating them. Family means so much, and this book is my homage to that. My dad, John Santopolo, would have loved that

I wrote a book about Italy, so I named many of the characters after family members in his honor: Giovanna, Vincenzo, Faustina, and Luciano are all for him.

My very last thanks go to Andrew, my Mercury, the cleverest and most mischievous god on Mount Olympus, and Laura Jane, our little Fortuna. Andrew, I will always be in awe of the fact that we found each other and grateful that I get to spend my life next to you. I couldn't have hoped for a more supportive, kind, generous partner—and a great copy editor, too! And Laura Jane, you are the future, you are our future. Everything I write always will be, in part, for you.

Stars in an Italian Sky

JILL SANTOPOLO

Discussion Guide

A Conversation with Jill Santopolo

Excerpt from *Everything After* by Jill Santopolo

BOOK
ENDS

PUTNAM
—EST. 1838—

Discussion Guide

1. What aspects of Giovanna and Vincenzo's and Cass and Luca's relationships do you think are the most important? The most challenging? Which relationship do you relate to more?

2. If Luca and Cass switched places with Vincenzo and Giovanna, do you think their love stories would have gone down different paths? Why or why not?

3. Who was your favorite character in the novel, and why?

4. Discuss the ways in which class and social standing played a part in both Giovanna and Vincenzo's, and Cass and Luca's relationships. Do you think Vincenzo was right to feel the way he did about abolishing Italian nobility? What about Giovanna? Did you empathize with one perspective more than the other?

5. Have you ever dated someone your family didn't approve of? If so, how did you handle that situation?

6. What was your favorite scene in the novel, and why?

7. If you could live in New York City, or Genoa, Italy, which

would you choose, and why? Have you visited or lived in either city, and if so, what was your experience like?

8. If you were Giovanna in 1946, would you have made the same life-changing decision to listen to her sister after everything that had happened between her and Vincenzo? Why or why not?

9. Do you think Vincenzo and Giovanna ultimately made the right decision in 2019? Why or why not? If you were Cass or Luca, how would you have reacted?

10. What were your thoughts on the ending?

A Conversation with Jill Santopolo

Although you've written three novels before, this is your first foray into historical fiction. What inspired you to write *Stars in an Italian Sky*?

The seed for *Stars in an Italian Sky* was planted in the summer of 2019 when my husband and I traveled to Italy for two weeks to visit family (we both have Italian roots). One side of his mother's family is descended from nobility, and a cousin of his talked to us about the institutional referendum that happened just after WWII in which the monarchy and nobility were abolished and the country became a republic. I was fascinated by the idea of that moment, when promised power is eliminated by popular vote, and started thinking about what that would be like, particularly if a member of the nobility had fallen in love with someone who was part of the working class. And then I realized that if I wanted to write that story, I would have to write historical fiction, so I dove into the research and fell in love with the genre.

What research did you perform to paint an accurate portrait of Genoa, Italy, during the 1940s? What were you most surprised to learn in your research?

The research was a lot more work than I expected, but a lot more fun than I expected, too—I read fiction books that were set in Italy in the

1940s; I read nonfiction books and articles about Italy and the area around Genoa, in particular during and after WWII; I used the archives of Italian newspapers and magazines to see what was being discussed in the media at that time; I went to fashion blogs dedicated to the time period; I interviewed people whose family members were alive then and listened to their stories and experiences; I asked questions to my grandmother, who was alive during the 1940s; I spoke to a historian who focuses on the region and watched the videos he sent me about that time in the area around Genoa and Saluzzo; I read travel guides about Genoa; and I used Google Maps to "walk" the streets with my characters. My husband and I also drove through Genoa while we were on our honeymoon, so I had those memories of the city to use for texture. And then my Italian publisher did an in-depth fact-check for me, sending historical train schedules and making sure my cultural references were accurate. One of the things I was most surprised to learn was that women made their own makeup during and after WWII by doing things like holding candles under a china plate and using the ash that formed as eye shadow.

Are Giovanna and Vincenzo based on real people? What about Cass and Luca? Where did you draw inspiration for these characters?

None of the characters are based on real people, but I did think a lot about my family—I'm descended from Italian shoemakers on my father's side and tried to imagine what their shop would have been like. I named Giovanna after my great-grandmother, Faustina after my great-aunt, and Vincenzo after my grandfather, mostly because I thought it would be a lovely way to honor them. I dedicated this book to my grandmother, on my mother's side, and Cass's relationship with and deep love for her grandmother is based on my relationship with my phenomenal Gram.

There are so many parallels between Vincenzo and Giovanna's and Cassandra and Luca's relationships, yet they also each feel distinct in their own special way. What do you think lies at the heart of each relationship's dynamic?

These relationships were formed a bit when my husband and I talked about how his family in Italy is descended from nobility and mine is descended from shoemakers. We noted that had we been alive generations earlier and fallen in love decades before in Italy, our relationship would have been a bit of a scandal. Decades later, in Vincenzo and Giovanna's time it might have been slightly less scandalous, but not quite encouraged. But now, with our families both having immigrated to the U.S. and flourished here, there was nothing at all odd about our marriage. I was thinking a lot about that as I wrote about Giovanna and Vincenzo and Cass and Luca—how time, location, and circumstances change how the same situation is seen. As far as the heart of each relationship—I think a feeling of belonging, of feeling at home with another person is what's at the heart of both relationships, but the times each couple lives in changes how they play out.

Family is such an important part of each of these character's lives. When it comes to romantic relationships, do you think love can be enough if your family doesn't approve?

I hope that love can be enough—and that if a couple feels so deeply about each other, their families will come around. In the end, I'd hope that families would want the people they love to be happy and would recognize that, especially if the reasons they disapprove of the match are about external factors.

The connection to mythology through Luca's paintings was so fun to explore. Do you have an affinity to mythology, and if so, do you have a favorite story or character?

I do! I've always loved reading mythological stories. As far as characters, I'm partial to Minerva/Athena. I love that a woman is the embodiment of wisdom in both Roman and Greek mythology. And as far as stories, there's one I included in *Stars in an Italian Sky* that is probably my favorite—the story of Pygmalion and Galatea, where a sculptor falls in love with a sculpture of a woman he made, and Aphrodite makes her real. I love that the story is echoed in *Pinocchio* and in *The Velveteen Rabbit*, how you can love something into reality.

Who was your favorite character to write, and why?

Definitely Giovanna because I got to follow her for so long and watch her grow and change so much.

What do you want readers to take away from *Stars in an Italian Sky*?

One thing I hope readers take away from all my books is the power and importance of love in all its forms—both romantic and familial. In *Stars in an Italian Sky* in particular, I hope they also take away the idea that there are always shades of gray and that the reasons we ascribe to other people's actions may not be true. There are always stories beneath the stories.

Without giving anything away, did you always know how the story would end?

Endings are the hardest for me! In all my books, the endings I start with are never quite the endings I end with. For this book, I always knew a few facts about the ending, but I rewrote it quite substantially two or three different times to get the order of events right so that it would (hopefully!) lead to an emotional crescendo.

What's next for you?

I'm working on the very first pages of a new novel right now that, like *Stars in an Italian Sky,* involves a past and present storyline. It's focused on two sets of sisters and two sets of love stories and tons and tons of secrets.

Keep reading for an exciting excerpt from

Everything After by Jill Santopolo.

Chapter 1

As she walked down Astor Place toward her office, Emily Gold rested her hand on her abdomen, trying to figure out if it felt different. If there was something new in there, a constellation of cells that would grow as she did, would end up as a tiny person with deep brown eyes like Ezra or wavy auburn hair like her.

Emily hadn't known she wanted a baby until she met Ezra. Then the idea of creating a child with him, of having another person living in this world who had his intelligence, his compassion running through their veins—it seemed like something she would have to do, the way she had to breathe, to blink, to swallow. And once she wanted it, once she knew it had to happen, she became immediately afraid that it wouldn't. That she couldn't. The fact that they'd put it off for a couple of years didn't help—Ezra had wanted to get a promotion first, a raise, an apartment, to make sure they'd be able to give this child everything they possibly could. Now the time was right. They'd been trying for seven months—months of hope and anticipation and disappointment. And now she was late. Only by a day, but still.

Every hour made it feel more real, more possible.

"Dr. Gold."

Emily had been walking up the steps to NYU's School of Global Public Health, and turned her head as she swiped her card key through the lock on the front of the building.

"Tessa," she said to the student looking up at her. "It's good to see you. I hadn't realized you were back."

Tessa smiled. Her eyes looked tired, but the grin was genuine. "I've been meaning to come by, but there was a lot to get settled."

"How's the baby?" Emily asked her.

"Zoe," Tessa said. "She's good. Mostly sleeps through the night now, which is awesome. My mom helped out a lot over the summer—Zoe and I went to Ohio while Chris was starting his new job here. But now we're back and it's just me and him and Zo. We've made it through our first week. I found a couple of freshmen who are up for babysitting while I'm at class. So far, so good."

Emily stepped aside so her friend Priya, another psychologist at the mental health center, could walk through the door. "I'm so glad, Tessa," she said. "If you need to talk, you know I'm here. I'm glad things are going well with you and Chris."

Emily didn't trust Chris, not after the way he'd initially reacted, not after the hours Tessa had spent in her office in tears. He'd seemed self-absorbed, not understanding what a pregnancy would mean for Tessa, not fully accepting his part in it. If Emily were Tessa's friend, she would've had some choice words to say about Chris. But as her therapist, she kept her mouth shut and helped Tessa with her side of the relationship, figuring out what she needed and how to communicate that. Something had worked, because Chris had come through in the end.

Tessa smiled again. "I'm glad, too." She laughed. "And happy I ran into you. But now it's time for Statistics for Social Research."

"Oof," Emily said. "You didn't give yourself a break with that one."

Tessa shrugged. "I figure it'll help with law school."

Tessa's dream was to be a human rights lawyer. She wore socks with Ruth Bader Ginsburg's face on them and had spent half a session once telling Emily about Amal Clooney's life story. Emily had enjoyed hearing it.

Two students walked into the building and Emily recognized one of them as her nine a.m.

"I should go," Emily said. "But I'm so glad to see you. Bring Zoe by some time."

Tessa hiked up her backpack. "I will," she said before she turned away.

Emily really hoped Tessa would be okay. When she'd come to the center last year, she'd been so petrified—of being pregnant, of telling her boyfriend, of telling her parents, of what this would mean for her life and her dreams and her future. Emily had helped her through all of it. She'd even gotten permission from the clinic's director to see Tessa as a long-term case. It was why she'd taken this job. She wanted to be there for these kids, the way she wished someone had been there for her, back when she was in college—someone more than her sister, Arielle. Luckily, later she'd found Dr. West, who changed her life and changed her path. She wondered, sometimes, if Dr. West found the job as difficult as she did.

Chapter 2

Before heading into her office, Emily filled her mug with herbal tea instead of coffee, something Arielle had said was better for fertility. Though the truth was, it was irrelevant. By this point, either she was already pregnant or she wasn't. She and Ezra had been tracking her cycle since their second wedding anniversary, when they moved into their new place and he was finally ready to start trying. Tracking her cycles together with Ezra was one of the benefits of marrying a doctor—everything about the human body was up for discussion. That was his area of expertise, after all. Hers was the human mind.

She wasn't sure how much longer her mind could take the crushing loss of hope each time her period started again, each time a month passed and the only thing growing inside her was disappointment. Seven months felt like forever. She'd been imagining this child for so long. For two years and seven months, to be exact, since she'd been ready to try right away. Which made each month that she wasn't pregnant even more excruciating. But perhaps this month would be different.

Emily sat down in her office and quickly reviewed her notes for her first patient, her fingers running along the pages as if they were playing scales on a piano. So many years later, she still couldn't shake the habit. She closed her notebook and let her hand stray to her abdomen again. If there was a baby in there, its brain was only starting to develop, not actually a real brain yet. Forty to forty-three days—that was when brain activity first sparked.

Kai walked into her office and sat down on the couch, holding one of the granola bars they always put out in the reception area. Free food, both to lure college students in and to help take care of them when they weren't caring for themselves. He looked over at the aquarium.

Emily had discovered years ago that watching fish swim seemed to relax people, or maybe it was the quiet burbling of the filter. Either way, her patients seemed to like it. And it gave them something to talk about when they were working up to what was really troubling them. It gave her something to look at, too, when she wasn't sure if she'd be able to hold it together, wasn't sure if she could be the anchor they needed her to be.

She quickly glanced at the framed quote on her desk. John Wesley: "Do all the good you can, by all the means you can, in all the ways you can, in all the places you can, at all the times you can, to all the people you can, as long as ever you can."

Then she cleared everything else from her mind as she focused on her patient. She wasn't going to let him down.

When I met your father, the first thing I noticed about him was his smile.

It appeared, slow and easy, across his face when he saw me walking toward him.

We were in a folk music club in the basement of an old church, the spring of my sophomore year. He offered me his chair and a beer. I offered to share the cup of popcorn I'd snagged on my way in.

We listened to a woman with a smoky voice sing about a crystal castle she'd build in the sky.

He called me his crystal queen.

Chapter 3

After Kai left, Emily heard a knock on her office door while she was writing up notes. Three staccato raps. She knew those raps; they meant "I. Love. You." Ezra had been knocking on her door like that for the last four and a half years; it began soon after they started dating, soon after she got her job at NYU, a few months before her twenty-ninth birthday. Originally, he'd said it meant "Em-il-y," but that changed three months in. It became "I. Love. You." A love that had only grown from there.

He knocked again.

Emily opened the door, and her worries about her patients, about whether she was pregnant, disappeared when she saw his face.

"Hey, love," he said, as he stepped into her office and took her into his arms. She lifted her face up for a kiss, and he brought his lips to hers.

"You feel so good," she told him, once they stopped kissing, when she leaned her head against his shoulder.

He smelled faintly of soap and cologne. She brought her finger up to his name, embroidered on the left side of his button-down, right above his heart, the letters that spelled *Dr. Ezra Gold*. A gift from his doctor parents when he completed residency, and a favorite of his.

"What happened?" she asked.

He taught one class a week in bioethics during NYU's spring semester, and otherwise practiced medicine at NYU's children's hospital, a mile and a half away, specializing in pediatric blood cancers. He and Emily had started working at NYU the same year, even though Ezra was four years older. His job needed more training than hers did. But he never quite got trained in how to handle when he was feeling overwhelmed by what he was facing, what his patients were facing. He had to figure out how to deal with that on his own. Sometimes he needed to leave the hospital, to jump in a cab for the nine-minute ride to Emily's office. Sometimes he needed a kiss to get through the rest of the day. Sometimes he needed to tell her what happened. Other times she had to be a detective, trying to figure out why he was so silent at home, what had hurt him so deeply.

"It hasn't been the best morning," he said, holding her tighter. "But better now that I'm here with you."

"Good," she told him, wondering if today was a day she'd have to dig, if he would let her in or push her away.

When they spoke for the very first time, in the elevator in the Global Public Health building, Emily had been surprised that Ezra noticed her. She'd seen him around—in the hallways, walking from the subway—and he always seemed absorbed in thought, as if the only world that existed was the one in his head. He wore round tortoise-shell glasses, which added to the sense that he was somehow separated from the world, looking at it through a window. And he kept to himself. Only a handful of people on the faculty knew anything about him other than his name.

Once they got together, Emily realized that Ezra's studious appearance, his quiet reserve, masked the heart of a doctor who felt deeply for his patients and their families, and who was always thinking about what he could do to make their lives easier, how he could practice medicine more ethically, not just to make their health outcomes better but their quality of life, too. He tried, tirelessly, to find trials his patients could be part of to improve their outcomes.

"Your husband is an angel," his patients' parents would tell her when she went to the hospital to pick him up at the end of a long day. She thought so, too—though those parents never saw the toll the job took on him. The nights he stayed awake staring at the ceiling afraid of the dreams that might come, the hours he spent inside his own head, unable to find the words to express how he felt. The worst was when one of his patients died, and he spiraled into self-doubt and silence. Sometimes for days.

"Don't dwell on failure," Emily had heard Ezra's father tell him when he felt that way. "Just learn from it." A sentiment that Ezra seemed to have internalized, like he did so many of his parents' beliefs.

What she told him, though, was that a death wasn't his failure. It was the world acting out its plans. He wasn't a god. He couldn't fend off the inevitable forever. But Ezra didn't see it that way. Emily wondered if it was easier to believe it was all in his power. It made failure harder, but it made everything else more meaningful.

"Want to talk about it?" she asked him, lifting her cheek off his shoulder.

Ezra shook his head, his wavy brown hair falling in front of his glasses. It somehow always seemed like it needed a trim. "I'd rather not," he said.

"You don't have to," she told him, brushing his hair out of his eyes, knowing he'd tell eventually, when he was ready.

It might take hours, days, sometimes even weeks, but she knew how to give him his space when he needed it. And she could usually comfort him when he was finally ready to talk. She could read people like she could read music, feeling the emotion between the notes, the way to tease the meaning from the melody with her fingers. She wondered, sometimes, if Ezra'd had to marry a therapist, if someone who hadn't been trained in psychology could've made a relationship work with him.

"Thank you," he said, and kissed her again.

"How about I come get you at the end of the day?" she asked. "Maybe we can walk home? Stop for dinner on the way?"

"Lady's choice," he told her. "I love you."

"I love you, too." She wove her fingers through his. "You have to head back now?"

"Now that I'm fortified, I'll be able to handle it all."

"Good." She knew this wouldn't be the end of it, but it was what he needed now, and she was happy to give it to him.

They kissed one last time, and Ezra left Emily's office. She stood at her second-floor window to watch him appear below her on Broadway, hailing a yellow cab amid the traffic and jumping inside. Sometimes she still couldn't believe that she and Ezra were married—that this beautiful, brilliant, broken man brought her more happiness than she'd felt in more than a decade. It made her strive to be better, to make sure she was a woman worthy of a man like that.

* * *

Arielle had argued with Emily when she told her, three years ago, that she was going to take Ezra's last name.

"But you've got a doctorate," Ari said. "You're one of the authors on a clinical study." Arielle had been particularly proud of her sister's by-line on that paper.

"You took Jack's name," Emily said. "Mom took Dad's. I don't see the problem."

"But I'm staying home with my kids," Ari said. "You're different."

"I'm not," Emily protested. But that wasn't the real reason she wanted to take his name. She didn't feel like Emily Solomon anymore; she wasn't who she used to be. Without music, with Ezra—she was someone new. And changing her name to Emily Gold—it felt right. It felt like she was taking ownership of the person she'd become.

Another student appeared in Emily's door frame. Emily looked up at her. Someone new.

"Come in," she said.

The girl sat down and looked at the fish tank.

"Is that a betta?" she asked.

"It is," Emily answered. "I'm Dr. Gold."

"I know," the girl said. "I'm Callie."

And they talked about fish until it was time for more serious matters.

iii

Your father taught me to play guitar.

"You know Dire Straits?" he asked. We were in my room. It was summer, and we'd both stayed in the city, a plan we hadn't made together but were both glad we'd chosen. He'd gotten a job working at a recording studio, I was folding and refolding shirts at a boutique that sold clothing neither one of us could afford. Our relationship had started slow, like a ballad, but then picked up speed the more we got to know each other. Weekly trips to the Postcrypt to listen to music together in March turned into drinks and dessert in April and walks through the city in May, where we talked about our families, our favorite books, our dreams, and our nightmares.

Soon we were hanging out in each other's dorms, studying for finals sprawled across each other's beds.

And then it was June, and we saw each other almost every day. One night, we were in his room, the window was open, the fan was on, but we still felt the warmth—sticky on our skin.

He didn't wait for my response about Dire Straits before he started playing.

But it was a song I knew, about Romeo on the streets serenading Juliet.

"*Indigo Girls,*" I told him. "*They cover this.*"

He stopped playing and laughed. "*Of course,*" he said.

"*What's that supposed to mean?*" I asked him.

But he was playing again.

I watched his fingers. I heard the chords, felt the notes vibrating inside me. And before long, I was singing with him. Our voices wove into each other. The whole world fell away. The heat and the humidity were gone. It was just me and him and the music. I was awash in it. We finished the song staring into the blacks of each other's eyes.

"*Wow,*" he said.

Soon he was behind me on the bed, his guitar on my lap, his legs on either side of mine, his fingers showing mine how to coax a chord out of the instrument, how to strum.

"*You're a natural.*" He kissed my neck as he said it.

And maybe I was. Or maybe it was just that everything with him felt natural.

Jill Santopolo is the *New York Times* and internationally bestselling author of *The Light We Lost* and *More Than Words*. Her work has been translated into more than thirty-five languages. She received a BA from Columbia University and an MFA from the Vermont College of Fine Arts. She is also the author of three successful children's and young-adult series and works as the associate publisher of Philomel Books. Santopolo travels the world to speak about writing and storytelling. She lives in New York City and Washington, D.C.

Visit Jill Santopolo Online
jillsantopolo.com
JillSantopoloAuthor
JillSantopolo

JILL
SANTOPOLO

"Santopolo is the true master of matters of the heart."
—Taylor Jenkins Reid

"Santopolo writes heartbreak like no other."
—Emily Giffin

"Nobody does page-turning, heart-wrenching love stories quite like Jill Santopolo."
—Rosie Walsh